The Scourge

Book One of the Brilliant Darkness Series

To Jim,

A.G. Henley

A. G. Henley

Thanks for helping me
sell out! :)

Seventeen-year-old Groundling, Fennel, is Sightless. She's never been able to see her lush forest home, but she knows its secrets. She knows how the shadows shift when she passes under a canopy of trees. She knows how to hide in the cool, damp caves when the Scourge comes. She knows how devious and arrogant the Groundlings' tree-dwelling neighbors, the Lofties, can be.

And she's always known this day would come—the day she faces the Scourge alone.

To RFH - for your love, support, and patience. And for finally reading it.

To ASH and WRH - for being the kind of people that great tales are told about.

CHAPTER ONE

I duck out of the storeroom and into the main cavern, stepping carefully across the uneven floor. My fingers ache from being trailed along the frigid stone walls for hours. Rubbing my hands together to generate warmth has all the effect of kindling a fire with chips of ice.

My footfalls echo in the stillness as I move down the passage toward the mouth of the cave, counting my paces as I go. The sun pours in, diluting the darkness. I can barely tell light from dark, but I know I'm almost out when I hear Eland's voice. He never ventures in alone. He hates the caves almost as much as he fears the Scourge.

"Let's go, Fennel," he calls. "The celebration's about to start, and I'm starving. There's roasted boar and fresh bread, bean and potato stew, blackberry pie–"

I laugh. "Is your stomach all you think about?"

"No, I think about lots of other things."

"Really? Like what?" I reach out toward his voice.

Eland's hand, grimy from digging up vegetables and herbs in the garden, finds mine. Grimy or not, the warmth is a relief. "Like how we'll trounce the Lofties in the competitions tomorrow."

I can't help smiling at his confidence. This is his first year to compete. He and the other twelve-year-old boys have talked of little else for weeks. Everyone looks forward to the Summer Solstice celebration for the feast, the dancing, and the chance to beat the Lofties—with spear and knife, if not bow and arrow. It's a highlight of the year, so different from the solemn Winter Solstice when the Exchange takes place.

The shadows shift as we pass under the canopy of trees. I wrap my hand around Eland's sapling-thin arm—roots and creeping weeds on the forest floor have sent me sprawling more often than I want to remember. We reach the clearing, the heart of our community, where a bonfire sizzles and sputters to life. People shout to each other as they make their way down the paths from the gardens and the water hole, their work done for the day. The luscious fragrance of gardenia winds through the air. Someone must have strung garlands as decorations.

Our home, like those of all the other Groundlings, nestles into the embrace of the towering greenheart trees circling the clearing. Eland pushes open the door of our shelter. Aloe, my foster mother and his natural mother, calls to us from inside.

"Come in here, Eland … are you presentable? Comb your hair and be sure you clean the muck out of those fingernails. Fennel? Did you finish in the caves?"

I move to Aloe's side, where I know her outstretched arm will be, and take her hand in mine. Her skin is weathered but warm, like the surface of the enormous clay cooking pot in the clearing that never quite cools off. She smells of rosemary, from working in the herb garden, and something else I can only liken to the scraps of pre-Fall metal we sometimes come across in the forest.

"There's plenty of blankets and firewood, but we could probably use more salt meat," I tell her.

"We can store what's left of the boar after the celebration. We're fortunate the hunting party came across such a large one, and so near to home. The Council is pleased."

"When will they meet?"

"Soon. Sable and Adder want to perform the ceremony before the Lofties arrive."

Aloe will join the Groundling Council of Three tonight. One more reason to look up to her. Aloe is the most capable person I know. I was given to her as an infant to foster because she's Sightless, like me. She taught me to rely on myself first, and others only when absolutely necessary. Her guidance made my childhood much easier.

"Can't we come, Mother?" Eland says through clenched teeth. He's combing his hair, but it sounds like he's stripping the bark off a dead tree. "We want to see you accepted into the Three."

"Try not to make yourself bald, my love. And no, you can't. The acceptance is private, like all meetings of the Council." She kisses him, and her stick taps away toward the door.

"Congratulations, Aloe," I say. "We're proud of you."

"As I am of you both, my children. I'll meet you later, at the celebration."

Eland follows her out to check on the preparations, mucky fingernails forgotten. The scent of burning wood and roasting meat rushes into my nose and throat as he opens the door. It makes my mouth water. Animated voices burst through the clearing like startled birds.

I wash my face and hands with the water from our basin and sit on my bed, a low wooden pallet along the wall. I work my fingers through my hair—the same color as the fertile soil of the gardens, I'm told—and a thrill runs through me. I wonder if I'll be asked to dance tonight.

When a boy asks a girl my age, seventeen years, to dance at the Summer Solstice celebration, it usually means he's singled her out as his partner—for life, not just for the dance. My best friend, Callistemon, is convinced Bear will ask me. I'm not so sure. We've all been friends since childhood, and I haven't noticed any change in how he treats me. Calli says she can tell by the way he looks at me now. I laugh, but it bothers me that I can't see what she means for myself.

I don't know if Bear will ask me, and I'm even less sure what I'll say if he does. He's courageous and loyal, and there's no boy I like better. But … maybe I'm just not ready to partner. Aloe didn't until she was a few years older. I don't really remember her partner, Eland's father, but people say they were happy.

I take special care with my hair all the same, twisting it into thin braids here and there, and tucking in the fresh wild flowers Aloe left by the basin. It can't hurt to look my best.

Eland crashes back through the door to fetch me, and I follow him out. The bonfire blazes now. The heat isn't necessary on such a warm evening, but a fire makes everything more festive. A group across the clearing from our shelter howls with laughter. Hearing the musicians warming up sends another jolt of anticipation through my body. Calli calls to me as Eland scampers off. She's talking before I even sit down.

"You look so pretty, Fenn. I love how you fixed your hair! I'm so nervous … do you think anyone will ask us to dance? Well, I already know who's going to ask you."

I cringe. "*Shh,* he might hear you."

"Relax. He's way over by the roasting pit. Oh, who do you think will ask me? What if no one does? I'd be so embarrassed … but I hope it's not Cricket. He's so serious. And short."

"There are worse things than being short and serious … like being chronically unwashed." We both snicker. Hare, one of the boys our age, never picked up the habit of bathing regularly.

"No danger there. I heard Hare's asking Clover," Calli says.

"Clover? Really?" She's been saying she won't partner with anyone since we were about seven.

"That's what I heard," she says, and I don't doubt her. Gossip is rampant.

More people enter the clearing now, greeting each other with high spirits. Calli and I stand when Rose stops to say hello. Her tinkly voice reminds me of the wind chimes we made as children using pebbles and bits of shell dredged up from the water hole. We touch her tidy round belly, which is as firm and warm as a healthy newborn's cheek. Not long ago, Rose and Jackal exchanged bonding bands, the leather strips partners wear around their arms as a physical sign of their commitment to each other. Soon after, they announced she was expecting and due when the trees finally shed their leaves. It's a good time of year to give birth. The baby will be too young to be taken up in the Exchange, this winter at least.

"She's so lucky," Calli says as Jack leads Rose off. "They seem so happy."

"For now," I say.

"I can't stand the suspense! I want someone to ask me to dance and get it over with!"

"Why? It's not like you have your heart set on partnering with someone in particular."

"I don't want to be the only one not asked, you know?"

I do know, although I think I'm more willing to suffer the humiliation of not being asked than to agree to partner for life with whoever might feel like asking me today.

"Here comes *Beaarr,*" Calli says, wickedness in her voice, "looks like he's bringing you an offering." I elbow her.

"I snuck a few slices of boar for you both. Be careful; it's still hot," Bear says, his voice a low and familiar rumble.

I blow on the meat and then test it out with a nibble. Delicious. Not many large animals are left on the forest floor, and hunting them is always a risk because of the Scourge, so boar's a special treat. The muscular texture and rich, smoky flavor evoke cherished memories of past feasts: music, dancing, rare carefree moments.

"Maybe this is your old friend, Fenn," Calli says, like she does every time we eat boar. I smile and agree, like I do every time she says it.

I was almost killed by an animal when we were about ten. We were playing hide-and-seek in the forest, and I was the seeker. Aloe made me memorize every path, bush, and tree in the area around our homes, so most of the time I could pinpoint where I was when we played. But on this day I was lost. As I wandered around hunting a familiar landmark, I heard what sounded like a gigantic boar snorting and charging toward me through the underbrush. Just before the animal reached me it squealed as if in pain and ran back the way it had come, leaving me shaking but alive. I don't know what caused it to turn around.

"So Bear, who will you ask to dance tonight?" Calli teases.

"Better worry about who's asking you," Bear says. "From what I hear, Cricket's got you in his sights. That is, if he can see you from way down there."

We laugh at Calli's tortured moans.

"Don't you think it's unfair that only boys can ask girls to dance?" I say. "Why can't it be the girls' choice for a change?"

"*Tradition*," Calli says, in a high-pitched imitation of our teacher, Bream's, voice.

"Our *traditions* protect us from the Scourge," Bear says in the same voice. He leans closer to me, the smell of toasted wood clinging to his hair, and murmurs, "Who would you ask, if you had the choice?"

I chew a mouthful of meat to buy time. A voice bellows right above us, saving me from having to answer. It's Calli's father, Fox. He isn't one of the Three, but he's sure to be eventually, when Sable or Adder either die or become too infirm to do their duties.

"Ready for tomorrow, Bear?" Fox sounds like he's had one too many cups of the spiced wine.

"I still want to know," Bear whispers to me, before pushing himself to his feet. "We'll do our best," he says to Fox. "I hear the Lofties have a new crop of–"

"Rumors, rumors," Fox says. "Pay no attention. We have the advantage, as always."

Soon they're debating which shape of knife is best to use in the fights, or what spear grip will produce the most accurate throw. Other men join them to strategize. Some of the younger children run around us, shrieking with excitement. I lean back on my hands, enjoying the sounds of the people enjoying themselves.

"Fenn?" Calli says.

"*Hmm?*"

"Aren't you scared?"

I know what she's asking about. Now that Aloe joined the Three, I'll take over her duty and collect the water for our people when the Scourge comes again. I spend hours in the caves every day stocking the storeroom with supplies and food so we're ready, but we'll still need water. I shrug, feigning confidence. "Aloe says protection is the gift of our Sightlessness."

Which may be true, but I'm still terrified. The sighted say the creatures' bodies are open in patches, weeping pus and thick, dark blood. Their deformed faces are masks of horror. They roam the forests, reeking of festering flesh, consuming anything living. People who survive the attacks become flesh-eaters themselves. Death is better.

I'm supposed to be safe from the Scourge, like Aloe, but I haven't been tested. I will be soon. To hear the agony of their hunger, smell their disease, feel their hot breath on my skin … the idea fills me with dread and loathing. But Aloe has never shown her fear to others, and neither will I.

"I won't be completely alone, anyway. I'll have my Keeper," I say. Calli snorts. The Lofties say the Keeper's job is to kill flesh-eaters and deter other fleshies—our nickname for the Scourge—from getting too close to me. But everyone knows the Keeper's really there to ensure the Lofties get their share of the water while the Scourge is here. Secretly I'm just happy *someone* will be with me, even if it's a Lofty in the trees. "Aloe insists her Keeper was important."

"*Self*-important," Calli mutters. "And devious. Don't trust them, Fenn." We all know the fate of Groundlings who cross Lofties. They're found with arrows in their chests. Or in their backs. It doesn't happen often, but it happens.

There's a rustling, more deliberate than the wind, in the leafy branches above our heads. I sit up.

"What is it?" Calli asks.

"The Lofties are here."

The talking and shrieking abruptly cease. The clearing is silent except for the chattering of the fire. Fox finally speaks, sounding stiff and formal—and more sober than I expected.

"Welcome. Please join us."

The woman who answers sounds equally uncomfortable. "Thank you. We brought food to contribute to the feast."

"Our Council hasn't arrived yet … so I'll just say a few words in their absence." Fox clears his throat and continues in his best speechmaking voice—the one Calli and I have heard many times when we were in trouble. "Groundlings and Lofties come together once a year on this day to feast, to dance, and to engage in friendly competition." I smile as some of the boys quietly scoff at the word *friendly*. "The Summer Solstice celebration is a reminder that every year given to us since the Fall of Civilization is a blessing, something for us to treasure. It's a time to reflect on the year that has passed, and to anticipate the year that will be. We honor those who came before us, our elders, many of whom gave their lives to ensure we would have a future." He pauses. "And we offer a prayer of protection for those who come after us—our children, and our children's children. May they always be safe from the Scourge."

The Lofty woman responds to Fox's traditional words of welcome with their customary response. "We appreciate the hospitality of our Groundling neighbors. We too pray for peace and protection, and for a year of prosperity for all forest-dwellers."

A respectful silence follows, promptly broken by Bear's less-than-respectful whisper that the Lofties will need a prayer of protection tomorrow. Calli giggles.

"What are the Lofties doing?" I ask as conversations around the fire slowly start up again.

Bear answers. "Standing around, looking like they'd rather be anywhere else. As usual."

"It's kind of sad. They come to the Summer Solstice celebration every year, but they never seem to have any fun," Calli says.

"They should invite us up to their little nests if they aren't comfortable down here," Bear says. "Wouldn't kill 'em."

"Why do we bother to celebrate together, when we all keep to ourselves?" I ask. "We can do that anytime."

"*Tradition*," Calli and Bear intone.

"Maybe it's time for a new tradition." I stand up, shaking out my skirt. "Where are they, exactly?"

"Over by my family's shelter," Calli says. "What are you doing, Fenn?"

Finding out who will be in those trees when the Scourge comes. I weave around the clusters of people, listening for voices I don't recognize. But I smell the Lofties before I hear them—the intense, slightly bitter resin of their homes, the greenheart trees.

"Welcome." My voice sounds too loud in my ears. "I'm Fennel. I'll be taking Aloe's place collecting water for our communities when the Scourge returns."

The Groundlings behind me fall silent again, their stares heavy on my shoulders. A Lofty speaks, his voice deep and gravelly.

"Fennel, it's Shrike. Has Aloe joined the Council then?" Shrike is Aloe's Keeper. She doesn't talk about him much, but I've always gotten the sense she thinks well of him.

"She was accepted this evening. She should be here soon." I worry the pocket of my dress with my fingers. "Shrike, could I … I'd like to meet my Keeper."

There's silence, then someone moves toward me, crunching leaves under their feet.

"This is Peregrine," Shrike says.

I hold out my hand. It stays extended in front of me for what seems a very long time. I think of myself frozen that way, a welcoming statue found years in the future by someone who happens across the clearing. Embarrassed, but determined not to show it, I thrust my hand out even further.

A hand finally brushes mine. I can tell it belongs to a man. There are calluses on the ends of his long fingers. This Lofty smells different from the others, more like … honeysuckle. I liked playing around the honeysuckle in the garden as a child, avoiding the preoccupied bees and soaking in the sweet, sunny scent. It's the fragrance of summer.

"Hello, Fennel."

I'm surprised. I pictured my Keeper middle-aged, like Shrike, but this Lofty doesn't sound much older than me. And while his hand is rough, his voice isn't. It's quiet, almost melodious. More like the calls of the warblers that wake us each morning than the predatory screech of the falcon he's named for. All the Lofty men are named for birds, while the women have ridiculous names like Sunbeam, Dewdrop, and Mist.

"Though I don't wish the Scourge to return," Aloe says from behind me, "they will. It's good that you've met."

"Congratulations on your acceptance into the Three," Shrike says. "You'll serve your community well."

"Thank you," she says.

Aloe's voice is different, gentler, the voice she reserves for Eland. She has a bond with this Lofty. I wonder if I'll have a similar bond with my rough-handed, soft-voiced Keeper.

"So," I say to Peregrine, "were you chosen because you're a good hunter? Aloe says Shrike is deadly, as deadly as she's ever known a man to be."

"I can use a bow and arrow."

"Ha, don't let him fool you. Peree's one of our best archers. We're counting on him tomorrow." Shrike sounds proud, like he's talking about his own son. Maybe he is. We don't know much about the Lofties.

Fox's voice booms across the clearing. "Come, eat, and let the dancing begin! We have some anxious boys here, waiting to find out if the girls they've had their eye on for the past year will dance with them." The crowd laughs, even a few of the Lofties. People all around the fire begin to talk normally again, and the music starts up. I'm relieved that the collective attention seems to have turned away from me.

I smile politely at my Keeper. "I'm sure we'll meet again, Peregrine, like Aloe said."

"Call me Peree. Everyone does."

I nod. "My friends call me Fenn."

The music starts up. I should go. Bear, or someone else, may be waiting to dance with me. Whether I want to or not. I turn away … and a mad idea grabs me.

Ask the Lofty to dance.

I hesitate. Is Aloe still nearby? Can she hear us? She's one of the Three now, tasked with managing our complicated relationship with the Lofties. There's no rule against dancing with them, but that's only because no one has ever tried. Aloe—not to mention the rest of my people—might be furious with me. I decide I don't care. At least I'll have made my own choice.

"Peree? Would you like to dance?" He doesn't say anything. I bite my bottom lip. "You know, dance? I'm not bad, really. I won't even step on your feet much."

"Lofties and Groundlings don't dance together."

"Why not?"

He's quiet again. "No idea. Tradition, I guess." I half expect him to say it in Bream's voice.

I hold my hand out, palm up this time, challenging him.

I never get an answer. Shrill birdcalls rip through the air—Lofty warning calls. The music dies, and for a moment the clearing is quiet. Then the screaming starts.

The Scourge is here.

CHAPTER TWO

I listen for the cries of the creatures, my hand still stuck out in front of me. I need to move, to get to the caves with everyone else. I map out the best way to get there in my head. *Run along the edge of the clearing*—avoid being trampled or knocked in the fire. I break for it, and someone grabs my hand. Peree.

"Come on."

He jams my arm under his and drags me around the fire. People careen off us, yelling to douse the flames, find children, gather up supplies. Someone shouts for help, but I can't stop with Peree towing me along.

"Fennel!" Eland yells, grasping my free arm. Peree's gone before I can thank him.

"Where's Aloe?" I shout.

"Over here!" Eland pulls me away from the spitting, hissing bonfire. "Mother, I've got her!"

"Get to the caves." Aloe's voice is calm, but weary. "I'll be there shortly."

I hang on to Eland's arm as we run. People jostle around us. The trail from the clearing to the mouth of the caves is endless.

"Almost there," Eland pants.

I hear a cry off the path; so weak I doubt anyone else can hear it. "Someone's hurt. Go on, I'll be right behind you."

"Fenn–"

"Go!" I push him and plow into the bushes. I could fall on whoever it is if I move too fast so I creep forward, sweeping my arms in front of me. A bush gropes me, tearing my skin. I hear the moan again, just in front of me.

"Fennel, thank the stars." It's Willow, one of the elders.

I lift her up gently and set her on her feet like a toddler. Clasping her frail body to me, I stagger back to the path. Willow whimpers in pain, and I slow to loosen my grip.

Then I hear them, crashing through the forest behind us, shrieking as they come.

I start to run, supporting Willow, trying to stay on the path. Hands seize me, and I cry out.

"I've got her!" Fox yells. He sweeps Willow into his arms and sprints forward, his feet pounding the path.

I run too, terrified I'll trip and fall. People call to me from the mouth of the cave, giving me a sound to aim for.

I hear the flesh-eaters just behind me now.

Then, warm arms and bodies catch me. I'm safe. Eland finds me and we hold each other. The people are quiet, listening to the creatures groan in the darkness outside the cave. Aloe's voice rises above their hungry cries.

"Come," she directs us.

And we do, following her through the passageway to the still, black cavity that will be our home until the Scourge leaves again.

Calli and I huddle together against the rock wall, shivering in our bedrolls. Groups of people around the main cavern confer in hushed voices, comparing escape stories as they warm themselves at small fires. It was a long, mostly sleepless night.

The Lofties usually give us more warning when the Scourge is near. It's their part of our uneasy bargain. We provide them with small game and skins, produce from our gardens, and access to the water. In return, they allow us to cut down certain trees for wood, and they warn us when the Scourge is coming so we can hide out in the caves. What they never do is offer to share the safety of their airy homes.

The caves are safe. The flesh-eaters don't come in—they don't seem to like dark, confined spaces any more than we do—but we can't leave either, until the Scourge is gone. They only move on when they've exhausted their food source, the animals—and humans—who rely on the fresh water to survive. Groundlings have tried over the years, but we've never been able to find another source of water. It's risky to explore very far from the caves, because we never know when the flesh-eaters will come. So we're stuck, with the Lofties, with the Scourge.

"I hate the caves," Calli says. "And I hate the fleshies. We never even got to dance."

I put my arms around her. "We'll dance again, when they're gone."

"I know Bear was going to ask you. You should've seen his face while you talked to that Lofty." She pulls the bedroll up under our chins. "We couldn't believe it when you went over there. You do the strangest things sometimes. Who was he, anyway?"

"My Keeper, Peree."

"Peree? What kind of bird is that?"

"Short for Peregrine."

"Oh. Well, what was he like?"

"I don't know; I barely spoke to him." I think of his callused hands and his musical voice. I won't tell her I asked him to dance. "What did he look like?"

"Tall, fair-haired, feathers sticking out all over the place. Looking down his nose at everyone. You know, like a Lofty. They all pretty much look the same. Ugh, I think my toes are frostbitten." She grabs my leg. "The Three are here."

We jump to our feet, and I feel Aloe take my hand. Sable, the oldest of the Three, speaks to me, his voice splintering like desiccated wood. He's been on the Council for as long as I can remember. Some call him Sable the Unstable, because he totters when he walks, and because there's been quiet speculation about how sound his mind is these days. Aloe said his time on the Council is probably limited, but he would stay on until she settles into her new role.

"I understand you rescued my mother last night, Fennel," Sable says.

"Fox really did. How *is* Willow?"

"Alive, thanks to you," he says. Aloe squeezes my hand, and my cheeks warm.

He continues in a clearer voice. "We were only able to bring in a little water last night, so I'm afraid we'll need you to collect three sacks today. I'm sorry to ask you to make more than one trip on your first day among the Scourge, but we have no choice."

"Three sacks," another man repeats, emphasizing each word. It's Adder, the last of the Council. His voice is raspy and harsh. I've always disliked it. I decided I didn't like Adder period when I heard he was unhappy that Aloe was chosen by the people to be one of the Three. "And don't let that Lofty Keeper talk you into any more than their equal share of the water. They'll not get one drop more than they're due—"

Aloe interrupts him. "She knows her duty. Are you ready, Fennel?" I nod. She embraces me, and whispers in my ear. "Don't forget—never forget—you are protected. The Scourge can't harm you. Remember that when you're afraid."

"I'm afraid now."

"Then remember it now."

She leads me to the passage that will take me back to the mouth of the cave. People touch me as I walk, murmuring good luck. Eland clings to me, followed by Calli. Her tears moisten my cheek.

"Here, Fennel." Bear's voice is even rougher than usual. He presses something silky into my hand, his fingers lingering on mine. "The foot of a rabbit, for luck." It's a charm, left over from the old days, before the Fall.

Then his hand is gone, and everyone is gone, and I stand alone in the passageway.

I start walking, rehearsing in my mind what I'll do when I leave the caves, as Aloe taught me. *Take the path to the clearing. Walk along the edge of the clearing. Find the sled track, and follow it down to the water hole, where the sled waits.* I go over the number of paces it should take to complete each part of my trip, repeating them to be sure I remember. Then I try to wipe my mind clean.

I try not to think of the cries of the creatures the night before. I try not to think of the many stories I've heard about the flesh-eaters tearing apart their victims, or the agonizing transformation into one of them—half human, half dead. Instead I focus on the cool, lumpy rock under my hand, or the musty smell of the passage, or how many steps I have left until I reach the mouth of the cave. Anything else.

But it's impossible.

My heart is a desperate animal, smashing against my rib cage. My shivering now has nothing to do with the cold. I sing—another trick Aloe taught me—but the closer I get to the mouth of the cave, the slower I walk and the softer I sing. Then I stop walking and singing altogether, trying to work up the courage to take the last few steps necessary to reach the sunlight.

Something's thrashing through the forest, coming closer. I hear shrieking, like the dying people of my imagination. I tuck the rabbit's foot into my pocket, and tug a scarf Aloe gave me up over my mouth and nose, preparing for the stench.

For a moment I wonder if my protection will hold, but I push the thought away. It's the gift of our Sightlessness, as I've always been told.

I think of Eland huddled in the gloom of the caves, eating the salty dried meat, waiting for his water ration. That does it. I take a deep breath, and step outside.

The creatures surge around me. Their howls pierce me. Even through the barrier of the scarf, I can smell their putrid breath. Something brushes my sleeve and I cry out, wrapping my arms tightly around my body like a shroud.

What if I'm not protected? What if everything I've been told about my Sightlessness—everything I've believed about myself—isn't true? The Scourge will consume me, as they have so many others. Or worse, I'll become like one of them, only knowing hunger, thirst, and the yearning for flesh. I yank the scarf down; it's suffocating. I wait, shuddering, for biting mouths and tearing hands to find me.

"Fennel–" The word drifts down from the trees.

A long moment passes before I can speak, and then my voice shakes. "Peree?"

"I'm right above you." He sounds steady, calm. "You're all right. Stay still; let me give you some space." Arrows zip across a bow. Two harrowing screams are followed by two thumps. "There, they've backed up a bit. Can you walk?"

I grew up in the forest. I know every path, and the position of every tree and bush. But I feel lost now, like someone moved all the familiar landmarks overnight. I take a step in what I hope is the right direction. The creatures follow, shifting to surround me again. My eyes sting from the smell of their rotting flesh. Singing under my breath, I take another cautious step. I don't want to stumble or fall. I don't want to do anything that might draw more of them to me.

"Watch yourself, there are bodies there," Peree says. "Step a little to your left … that's it." He follows me through the trees above, using the Lofties' well-maintained wooden walkways. They clear the lower branches up to the height of two grown men, so the walkways are too far up for humans—and more importantly, half-dead humans—to reach by climbing.

There are more creatures coming, hurtling toward me through the trees. Panic almost takes me again. I need to focus on something, anything, other than the flesh-eaters pressing in.

I call to Peree. "They're keeping their distance?"

"Yes, but if they don't I'll take out a few more. Keep walking; you're almost to the clearing now. It's to your left—"

"I know where it is." I might be terrified and disoriented, but I don't need a Lofty to give me directions in the forest.

I hear creatures dart at me, stopping right before they reach me. Others pace alongside. If I were to run they would chase, quick as the fleetest animals. In the rare moments they're quiet, I hear their tongues searching. The sighted say many of the creatures don't really have mouths anymore, only gaping, seeping holes in what were once their very human faces. My stomach contracts, pushing up the little breakfast I managed to eat. I put my hands on my knees, and saliva pools in my mouth.

"Have you ever heard of a tiger?" Peree asks.

I swallow hard. "A what?"

"Hold still." An arrow whistles by, followed by another thump. "A tiger, it's an animal." He sounds relaxed, like we're sitting and chatting over a meal, instead of having a semi-shouted conversation from the ground to the trees, overheard by the creatures and who knows how many Lofties.

"*Uh*, no, I don't think so."

"They were big cats, amazing hunters, graceful and beautiful, and they had a wild scream that would put the fleshies to shame."

I wince as a creature shrieks at my side. "That's hard to imagine."

"For me as well." His voice is grim. "Are you able to see colors at all?"

"No, but I've heard some colors are warmer, like red, and some cooler, like blue, with others in between. So that's how I picture them, as degrees of heat." It snowed a few seasons ago. I guessed the soft, frosty flakes must be blue—to Calli's everlasting amusement.

"Well, tigers would be warm, like a fire you don't want to get too close to. They're orange, with black marks all over their bodies. In ancient times, the tiger was chosen by the gods to protect humans. He did it so well, he was given three marks across his forehead to represent great battles he won against three evil animals. When the tiger won a final time, saving the human race, the gods placed a mark down his forehead, intersecting the others. They formed a word, 'King,' in the ancient people's language. The word could be seen on all tigers from then on."

I start walking again, following the line of trees circling the clearing. A branch creaks above my head. The Lofties leave spaces between some trees as firebreaks. Peree must have swung across a gap.

"I wish the gods would send an animal to fight the Scourge," I say. "How do you know about tigers?"

"My mother told me—my foster mother. She knew a lot of stories from before and after the Fall. Stories about animals, and strange tales of our ancestors who lived in the City, in homes as tall as the tops of mountain peaks, and taller."

"Our teacher told us about the City," I say. "He said it was a nasty, crowded place, full of evil people. He told us that's where the Scourge was born."

"Mother never said any of that, only that it was large and lit up at night by specks of light, like mists of fireflies."

"You said she *knew* those stories. Is she …?"

He's silent.

"I'm sorry. How did it happen?"

I hear him load his bow. Another thump. The creatures howl in response. "The sled track's in front of you," he says.

I know that, but I don't say it this time.

I'm amazed I made it this far. I was very close to losing my nerve and running back to the cave—until I heard Peree call to me from the trees. His arrows discouraged the flesh-eaters, and his story about the tigers distracted me. I'm beginning to understand why Aloe insists our Keepers are important.

I reach out to find the smooth wooden rails of the sled track, praying I don't touch any of the creatures hovering around me. I'll drag the sled and heavy oilskin sacks of water up the steep tracks, while doing my best to ignore the enraged creatures. This will be the most physically difficult part of the work. I can't pull more than two bags in the sled each time, so I have to make three trips today: three sacks of water for us and three for the Lofties. Aloe said there will be more fleshies by the water hole.

The air is still temperate for summer, but I'm sweating like the sun's been breathing on me for hours. I wipe my face, trying to pull myself together.

"Are you all right?" Peree asks.

"No."

"You've done well so far," he says. "Not many of the Sightless are brave enough to take more than a few steps among the flesh-eaters the first time. Shrike told me one woman refused to do her duty at all, and the people suffered for years because of her cowardice."

I've heard of this Groundling. She took her own life. I'm ashamed for her, but I bristle at his words. How dare a Lofty criticize any Groundling from the perfect safety of his trees, much less a Groundling who's Sightless and faces the Scourge alone? I'm about to tell him what he can do with his praise, when I remember Calli's warning. I doubt any Lofty would kill their one source for fresh water, but I don't want to tempt Peree. I swallow my anger, grimacing at the bitter taste.

I stalk away, following the sled track, leaving him well behind me in the trees. Under the low moans of the creatures, I hear gentle waves breaking on the shore and a bird trilling in the forest. Others join it, creating a joyful chorus of avian voices. For a moment the world feels peaceful and safe.

But only for a moment.

The flesh-eaters swarm around me. The small group that followed me through the forest was like nothing compared to this onslaught—the first crack of lightning before an electrical storm. Their rage and hunger grip me. I fall to my knees, my hands over my ears.

One time I asked Aloe why she still fears the creatures, after all the years she's walked among them. She told me she no longer fears the Scourge, she fears her own fear. Now I understand. I curl up on the muddy ground and drift away for a time, lost in a place darker than the deepest, blackest cave.

After some time I hear something other than the terrible screams. Peree, shouting my name over and over. I ignore him. The cave in my mind is safe. But he keeps calling.

Go away. Go away and leave me.

He doesn't.

I have to get up. For Eland, Aloe, Calli, Bear, Fox, Rose and her baby. I hear the pleas of my people, each one in turn. Trapped in the caves, waiting for me to return with their life-sustaining water. Relying on me. I can't fail. All these thoughts echo in my mind, and somehow, I'm standing again.

"Fennel! Are you all right?"

I raise my hand, and stagger down the slope to the water's edge, the creatures following me like a fetid fog. Peree keeps shooting. The thumps mean one less nightmare I'll have tonight, but I shrink from the thought of the bodies piling up, bodies that were once human. I grope along the end of the track until my hand finds the sled. Inside are two oilskin sacks.

I fill them, secure the tops, and roll them up onto the sled. Then I shuffle to the front to secure myself in the harness. The sacks were made to hold as much water as I can pull with the sled, but I still struggle. When I rehearsed with Aloe I was fresh and unafraid, not exhausted and petrified as I am now. I pull the sled forward a few feet, and have to stop to rest. I try again, straining as hard as I can in the harness, but the sled barely budges.

If I can't make it up the hill, I'll have to unload a sack. Which means I'll also have to make twice as many trips as I now face. I put my hands on my knees again and choke back tears.

Peree calls to me. "Fenn, listen to me. You can do this. You have the strength. Focus on taking a few steps forward. Just a few, then you can rest. Pull the sled."

I pull.

"That's it, and again."

I pull again. I do what he says, and focus on the next few steps. Step. Pull. Step. Pull. The sled inches up the hill, the water sloshing in the sacks behind me. I pray they don't fall out.

"Good Fenn, very good, not much farther. Bring the sled to the end of the track. I'll lower the ropes."

Guided by his voice, I reach up for the ropes, and tie them to the sacks. He hoists them into the trees. The Lofties will deliver our portion to us at the mouth of the caves after nightfall, when it's safer. The flesh-eaters don't seem to see as well at night. I start again, skimming the empty sled back down the tracks, trying to ignore the creatures surging around me. I fill two more sacks and load them on the sled. Step. Pull. Step. Pull.

Peree talks to me as I rest, my back against the side of the sled and my head in my hands, but I don't register what he says. When he finishes lifting the sacks up, I haul the sled back down to the water. I focus on the rhythm of the work as much as I can, trying to pretend I'm in the quiet caves, stocking the storeroom. But it's not the same, not by a long shot.

When I finally finish, I step out of the harness and stumble back toward the clearing. The creatures still follow, but there are fewer now. Peree follows, too. I speed up when I reach the clearing. The trees on the other side are all that separate me from Aloe and Eland—from safety.

The flesh-eaters seem to sense my desperation as I near the caves. They encircle me again. Aloe calls from the entrance, and I dive into the darkness. She pulls me into her arms.

"Brave, brave girl," she croons, stroking my hair. I let her soothe me, grateful to be alive. The scent of death recedes as the Scourge melts back into the forest.

"Peree," Aloe calls. "Tell Breeze we'll collect our water at dusk."

"I'll tell her. I'll see you in the morning, Fenn."

The morning. When I'll have to do it all again. I crumple in Aloe's arms, and the tears flow.

I wake before dawn. I don't know how I know what time of day it is this deep in the caves, but I do. I give no sign I'm awake. I don't want the day to find me.

Adder met Aloe and me in the passage as we came in last night, already hurling questions at me. Did I fill six sacks of water? How many of the flesh-eaters did there seem to be? Did I hear any Lofties other than Peree?

Aloe guided me past him. "Later," she said.

Calli and Bear grabbed me next, hugging me to them. Eland drove into us so hard we all crashed to the stone floor of the cave. Our shouts caused others to come running, thinking there had been a cave-in.

Once I was seated, people brought me food and water. They touched me, speaking in whispers, sounding … reverential. My protection from the creatures was confirmed, and it gave them a new respect for me. Some asked questions about the Scourge, or about my Keeper, and I answered as well as I could. But no matter what else they asked, everyone wanted to know the same thing in the end: did the flesh-eaters show any signs of leaving?

The Scourge typically stays for two or three days, but they could stay longer. Sometimes even a week or more. The elders didn't speak of those times.

A week. I'd been through one day.

I won't think about it. One step at a time, one minute at a time.

Before we fell asleep, Eland asked me what it was really like to face the flesh-eaters. He seemed to sense I was holding back with other people, and he was right. But I wouldn't tell him the truth either. Because the more I thought about it, the more shameful the truth became.

I was afraid of the Scourge, and of my own fear, as Aloe had been. Dreadfully afraid. The only thing that forced me to my feet when I was crushed by my fear, persuaded me to move again when I was paralyzed by it, was a Lofty. A *Lofty*—oppressive and superior. They keep us in our place, literally, with their bows and arrows. But I wouldn't have done my duty without Peree talking me through it. I would have failed my people, and myself.

And what about Peree? He's kind. Concerned. Funny, even. Things Lofties aren't supposed to be. I'm not supposed to like him.

So I told Eland a different truth. I told him Aloe was wrong. Protection from the Scourge isn't the gift of our Sightlessness. It's all part of the same curse.

I think about this as he sleeps beside me, and I wonder how I'll survive the day.

CHAPTER THREE

I tremble as I approach the mouth of the cave. Invisible hands—rotting, diseased, and smelling of death—clench my throat. I stroke the velvety rabbit's foot in my pocket to calm myself, and step out into the sun.

Birds call from high in the treetops, and the wind plays with my hair, but otherwise it's quiet. I take a few tentative steps toward the tree line, hoping Peree is waiting.

"Fenn."

The compression in my chest loosens a little when I hear his voice. "Where are they? Are they gone?"

"No. You'd better start moving toward the clearing."

I stand still, struggling with my cowardice. He's right. I might as well get as far along as I can before they find me—I have to make at least two trips with the sled today—but I still don't move. I don't want to admit how much I was hoping the flesh-eaters had gone overnight. And I don't want to admit how happy I am Peree's here with me again.

"You okay?" he asks.

"Not really."

"I'm sorry. I wish–"

"What?" *What does a Lofty wish for?*

Branches snap in the forest in front of me as something hurtles through the underbrush. Many somethings. I start trembling again.

"I wish the damn things would go burn in whatever hell they came from," he says, as the creatures explode out of the trees. "Don't move."

Bodies fall all around me, pierced by Peree's arrows. I try to block out the sickening smell, and the hideous screams, while a detached part of my mind admires the swiftness of his archery. The arrows don't seem to let up, as if he's found a way to loose them without the use of his bow. I picture them shooting from his mouth, the way we spit watermelon seeds in the summer, and a hysterical giggle escapes me.

"Okay, I cleared a little space. You can go now," he calls. "Watch it, though. There are a few of them on the ground to your right, and one behind you ... are you laughing?" I tell him what I pictured, and he chuckles. "Speaking of spitting, have you ever heard of a camel?"

"Another strange beast?" I move forward, my hands outstretched to find the familiar tree trunks along the path to the clearing. I dread finding something else, like the dripping flesh of the creatures. "What color are these?"

"Nothing like tigers. Camels were supposed to be a light brown, same as the sands of the deserts where they lived."

"Deserts?"

"Hot, sandy places with no trees or grasses, and little water."

"Sounds idyllic," I say sarcastically. "But maybe no water means no Scourge?"

"Then again, no water means nothing to drink, and nothing to water crops with."

I raise an eyebrow. What would a Lofty know about watering crops? It's not like they've ever tried—

A scream rips the air beside me. I slap my hands over my ears. A second later there's a muffled thump. I shiver and move forward again, into the clearing.

"Camels," Peree continues, "were odd looking, with parts from many different animals, like the ears of a mouse, the coat of a sheep, and the nose of a rabbit."

"Sheep?" Mice and rabbits abound in the woods, thanks to being small and easily hidden from the flesh-eaters, but I have no idea what a sheep is.

"Sheep ... are a story for another day. Camels were interesting animals. They stored nutrients in great humps on their backs to use when food was scarce, and they could go a long time without fresh water."

"And the spitting?" An arrow parts the air in front of my face, and I jerk back. "Remember, no water for anyone if you kill me," I joke weakly.

"Sorry, I was demonstrating the purpose of camel spit. It was a warning, like my arrows, for others to back off. Although it wasn't spit so much as, well, stomach contents." He sounds like he might regret having brought it up.

"Humped backs *and* projectile vomiting? Lovely." I reach the far side of the clearing, behind Calli's shelter, and walk to the beginning of the sled track. The creatures follow, of course. "Did your mother tell you about these ... what are they called again?"

"Camels."

"How did she know so much about animals?"

"She knew a lot about a lot of things, but she never said how she learned it all. I think my father knew, but he's never told me either. He doesn't really talk about Mother now."

I remember he said he was fostered, mostly because he told me so casually. The subject of fostering isn't really taboo among Groundlings; we just avoid talking about it. We don't talk much about the Exchange, either. It only reminds us why we hate the Lofties.

As Bream is fond of telling us, the Scourge consumed countless people after the Fall, generations ago. The scattered, frightened survivors saw that birds and tree-dwelling animals were safe. So they took to the trees, building homes in the tops, complete with rope ladders that could be raised when the flesh-eaters came. They fashioned bows and arrows and learned to use them with lethal accuracy to provide food and to protect themselves. But the trees were crowded and food was scarce. Resources had to be protected. People with dark coloring were arbitrarily forced to the forest floor to become Groundlings. The Exchange began soon after.

Once a year all the weaned Groundling and Lofty babies are sorted. The fair-haired, light-eyed children are taken by the Lofties to live high above the ground, in the sunlit warmth and security of their tree-top aeries. The dark babies are taken by us, to live in fear of the Scourge.

I was a Lofty baby, born with the wrong coloring, and without sight. I often wonder who my natural parents were. If they were relieved to see me go. Raising a Sightless child in the branches of trees can't be an easy prospect.

Peree swings between two trees, the branch he hangs from groaning under his weight. "There's the track ... but you know that already."

The sled's at the top of the track, where I left it yesterday. I pick up the harness and begin dragging. The bottom grates against the wooden tracks.

Almost instinctively I know the noise is attracting attention of the wrong kind. The hair on my arms stands up as if preparing to run.

"Here they come," Peree says bleakly.

Flesh-eaters throng around me like flies on a carcass, and fear shoots through the top of my head, blocking out almost any other thought or feeling. It's all I can do not to sink under the weight of it. I sing under my breath, a song the men sing as they prepare for hunts, meant to build courage. The whistling of arrows and the sound of bodies hitting the ground are my accompaniment.

I pull the empty sled down to the water's edge and fill the first sack while the water laps around my ankles. It's cool and enticing. I want to swim out. All Groundlings can swim, and I'm no exception, but as far as I know the creatures can't. One survivor supposedly escaped the flesh-eaters by treading water for hours before slipping safely back onto land after nightfall.

I've never swum alone, but I think about trying it now. I take a few steps farther into the water, the sack slipping out of my hand. The urge to dive in is powerful. After a moment I grasp the sack more firmly, and turn around.

Dragging the sled, with the sounds and smells of the creatures fueling my fear, is almost unendurable. I want to cry, or scream, or commit some terrible act of violence as I pull. But each time I near the top of the hill, Peree's calm voice—equal parts encouraging, coaxing, and soothing—keeps me moving forward. Still, by the time I tie off the last sack, I feel like one of the creatures—miserable, and mostly dead.

I trudge back through the forest to the caves. Peree speaks as I step into the darkness. I'd almost forgotten he followed me.

"See you in the morning."

More to myself than to him, I mutter, "I hope not."

I sit with Calli and Eland later, the rough wall jabbing into our backs. Dinner is dried rabbit and rehydrated beans from the storeroom. I should eat to keep up my strength, but I'm not hungry. The dense, wrinkled texture of the meat is how I imagine the creatures' skin feels. When I try to swallow it, I gag.

"Bream was even more boring today than usual," Calli complains. Eland snorts in agreement. "Between the darkness and his voice, I barely stayed awake. Bear kept poking me when I drifted off, thank the stars."

"He was talking about the Fall *again*," Eland moans.

We could all recite Bream's rotating lectures about the Fall of Civilization—and we sometimes did when we were confident we wouldn't be overheard mocking him. But I have to admit that experiencing the cause of the Fall firsthand over the last two days gave me a new appreciation for the terror our ancestors must have felt as the Scourge overtook them, turning them one by one into the vast numbers of creatures that now roam the earth.

"Have you ever noticed that he almost seems happy about it? Like we brought it on ourselves or something?" Calli's voice is pitched low. "Sometimes I wonder if he thinks we all deserve to be, you know, consumed."

"Calli!" Eland says, sounding scandalized.

"Well, he *is* obsessed!"

"Aren't we all?" I say. "Without the Scourge we wouldn't have to be afraid anymore. We wouldn't have to hide in these caves. We wouldn't even have to live on the ground. We could live in the trees, or in the City, or even in deserts, if we wanted. Maybe we could find a camel, or a tiger–"

"What? What are deserts? And tigers? What are you talking about, Fenn?" Calli asks.

I feel them staring at me, and I wish I hadn't said anything. Suddenly, loud voices ricochet across the cave.

"They cheated us, I tell you!" Adder shouts.

"We can't be sure of that," Fox says. His voice is calm. More calm than Adder's, anyway.

"The sacks aren't full! What else could it be?"

"Where's Fennel? We should ask her what happened." It's Aloe.

I stand, willing my tired legs not to wobble, hoping I look stronger than I feel. "Over here."

Adder reaches me first, moving so silently I'm sure he must have slithered. "Did you fill all four sacks today?"

"Yes." I try to keep my voice even, but a defensive note creeps in. People gather around, their whispers reverberating against the walls of rock.

"All the way to the top?" Sable asks. "Each of them?"

I hesitate. Between fighting my fear of the creatures, and resisting the urge to swim away from them, I can't remember whether I did or not.

"Fennel," Aloe says, "I know you did your very best. But the sacks the Lofties brought to us were only three-quarters full. To the best of your knowledge, did you fill them all the way up?"

"I don't know. I think so."

"You see?" Adder explodes. "They're cheating us, pulling off extra water! Fennel, tomorrow you'll collect one sack for us. Don't give it to the Lofty Keeper to hold. Drag it back here instead."

"So you'll put us on water rations to punish the Lofties?" Fox still sounds composed, but there's a sharp edge to his voice.

"I'll do what it takes to show them we won't be taken advantage of," Adder says.

"We should discuss this. The girl isn't sure," Sable says.

"There's nothing to discuss! We won't tolerate Lofty deceit."

"Adder, Sable, we should speak somewhere more private." Aloe's voice holds a warning. The crowd has grown. She squeezes my shoulder reassuringly before the Three move away. People disperse, muttering in worried voices.

I sink back down to the freezing floor. My one responsibility was to fill the bags and deliver them to the Lofties. Did I fill them completely? Could I have been so distracted that I only filled them part of the way? Wouldn't Peree have pointed it out if I had? How could I have failed to do the one thing that was expected of me? Calli and Eland go back to their meals, but I push the rest of mine aside. What little appetite I had is gone now. Someone drops down next to us.

"Damn Lofties," Bear says. "Stealing from us—after all you went through to collect water for them."

"What do you think happened, Fenn?" Calli asks. "Could the sacks have leaked somehow?"

I shrug, feeling helpless. How can I explain my state of mind while I was filling and tying those sacks? I can't, not without admitting I was almost paralyzed with fear, dependent on the voice of a Lofty to pull me through.

"We all know Fenn did her duty well, as she always has," Bear says, patting my back. I'm touched by his unquestioning faith, even as it causes fresh guilt to rip through me. I smile a half-smile at him. "It was probably that Lofty Keeper of yours. Wouldn't be surprised if he quenched his own thirst before delivering the sacks, then blamed it on you."

My smile fades. "Peree wouldn't do that."

27

"I didn't like the look of him," he continues. "Looked like he'd cheat his own mother out of her ration if he got the chance."

"Don't say that about him." My voice is harsh, indignant; it surprises everyone, including me. "He wouldn't steal the water, or blame me. And his mother's dead. She was taken by the Scourge."

I can almost see Calli shoot Bear a warning glance. "Okay, okay, we believe you," she says.

My friends soon start talking again, but I don't join in. I pull my knees up and bury my face in my skirt, feeling awful. An undercurrent of unrest ripples through the cave, moving from group to group, riding the flickering light of the torches.

The Three decide I'll fill only one bag the next day, for us. They figure that's all I can carry back with me, and I'm not going to argue. Aloe walks with me through the passage to the mouth of the cave, her stick tapping like a heartbeat. She gives me a message to pass on to Peree: The Groundling Council of Three will allow me to resume collecting water for the Lofties when they receive an official apology from the Lofty Council for the theft of our ration.

"What if I … what if …" I can't admit my doubts out loud.

"I tried to explain to the others how difficult the first few days among the creatures are. That you may not be at all certain what you did or didn't do. But Adder would not be swayed, and in the end Sable agreed, to pacify him. I was outvoted." She sounds so tired.

"But this is going to antagonize the Lofties!"

"I know. Adder seems determined to start something with them, something that won't end well for either side."

"What should I do, then?"

I feel her draw herself up to her full height. "Your duty, as we all must."

She embraces me at the mouth of the cave. I hang on to her for a moment, like I used to when I was frightened by a thunderstorm, or by stories the older children told of the flesh-eaters. But instead of pulling me into the comfort of her thin chest like she would have then, she presses me away.

"Be safe, child."

Despite her words, I think my childhood is now behind me.

I enter the forest, wondering when and how to give Peree the Council's message. Do I get our water and then tell him? Or tell him first? What's the protocol for picking a fight? Or did the Lofties already pick one by stealing our water?

"Good morning," Peree calls. "No sightings of fleshies in the forest this morning. We might be in luck."

"Really? They're gone?" If the Scourge left, maybe it will smooth over the conflict. The caves seem to drive people to do foolish, reckless things. Daylight rights their sense of perspective.

"No, they're by the water hole. I meant you should be able to get a little farther without drawing their attention."

"Oh."

"But I have a surprise for you." He sounds excited, his voice higher than normal.

I have a surprise for you, too, and it's not a good one. "What is it?"

"You'll see."

"I'll see? That *is* a surprise." It's a bad joke, I know. He groans, and I laugh, until I remember what I'm about to do. I walk on in silence.

It's quiet—quiet enough to hear the birds singing in the trees far above. It's also sweltering. Full summer arrived while we hid in the caves. I blot my forehead with my sleeve, and wonder if it's any cooler in the trees. I ask him without thinking: "What's it like up there?"

He hesitates. "Leafy."

I flush; of course a Lofty won't tell me anything about his beloved trees. After a moment he asks, "What's it like down there?"

"Hot," I mutter as I move to the front of the sled to strap the harness on. I take off down the track.

"Fenn, wait—your surprise! Reach inside the sled."

I shove my hand in the back. All I find is a coil of scratchy rope. I hold it up questioningly.

"There's a loop at the end," he says. "Put it around your waist."

"Why?"

"Yesterday you looked like you wanted to swim. I've got the other end tied up here. You can swim out for as long as you like, and when you're ready to come in, I'll pull you back to shore."

I move my hand up the rope. Sure enough, it's hanging from the trees. I give it a tug. Feels secure.

29

"Really? You would do that?" I ask him. I doubt the other Lofties would be thrilled about Peree helping me take a swim while they wait for their water. I don't even want to think about what my Council would say. "Did you get permission?"

"What they don't know won't hurt them."

I'm astonished at his daring, touched by his thoughtfulness, guilty I'm even considering it, and more than a little worried we'll be caught. But the temptation of escaping the heat, the tension, and especially the fleshies is more than I can resist. I throw the rope over me and secure it around my waist, grab the sled, and hurry down the hill to the water's edge.

The creatures surround me, but I dart past them. I drop the sled at the end of the track and kick off my shoes. When the water reaches my torso I spread my arms wide and dive forward, the rope trailing behind me. It's cool, but not cold. Blissful.

I swim out, using a strong overhand stroke, putting a little distance between myself and the shore. Then I stop, tread water, and listen behind me. The flesh-eaters sound distant already. So it's true, they don't swim. I laugh like a child who got away with something naughty, and turn over to float on my back. With my ears underwater, their cries are muffled. I lay like that, basking in the warmth and the relative silence.

I swim around, flipping from my front to my back, careful to keep the rope from tangling around me. Whenever I feel like escaping the noisy reminder of what waits for me on the shore, I dive underwater. My dress is waterlogged and heavy. I want to take it off, but of course I can't. Not with a male Lofty audience on shore.

What possessed Peree to arrange this treat for me? Was he only being nice? Was it a bribe? I bolt up at the thought. Did he do it so he'd have something to hold over my head? Like, I have to bring the Lofties extra water or he'll tell about the swim? Why did I trust him so readily? What am I doing enjoying a swim, anyway, while my community holes up in the caves, waiting for water?

Diving again, I kick toward the bottom. The grasses slip through my grasping fingers. I hold my breath and fight to remain in the safe, alien world for as long as I can. When I start to feel light-headed, I surge back up to the surface, gasping. Then I tug on the rope to tell Peree I'm ready to come back. Even though I'm not.

The rope tightens around me, towing me in. I don't resist, but I don't help either. The cries of the creatures swell, and my anxiety surges apace.

What will Peree ask for in return for this reprieve? My feet graze the sandy bottom, and I stand up and loosen the loop of rope. One of the creatures moans, panting its reeking breath in my face. *Welcome back.*

I throw my end of the rope in the sled, then fill one of the empty sacks and load it. Water streams from my sopping dress as I haul the sled to the top of the hill.

Peree calls to me from the trees. "How was your swim?"

No matter what the consequences, I owe him a sincere thank-you. "Wet, and wonderful. You have no idea how wonderful. I feel human again for the first time since the Scourge came. Thank you, Peree."

"You're welcome," he says, sounding pleased. "Hey—why did you only fill one sack? Now you'll have to make extra trips."

I stiffen. Here it comes. "How many sacks do you need?"

"Normal ration. Two."

My body relaxes. So Peree didn't arrange the swim as some kind of bribe. He isn't asking for a favor. He wanted me to be able to escape the flesh-eaters for a few minutes, to swim on a hot day and enjoy myself.

The Three will be furious with me if I don't follow their directive and give him their message. But how can I tell Peree now that there will be no water for the Lofties at all? That he, or someone he cares about, will have to suffer?

I can't.

I hope I look genuine as I smack my head, and smile up at him. "With the excitement of the swim and everything I forgot to fill the second sack! Here, take this one up and I'll go fill two more. My Council only asked for one sack, but we need it before dark. I'll take it back with me."

"Take it back with you? How?"

"I'll drag it. So let me fill two more, and we can be on our way."

"I don't get it. Why–"

"Peree, please, I need to move." It's true; the creatures are pressing in. Something brushes my ankle and I swallow a scream. Arrows buzz past me. Peree still sounds puzzled when he tells me I can move.

I hurry back to the water. I don't want to lie to Peree any more than I have to, after what he did for me. I still can't believe it. It was a simple gesture—he knew I wanted to swim, and he arranged it so I could—but I've never heard thoughtfulness toward Groundlings mentioned as a common Lofty trait. Who is this Keeper of mine?

31

I fill the bags, deliver one to him, and yank the other onto the ground behind me. It's unwieldy, but not impossible to pull.

"If you have to take the sack back now, why don't you let me bring it up and carry it for you?" he asks.

Not a chance. This is the one part of the Three's orders I'm actually following, so I'm following it to the letter. "No thanks, I'll manage."

We set off back toward the clearing, a smaller group of the creatures following. Struggling to drag the sack behind me, I'm thankful for my cool, wet clothes. But I feel sick, thinking about how to tell Aloe I disobeyed the Three's order.

Peree's been quiet, walking along above me. Suddenly he says, "Have you ever heard of a water dragon?" I haven't, of course. "It's kind of a lizard. You remind me of one."

The branch I'm wrestling out of my way almost decapitates me as I let it go prematurely. "What? You're saying I'm like a lizard?"

"No, I ... well ... okay, I am. While you were swimming I was thinking about ... admiring ... your capabilities."

I throw out an arm, then snatch it back to the safety of my side. "My capabilities? Which ones? Being slimy, or good at scurrying up trees?"

"Lizards aren't slimy, they're dry and scaly, like snakes."

"*Scaly?*" I sputter.

"And by capabilities, I mean how you do your duty without complaint. How you find your way with no hesitation. You swim like a, well, like a water dragon. I wouldn't be surprised if you could scurry up a tree—you do everything else better than most sighted people."

I feel blood rushing to my cheeks. I'm not used to praise like this. And certainly not from a Lofty. "Oh. Thank you."

"No hesitation, no stammering. See, you even take compliments well," he teases.

"I'm just so used to them," I joke, "hearing them *all* the time like I do."

He groans. "Ah, there it is, the conceit. I knew there was a dark underbelly to all that excessive competence."

I smile and start walking again, following the path out of the clearing, toward the caves, counting my paces. The creatures match my steps.

"You don't need a Keeper, you know. You do fine on your own." Peree sounds disappointed, like he wishes that wasn't true.

"No, I don't." I want to leave it at that, but after everything he said, it doesn't seem fair. "Your voice, it gets me through the day. Knowing you're there, it's what keeps me going." I wonder if I've just thrust my face into a wall of fire, or if it only feels that way.

"You failed to mention my unparalleled skills with a bow and arrow."

I snort. "Now who's conceited? But yes, body count is an undeniable part of your charm. And what would I do without a Keeper to keep me honest?" I'm teasing, but my face flames again. I'm being anything but honest today.

"There *is* that."

I leave the semi-darkness of the trees and step into the sunlight. The cave mouth should be a few paces in front of me. "Thank you. For the swim, and for calling me a lizard."

He chuckles. "You're welcome. I'll see you–"

"In the morning," I finish. But I'm not so sure. I'm not sure I'll live to see the morning after the Three discover my duplicity.

CHAPTER FOUR

The sun sets somewhere outside the perpetual night of the caves. I lie awake, wondering what will happen when the Three find out I gave the Lofties water. I thought about trying to explain myself to Aloe, but in the end, I didn't. I disobeyed the Council's orders, and hers in particular. I didn't do my duty. That's something Aloe would never understand.

Still, I can't quite bring myself to regret it. The swim was incredibly rejuvenating, for one thing. And Peree probably broke a half-dozen Lofty rules to set it up for me. But the real reason I disobeyed was that I disagreed with the Three's decision to cut off the Lofties' water. I don't know how those sacks of water ended up being less than full, but I don't believe the Lofties had anything to do with it. I'm not going to condemn them to thirst for something they didn't do, whatever the Council says.

I lie with one arm pillowing my head, and listen to the people settle in for the night. I wonder what Peree's doing, if he's sleeping. I wonder about his family, if he has many friends, if he's already partnered, or intended for someone. I didn't think of that possibility when I asked him to dance at the Summer Solstice. I asked on a whim. What would it have felt like to have his bow-callused hands on my waist, leading me around the fire?

I frown. Dancing, and particularly dancing with a Lofty, isn't on the agenda now or anytime soon. Surviving the Three is, and so is getting through another day of the Scourge. The creatures should be leaving soon. Unless they don't. The unpredictability of their behavior is what makes staying in the caves so frustrating—we have no control. The darkness and deprivation is difficult, and each day that passes creates a greater strain on the people. Not to mention on our stores of food and supplies.

I hear footsteps, and the quiet tapping of a cane. Aloe.

"Fennel," she says, and I know she knows of my deceit. I don't even pretend to be asleep. "Come with me. Now."

I rise and follow the sound of her stick, trying to avoid the small groups of sleeping people. I'm nervous, but resigned. I made a decision. I'll have to live with the consequences.

Aloe doesn't speak as she leads me into one of the passages off the main cave. It's even darker here, and colder. I'm wrapped in an extra blanket from the storeroom, and I burrow into it, my hands trembling. I sense the low-but-concentrated light of a torch ahead. Whispering voices fall silent as we approach.

"Fennel, did you give your Keeper our message?" Sable asks. He sounds as unfazed as always, but there's an unexpected note in his voice, like stepping into what you think is lukewarm water and finding it's chilled.

I take a deep breath. "No."

"Why not?"

"I wasn't sure I'd filled those sacks to the top. I didn't think it was fair to accuse the Lofties of stealing the water, when it might have been my mistake."

"So you deliberately disobeyed our orders?" Adder almost hisses. I think it's fairly clear that's the situation, so I don't answer. "How much water did you give them?"

"What they asked for—two sacks," I say.

They all gasp. "Two? Two sacks?" Aloe says. "When you only brought one to us?"

I hadn't thought about how that would sound. "I was following the rest of your orders, to bring one sack back with me—"

"You bring more water to the Lofties than to your own people?" Adder says. "Are the flesh-eaters affecting your mind?"

"No!" My shout rockets back and forth across the narrow passageway. Adder touched a nerve. The Scourge has been known to drive people mad from seconds of exposure, and I've had more than my fair share of intimate contact with the creatures in the last few days.

"Why did you act against our wishes?" Aloe asks.

I think of telling them about Peree's gift to me. I want to explain how much that swim meant, how it helped return me to myself, so I could do my duty for my people. But if the Lofties hear about it, Peree could be punished. He might be replaced as my Keeper. And I'm not sure I'm ready to admit, even to myself, how much I already rely on him being in those trees.

I reach for Aloe's hand, but I can't find it. I turn my palm up in a gesture of pleading. "I did what I thought was right."

There's a sound behind me, in the tunnel.

"Who's there?" Sable calls. Footsteps shuffle away.

"Stop!" Adder demands, moving toward the sound. There's a short scuffle, then two sets of footsteps come back.

"What's this about?" Sable asks.

"I thought she knew something about when they were leaving," a familiar wheedling voice says.

It's Thistle, a middle-aged woman who helps with the washing and repairing of the community's clothing. She isn't well suited for laundering—she's known to be careless and prone to laziness—but she enjoys her duties. The constant stream of people dropping off and picking up their washing means she's never short on gossip. I'm not surprised to find her eavesdropping on a meeting of the Three in the middle of the night, in the black of a frigid tunnel.

"The Council always lets the community know when the Scourge shows signs of leaving," Aloe says, her voice stern. "You know that."

"Yes, but there's been talk. Rumors that the Lofties are taking our water because they know the flesh-eaters aren't leaving quickly this time," Thistle says. "I thought Fennel might know more."

"The girl doesn't know anything," Adder says coldly. "But you, on the other hand, know better than to snoop around, listening to the Council's private proceedings."

"We'll inform the people the moment we have news of the Scourge's departure, as always," Sable soothes. "Now come with me." He and Thistle walk back along the passageway, toward the main cave.

"She'll talk," Aloe mutters as their footsteps fade. "The community will know everything we said by breakfast."

"I hope you're proud of yourself," Adder says to me. "They'll know of your disobedience and deceit now. We'll discuss an appropriate punishment for you, but in the meantime you might want to sleep. I have a feeling you'll need every bit of your strength tomorrow."

I nod and follow them back down the passage. When we reach the cave, I call to Aloe in a low voice.

"I'll speak with you in the morning," she says. Her voice is flat, but I hear a hint of regret. I creep back to my bedroll, where I lie awake again, wondering what the morning will bring.

"You better wake up." Eland's voice drifts through my troubled dreams. I try to roll over. "Come on, Fenn, wake up. This is serious."

"What happened last night?" Calli says from my other side.

I want to pull my bedroll over my head and block them out, but instead I reluctantly sit up. "What did you hear?"

"We heard the Three told you not to get water for the Lofties yesterday, but you did anyway. We heard you're giving them extra water because somehow you know the flesh-eaters aren't leaving. And we heard," her voice drops lower, "you gave the Lofties more water than you brought us, but we knew that part wasn't true."

"That's about the only part that *is* true." I raise myself up to my elbows. "So Thistle and her prying nose and big ears overheard, and now everyone knows?"

"Yes, but that's not all," Eland says.

"What now?" Neither of them answers. "What is it?"

"You tell her," Calli says, her voice breaking.

"Jackal snuck out of the caves this morning and set a fire under one of the Lofty walkways," Eland says.

"What?" I shoot all the way up, the bedroll dropping off my shoulders.

"They shot and killed him." Calli whimpers. "And when Rose heard, she sort of lost her mind and ran out to look for him. She hasn't come back. Aloe went after her, but she couldn't find her."

"They're both gone?" I ask.

"Mother thinks so," Eland says.

Nausea grips me, like I swallowed one of the nasty brews our herbalist, Marjoram, concocts. Rose, Jackal, and their unborn child. I can still feel the warm swell of Rose's belly under my hand. "This is my fault."

"No, it's not," Eland says, squeezing my shoulders. "No one made Jack go out there. He took being in the caves really hard, because of Rose and the baby and all. He kept saying he wished he could make the Lofties pay for their theft. I guess this was how he decided to do it."

"But if I'd done exactly what the Three told me to do, maybe he wouldn't have felt like he needed to set the fire."

"Why *didn't* you do what they said?" Calli asks gently.

"I didn't think it was fair. I didn't think the Lofties stole the water." I try to explain my actions without telling them about Peree and the swim. My excuse sounds as weak this time as it did with the Three. Given the consequences, no explanation will be good enough now.

"Adder's furious," Eland says. "I thought his head was going to pop off when he heard about Jack and Rose. He chucked his cup against the wall. Barely missed Bream."

"Were any Lofties hurt in the fire?"

"No, they put it out with their water," Calli says.

Was that an accusatory note in her voice? "Then why did they kill Jackal?"

"Ask your Keeper," she says. "Father said he was the shooter. Looks like he proved how good he was with a bow and arrow."

Peree shot Jackal? The grief intensifies, clarified by anger. How could he kill a defenseless Groundling, especially when his people had the water—water I'd provided them with—to put out the fire? How could he do it? And why did I ever think I could trust him?

After breakfast Sable makes a solemn announcement about the deaths of Jackal and Rose. Amid quiet sobs, he reminds us we need to be strong during the difficult times when the Scourge is here, to stick together, and to trust in the Three to make the decisions that will be best for the community. He urges us not to take matters into our own hands like Jackal did. Then he calls me up to the front.

People move out of my path, murmuring. Some voices sound angry, some sympathetic. I keep my head up, but my heart stutters, and sweat musters under my arms.

"Fennel—being honored with Sightlessness and thus protected from the Scourge, you have more responsibility than most of your peers. Normally you perform your duties in a manner that makes our community proud. Yesterday, however, you displayed a serious lapse of judgment that may have contributed to the deaths of several Groundlings. I know you regret this lapse, and I know you will not allow it to happen again." I nod, not trusting my voice. "Still, there must be punishment," Sable says. "Today you will collect six sacks of water and transport them here without assistance. You will not collect any for the Lofties." He pauses. The crowd is silent. The torches on the wall flicker and crack. "And you will spend the night in the forest, among the Scourge, as a reminder that you can either stand together with your community … or you will stand alone."

Shocked murmurs roll through the cave.

"Do you understand what's expected of you?" I nod again. "Then go and perform your duty."

I'm burning with guilt, anger, and fear, but I must obey the decision of the Three. Legs trembling, I push through the silent stares to the tunnel entrance. As I step into the dark passageway, someone presses a pouch into my hand.

"Bread, dried meat, and herbs—from Mother," Eland whispers in my ear. He sounds like he's crying. I kiss his cheek and thank him, then I walk until the tunnel swallows me, hiding my own tears in its familiar, comforting blackness.

I sit at the entrance to the caves, my back against the sun-warmed wall. Flesh-eaters pace outside, shrieking and howling at me. They're hungry as always. I'm torturing them—intentionally—by sitting just out of their reach.

I should go; it's going to be a long day. I have no idea whether Peree will be waiting for me, or what he'll say, but it doesn't matter. I've already decided I'll collect the six sacks of water without his help. After last night, it's obvious I can't trust him, as much as I had hoped otherwise.

I wipe away my tears, stand up, and march into the sunlight toward the forest. The creatures scream all around me. I scream back, until it occurs to me I must look mad having a shouting match with a pack of half-humans. I stop, and realize Peree's yelling, too. I can barely hear him over the flesh-eaters' furious noise.

"Fennel! I need to talk to you."

"Go away," I shout, and continue on to the clearing. Sweat trickles down the back of my neck. It's steaming, even at this early hour.

He follows me through the trees. "I didn't want to shoot him; it was my duty. I was the lookout this morning–"

"Your duty? To kill an unarmed man? He was frustrated from staying in the caves for days. He didn't do any real harm!"

The creatures groan. I notice, not for the first time, that the more upset I am, the more agitated they become.

"Did you know his partner was pregnant?" I say. "And that she left the caves to find him, and that she was taken by–" I choke on my tears. I don't want to completely break down again.

"I heard," he says. "I'm sorry."

"Sure you are," I say. "You Lofties are known for your compassion, aren't you? Always looking out for us, up in your safe little nests. More like looking *down* on us." I'm going too far, but I can't seem to stop now that I've started. "Why are you even pretending to be my friend, with your swim and your compliments? You said I don't need a Keeper, and now I don't want one. Stop following me around. Leave me alone."

"I can't do that." His voice is low.

"And I can't do anything to stop you, can I? Then do what you have to, but you might not want to exert yourself too much. You won't be getting any water from us today."

"We anticipated that."

"Aren't you the clever ones." I clamp my lips shut. I'm probably close to getting shot, too.

It's time to get to work anyway; I'm at the sled track. I grab the sled and run down the hill with it, hoping to have several trips completed before the temperature goes from steaming to blazing. The scraping of the sled along the track brings a fresh wave of creatures to me.

Once, while searching for a patch of wildberry bushes in the forest, I put my foot through the rotting carcass of an animal. The foul odor clung to my shoe for days. This stench is much, much worse. It's going to be a very long day, and an even longer night.

Sometime later I collapse in the clearing, our deserted shelters all around me. I've made four trips to the caves, dragging the loaded sacks behind me, but I still have two more trips to make and I'm coming to the end of my mental and physical reserves of energy. I want nothing more than to lie down and go to sleep. As if I could, with the sickening cloud of creatures around me.

Peree still follows. He hasn't tried to talk to me again, but I hear him up there. Whenever the creatures crowd me he clears some space with his arrows. I don't even stop walking as he shoots. *What's the death of another Groundling to him?* I think bitterly.

I ease my leather slipper off and touch the angry blister on my heel. Moisture bursts out, and one of the creatures moans hungrily. I shove my shoe back on, disgusted, and limp into our shelter.

The creatures follow me in. There's no way to secure the door against them. I've fetched items from other people's homes in the past few days since the Scourge came—favorite toys, water sacks, winter clothes, Bear's extra spear—but I haven't been inside ours. Something about having the creatures in our home makes me feel even more revolted. I won't be able to sleep here tonight. I go back out and press my forehead to the wall. Spreading my fingers wide against the warm wood, I search for the will to collect the last two sacks.

A creature moans close by. I turn my face away, too tired to move any farther. It moans again, but this time it sounds like … more than a moan. I stumble away and fall, skinning the palms of my hands.

"Are you all right?" Peree yells.

I forget I'm not speaking to him. "Do you see the creature that was next to me just then, when I was by the shelter? Does it look any different?"

"They all look the same," he says. "Repulsive."

"Please, Peree, look closely! Do any of them seem, I don't know, newer maybe?" I can't tell him what I'm thinking. It's too horrible to say out loud.

"Newer? What are you getting at, Fennel?"

"Do any of them have long, curly brown hair?"

"Not that I see. Some of them have wisps of grayish-looking hair; most don't have any at all. Why, what's going on?"

I hold my stinging hands to keep them from shaking. "Nothing, I must be hearing things."

But I wasn't.

One of the creatures spoke. It said, *Help me.*

And it sounded exactly like Rose.

CHAPTER FIVE

I'm back at the top of the sled track, two more sacks filled and delivered. My feet are bare, shoes discarded somewhere along the path. I lean against a tree trunk, waiting for the sun to suck the most intense heat with it below the horizon before I venture to the water hole to drink. The food Eland and Aloe gave me is long gone. I'm numb from fatigue and hunger. The idea of spending the night among the flesh-eaters isn't even that frightening anymore.

I stagger down to the water, fall on my hands and knees, and drink like an animal. As I clean my filthy face and hands, I can tell my skin will be swollen with sunburn by morning. The creatures hover, shuffling and chewing their tongues. When will they go? I haven't heard the sounds of a single animal since the Scourge came. What could they be feeding on? I hear Jack's easy laugh and Rose's tinkly voice in my mind, and I cringe. I haven't heard … what I thought I heard … again. It's almost a relief to be surrounded by the flesh-eaters' shrieks and groans.

After drinking my fill, I drag myself back up the hill to the tree I was lying against before. It's as good a place as any. I push together some leaves and brush to make a pillow, curl up, and almost instantly I'm asleep.

Something hits my head. I push myself up, confused.

"Fennel," Peree says, "listen!"

I do, and fear crashes through me. A crowd of howling creatures encircles me. I pull my legs up under my chin, making myself smaller. "What are they doing? What's happening?"

"Ever since you fell asleep they've been coming, gathering around you. They seem more aggressive. My arrows weren't keeping them back, so I've been throwing things to wake you up. You need to go back to the caves."

"Can't," I mumble. "Punished. Have to stay out here." I try to stand, but I sink back down. My eyes sting like I've been rubbing dirt into them, and Peree's voice sounds like it's percolating from underwater. My cheek drops onto my arms.

"Try," he pleads. "Try to stay awake. I'll tell you a story."

"More animals? Won't be enough, too tired … "

I'm walking on top of the water. I have an expansive, majestic pair of wings sprouting from the middle of my back. I can always "see" in my dreams, although I don't know if what I picture is the same as what the sighted see. My wings begin to flap and I take off, low and slow, my feet skimming the surface. I revel in the speed, and the freedom. I'm starting to gain altitude, when I hear a shout from the shore. Something strikes my beautiful wing, and I crash into the water.

My right arm throbs. "Quit throwing things, Peree! Let me be!"

"It wasn't me. Were you … bitten?" Horror strangles his voice.

I touch my arm. It's not bleeding, but it hurts like hell. My voice shakes as I answer him. "I think I was, maybe."

I pull myself up against the tree and almost topple over. The flesh-eaters scream at the sudden movement. I start to pace, my hand over the bite, but it's hard to pace when you're surrounded.

"How do you feel?" Peree's voice is hollow now. "Any … different?"

Am I changing? I'm sick and dizzy with exhaustion, but I still feel like me. For now. "My arm hurts. How fast do you think it happens?"

"I've never seen someone change, but I've heard it's quick."

"I've heard that too," I say.

"It's like your protection faded when you fell asleep. Did Aloe say that could happen?"

"No, but I don't think she ever slept with the fleshies." Blood pounds in my ears, distorting the cries of the creatures. I realize I'm about to faint. I lodge myself against the tree and jam my head between my legs. When the fuzziness clears away a little, I straighten up slowly. "I'm scared, Peree." A sob sticks in my throat.

"It's all right, it's going to be all right." His voice sounds different now, calmer. "You can come up here."

"What?"

"I'll pull you up with the rope."

"But what if I change? What if I come after you?"

"I'll take care of it." His voice sounds steady, but like he's struggling to keep it that way. He's telling me he'll kill me, and all I feel is relief: I can't live as one of the Scourge. It's my worst nightmare.

"Isn't it against your rules? To allow a Groundling in the trees?" Not to mention someone who's about to become a flesh-eater.

"It can't be helped. I can't let the Water Bearer be taken."

That distracts me from the terror clawing away at my insides. "What did you call me?"

"Water Bearer. It's our name for you."

"Was Aloe called that, too?" I'm saying whatever pops in my head, putting off the decision, waiting to find out if I'll change. I still don't feel any different.

"Yes."

"I didn't know we had a name."

"Maybe Shrike wasn't as chatty as I seem to be. What do you want to do? More of them are coming."

I hear the new ones, moaning and panting as they get closer. That's it. I can't think the consequences through. All I know is if I'm going to change, I want Peree to be able to put an arrow in my chest, or some other essential body part. I want him to ensure I'm deader than dead.

"Send down the rope."

Boards creak under his feet. "I'm making a loop in it, like when you swam. Can you climb into the sled?"

I feel around for it and fall, more than climb, inside. When I stand, I can tell the creatures have moved in around me.

"Here it comes," he says, "reach up and grab for it. I don't want to bring one of them up instead."

I find the loop and pull it over my head, then under my arms. "Okay."

The flesh-eaters shriek as I start to ascend. I accidentally kick one of them as I go up, and I take a perverse pleasure in hearing it grunt—hopefully in pain. The feeling of hanging in midair is unfamiliar and scary, but despite everything, also strangely exhilarating. I'm flying, like in my dream.

"Swing your legs, I'll pull you in," Peree says.

I do what he says, aiming for his voice, and scramble onto the walkway. I end up flush against his body, my face against his warm chest, my arms around his waist. I drop my hands, and he takes a step back, clearing his throat.

Relief surges through me, diluting the fear. I'm in the trees—safe from the Scourge. Then the walkway sways, and abruptly I feel vulnerable again. I'm in the trees—in Lofty territory. I have little fear of moving around on the ground most of the time, but this is different. There's no map in my head of these walkways, and I know nothing of Lofty ways. I stand very still, afraid a step in any direction will cause me to plunge to the ground, or into some unknown trap.

"What is it?" Peree asks. "Do you feel different?"

"I don't–" *I don't like asking for help.* "Is there something to hold on to?"

"Oh, of course." He steps beside me and takes my hand. "Let me see your arm … There's a bite-shaped mark, but the skin isn't broken. I'll wrap it." He tears some sort of cloth and binds my arm.

"Shouldn't I be feeling something by now, if I was going to change?"

"Maybe. I don't know. I think so." He takes a step closer. "You don't look any different. No, I take that back, you look beat. Let's sit."

He guides me down the walkway to a small seat—rough wood planking secured against the trunk of an enormous tree from the feel of it. I hear the rattle of his bow on the walkway as he sits down a few feet from me. The pungent smell of the greenheart trees, always strong on the ground, is even more potent up here. No wonder the Lofties all smell like them—except Peree, with his honeysuckle scent.

"What now?" I ask.

"We wait. Are you hungry?"

"Starving."

"Here, I have some bread, berries, and squirrel meat."

He puts a cloth in my hand, with the food wrapped inside. I want to devour it, but I nibble instead. This may be the only food he has. When the weakness and hunger pangs subside a little, I wrap up the rest of his food and hand it back.

His callused thumb slides across my fingers as he takes the packet. "So many scars."

I shrug, embarrassed. "My hands see for me, but they pay a price."

We sit in silence for a few minutes. Waiting. I'm conscious of his eyes on me, watching me, looking for any signs of the change.

"How do you feel now?" he asks.

"The same. My arm doesn't hurt as much."

I hear him exhale. "Maybe we're in the clear. That flesh-eater just wanted to see how you tasted before it dug in." There's the sound of a smile in his voice.

I make a face. "Probably like salt meat. It's practically all we eat in the caves. Keep your bow close anyway."

I allow myself to relax a little as time creeps by, and to listen with more interest to the sounds in the trees. Branches creak, the flesh-eaters roam around below us, but I can't hear the sounds of any Lofties. "I hope no one can see us," I say.

"Not likely. *I* can barely see you now that the sun's gone down. And no one sleeps this low to the ground." From his tone, it sounds like that should somehow be obvious to me.

"How would I know? It's not like I've ever been up here before." It's not like *any* Groundling has ever been up here before. "So where *do* you sleep?"

"Much farther up—our homes, the kitchens, the workplaces—everything is high up. This is only a little outpost. No one comes down here, except to access the water hole when the flesh-eaters aren't around. Hey, are you thirsty?" He changes the subject quickly, like he doesn't want to leave an opening for me to ask more questions about their community.

Guilt trickles through me, thinking of all the water I lapped up earlier. "I'm okay. You?"

"It's manageable. We've learned to conserve our water rations when the fleshies are here."

I wonder if that means the Three have punished the Lofties before by withholding their water. I'd never heard that. Then again, when the Scourge came before, I was doing lessons or playing with the other children in the caves, not following every decision of the Council. A cooling wind blows through the branches, lifting the ends of my sweat-and-dirt-matted hair. I face the breeze and breathe deeply, preparing to ask him the questions that I've been asking myself all day: "Peree, why did you shoot Jackal? Couldn't you have put the fire out and let him go back to the caves? Did you have to kill him?"

"Yes, I did have to kill him," he says, his voice hard.

"Why? Because it was your *duty?*"

"He started it, remember? But no, not because it was my duty. He was being consumed."

"By the fire?"

"By the Scourge."

"What? No one said Jackal was in danger from the flesh-eaters. I heard he set the fire and you shot him as punishment," I say.

"Shrike told your Council exactly what happened."

"Which of the Three did he tell?"

"The one named for a snake."

"Adder. That's not the story he told us."

"And yet it's the truth," Peree says. "Believe me, Fenn, I didn't want to kill the man, but I couldn't let the Scourge take him any more than I could let them take you. Shooting him was the only humane thing I could do."

I'm torn. Everything I've been raised to believe urges me not to believe a Lofty. But I want to believe him. Peree's version of what happened is exactly how I would expect him to act. Look what he did for me. And why am I unsurprised to hear Adder might have lied, especially if the lie placed the Lofties in an even worse light in the eyes of the community? If I told them Peree's side of the story, it would be his word against Adder's. No one would even consider taking the word of a Lofty over the word of one of the Three. Except me.

"I believe you," I whisper.

"Thank you."

I listen to the moans of the creatures below. There are less of them now. They've dispersed since Peree pulled me up, like they have no interest in us as long as we're in the trees. Lucky Lofties. I push away the burst of resentment I feel, reminding myself that a Lofty probably saved my life. I owe him. Again.

"I don't think I would've survived down there."

His laugh is sharp. "We may not survive up here if anyone finds out I let you come up."

"You said no one could see us!"

"It's not likely, but still possible."

I frown. "I'm sorry I put you in this position."

"I invited you up, remember? I put myself in this position."

"And the Three put us both here." My resentment flares again. "What happens if your Council finds out?"

"Oh, I'd be punished."

"What would they do?"

"Probably give me the same punishment as you," he says. I chuckle, assuming he's joking. "It happened to my mother."

My grin disappears. Sending someone without protection to spend the night among the flesh-eaters isn't a punishment in our community, it's a death sentence. Permanent banishment—severing a person's ties to their life and setting them adrift in the forest with the Scourge—is reserved for only truly serious infractions, like intentionally taking a life. What did Peree's mother *do*?

"Is that how she died?" I ask.

"Believe it or not, she survived."

"How?"

"It's a long story. Sure you wouldn't rather get some sleep?"

I'm worn out, but I've only heard a few stories of sighted people who survive the Scourge, and most were from before I was born. None were about Lofties. Hazily, I realize *I* almost didn't survive this time. Could the Three possibly have known my protection would fail when I fell asleep? Did Aloe know? She wouldn't have allowed my punishment then, would she? I rest my head against the gnarled tree bark, too tired to contemplate all the possibilities.

"I'd like to hear it," I say.

Peree's voice drifts across the narrow, dark space between us. "From what I've heard, Mother was always asking questions as a girl: why we have to stay in the trees; why we can't walk on the ground or swim in the water; why we don't allow Groundlings in the trees; why we always hide when the Scourge comes. She asked hard questions, and she didn't like the answers she got. As she grew up, she went looking for different answers."

"What did she do?"

"She started leaving the trees without permission, to take walks on the ground."

"Really? Why?" The Lofties didn't leave the safety of the trees other than to bathe or to collect water when the Scourge was gone. They usually kept it short, and hurried back up like panicked squirrels when the task was done. Of course, we wouldn't allow them to stay on the ground for long, either.

"Shrike said at first she wanted to prove she could. Then she wanted to prove we *all* could—leave the trees, spend time on the ground—when the Scourge wasn't here. The Council was livid when they found out what she was doing. They talked to her, reasoned with her, threatened her. They even gave me to her to foster, hoping being a mother would tame her. They were wrong. She was a good mother—kind, caring—but being a mother didn't stop her. My parents had to give up a baby in the Exchange a few years after they got me. Mother supposedly left the trees even more often after that. My father said he worried constantly, that she might be consumed by the Scourge, or grabbed by a Groun–" He stops, as if he remembered who he's talking to.

I'm startled. I never considered the Lofties might be afraid of us. *They* were the ones lurking in the trees with their bows and arrows, shooting people at will. Then again, I thought, we creep around on the ground with our spears, superior hunting skills, and fire-setting torches. Maybe I could understand their concern, a little.

"Anyway," Peree hurries on, "the Council lost patience with her. They said if she was so comfortable on the ground, she could stay and see how she liked it." His voice is harder now, more bitter. "The punishment was meant to be for one night, but she was gone more than a week."

I almost choke. "A week? Where did she go?"

"I don't know, she wouldn't talk about it. Mother was different when she came back, more serious. She did her work, didn't ask questions anymore. The Council figured they'd found a cure for her curiosity."

"What did you think?"

"It seemed like she was waiting for something, something that never happened. She was always watching the ground … My parents began to quarrel. One night, they had a fierce argument. I remember being cold. I wanted them to lie down; it was warmer when we all slept together. Then, sometime during the night, she hugged me, and told me she loved me. The next morning she was gone. I think about that night, and I wish I'd done something, anything, other than rolling over and going back to sleep." Peree sounds … vulnerable. Like a child. My heart breaks for him.

"I'm sorry," I murmur.

"I wish I knew what was so important on the ground that she'd leave, give up her life, because of it. I've been looking down ever since, hoping to figure it out."

"What was her name?" I ask.

"Blaze, and it fit her well. She had red-blonde hair, like tendrils of flames. She was beautiful."

"And brave, from the sound of it."

"Maybe even reckless."

I shake my head. "I don't know what I would've done if Aloe had suddenly disappeared."

"You're close to her, then?"

"I thought I was, but now I don't know. Things have been different between us since the Scourge came."

"How so?"

I shrug. "She hasn't been talking to me. It seems like she's distancing herself–"

"Right when you need her most."

I nod, gratified that Peree understands how I'm feeling. I'm angry. Angry at the Council for punishing me in front of the whole community, and angry at Aloe for going along with it without even talking to me. Ever since she joined the Three I feel like I don't know her at all. "Peree, do you know who my natural parents are? I thought someone might remember when I was born, because of my Sightlessness."

"I don't know … you're about seventeen?" I nod in answer. "That's what Shrike said. I would have been pretty young when you were given up."

"Is Shrike your father?" I ask. "I thought he might be when we first met. He sounded so proud of you."

"He just wanted credit for his coaching abilities," Peree says, his voice warm again. "He's impressed with you. He thinks you'll be a strong, reliable Water Bearer, like Aloe. Others agree."

I flush at the compliment. "I'm not sure *my* people have so much faith in me." My voice drops. "I'm not sure I have that much faith in myself. When do you think the Scourge will go?"

"I wish I knew. It can't be much longer though, can it? Speaking of the creatures, let me see the bite." I offer my arm to him. He unwraps the bandage and moves closer to look at it with only the illumination of the moon. "How does it feel?"

"It still aches, but not bad. Why do you think I didn't change?"

"Because you're protected? Because it didn't break the skin? I don't know, and I don't care. I'm just glad I don't need this anymore." I hear him sheath a knife that I didn't know he had. The sound is chilling. He rewraps my arm. "So, why did you ask me about the fleshies' hair?"

I fidget with the worn hem of my dress, reluctant to tell him what I heard.

"What is it, Fenn? What happened down there?"

"You'll think I'm crazy."

"I won't. Tell me." He leans closer. That succulent, honeysuckle smell again.

The words tumble out. "I thought I heard one of them speak to me. She asked me for help. It sounded like the partner of the man you shot."

He whistles softly. "Are you sure? Could you have misheard?"

"Maybe." I draw my knees up under my dress, hugging them to my body. We always thought someone couldn't change back, once they began to change. But what if that was Rose I heard? Could we have saved her? Does it take longer to change than we think? Does that mean there's still a chance *I* could change? I touch my arm.

"Will you tell Aloe?" Peree asks. I'm not sure if he means about Rose, or the bite.

"I don't know. I don't know what any of it means yet." *And I don't know if I can trust Aloe anymore.* I'm ashamed by the thought. Of course I can still trust her. Can't I?

"Our Councils will need to know if you hear anything like that again. It might mean something's changing with the Scourge."

I rest my chin on my knees and rub my eyes. They're even grittier now.

"You should sleep," he says. "Would you like me to tell you a story? A bedtime story?"

I smile, and slide down to lie on my side, resting my head on my good arm. "What animal will it be this time? You said you'd tell me about the sheep."

He laughs. "I have a different story in mind. This was one of my mother's favorites. Have you heard of a cassowary?"

"Tell me." I close my eyes, listening to the hum of the crickets in the trees. The fleshies don't bother *them*, either. Lucky Lofties, lucky bugs.

"The cassowary was a bird, an unusual bird, that once lived in the forests. It had thick black feathers on its body; a bare, bright-blue head and neck; and it wore a crown. It was as tall as a person, fast, and a fighter, but it couldn't fly. It made its home on the ground."

"A fighting, flightless bird as big as a person?" I snort. "That's impossible."

"Maybe so. It's a story. Who knows which ones are true and which aren't? But this is the story Mother told me." He settles back against the tree next to me. "There once was a hunter who could take down any animal in the forest. He would sit quietly in the trees for days, waiting for prey. At first the animals avoided him, but eventually they forgot he was there. When they came a little too close, he'd raise his bow and arrow and strike.

"One day, the hunter went into the forest to hunt for game. He found a tall tree next to a water hole, and prepared himself for a long wait. At midnight, five giant cassowaries came to the edge of the water hole and circled around it, dancing. Very slowly, the hunter took aim. Suddenly, all five birds slipped off their feather coats, revealing five beautiful sisters. The hunter, who'd trained himself to be completely still while hunting, shook at the sight. The youngest woman was so beautiful, he knew he must have her as his partner. At midnight the next night, the cassowaries came to the water hole again. The hunter watched as they once again removed their coats of feathers. When the youngest sister swam away across the pond, he left the trees and stole her coat.

"After their swim, the women returned, and the youngest sister realized her coat of feathers was missing. Her sisters tried to help her find it, but they were sleepy and wanted to go home. The youngest sister told them to go. 'I will return when I find my coat,' she said. After her sisters left, the hunter approached the girl, her coat in his hand. 'Please give it back,' the girl said. The hunter shook his head, and began to walk away. The girl followed, pleading with him to return her feathers. He led her far away, to his home. When they reached it, she fell down, tired to the bone.

"The young woman woke up days later, and the hunter cared for her needs. But she only wanted her coat of feathers. 'It's lost,' he told her. The cassowary woman decided to stay with the hunter until she was strong again. But slowly, slowly, the girl forgot about her life as a bird. When the hunter eventually asked her to partner with him, she agreed. And soon after, she had a child. For several years, the hunter and the cassowary woman lived together with their son. And she was happy.

"One day, while the young woman was cleaning their home, she discovered a box hidden in a hole in the floor. She pulled the box out, opened it, and found her coat of cassowary feathers inside. As she stroked the black feathers, the woman remembered she had once been a bird, living free with her sisters. She slipped the coat on and instantly turned into a cassowary again. Flapping her wings with joy, she raced outside as her family was coming home from the forest. The little boy pointed to the cassowary as it flew away. The hunter knew her immediately. He shouted, 'Please, don't go!' But his words came too late. The cassowary woman had remembered who she really was." Peree stops. The crickets are silent too, as if they were listening.

"Such a strange story," I slur, already half asleep.

I dream of flying again. But this time when I take to the air, my head and neck are a brilliant blue, my feathers a glossy black. And nothing impedes my powerful wings as I soar across the sparkling water.

I wake to the sound of birds calling to each other. My head rests on something soft. Suddenly remembering I'm in the trees, I jump up. The walkway creaks and sways under my feet. I throw out my arms in panic, but then Peree's there.

He grips my arms, steadying me. "Easy, you're all right." His voice is husky with sleep, his hands warm against my chilled skin.

"I need to go, I need to get down. Someone might see us."

"It's early, no one's awake yet."

"Still." I was so frightened and exhausted last night; I would have gone anywhere the Scourge wasn't. Now that I'm safe, well-rested—and still human—being in the trees feels very wrong.

His hands stay on my arms. "Was it that bad, then, spending the night with me?"

I laugh nervously, and turn my back to him, finding a rope handrail running above the edge of the walkway. I hold it with both hands to settle myself. Peree stands behind me and places his hands on top of mine. My heart lurches, but I don't move away.

Instead, I turn my hands over and braid my fingers through his. Scars covering calluses covering scars. I listen for sounds of the flesh-eaters below, but I only hear birds singing in the swaying branches.

"I should go," I say again.

He leads me down the walkway and helps me loop the rope around myself. I wait for him to say something, anything, but he doesn't. As he lowers me down, I don't feel like I'm flying so much as falling. And instead of being happy when my feet finally touch the ground, I'm disappointed. I want to be up in the trees again, with him.

CHAPTER SIX

Two days later, and the Scourge is still here.

The community is meeting, trying to decide what to do. I sit with Bear in my usual spot, leaning back against the rock wall. I'm only half-listening. It doesn't matter what they decide; I'll still have to collect the water.

Unbelievably, no one discovered I spent the night in the trees. I slunk back to the cave that morning, the bite wrapped and hidden under the sleeve of my dress. Unsure what kind of reception I would receive, I was astonished when the Three publicly forgave me. Grudges lead to hostilities that a small community like ours can't afford, Aloe explained. I try to let go of *my* hard feelings, too, but it's not easy.

I think often about my night in the trees, but Peree and I don't talk about it as I collect the water. He finally tells me the story of sheep—dim creatures that gave their wooly coats to make warm clothes for people in cold climates—but he seems more distant, making me wonder if I dreamed the moment when we touched. I want to ask Calli what she thinks, but I don't dare.

Sable's droning on about how the Scourge has stayed this long before; how we should remain strong and wait them out. I lean my head against the wall, and close my eyes. Even after a full night of sleep, I'm exhausted. I drift off, until I hear my name.

"Fennel can't keep bringing us water—look at her," a woman is saying. It's Pinion. I can hear people twisting around to stare at me. "She's done in! We're on restricted rations as it is. What will we do if she can't collect the water anymore?"

"Then I will collect the water, as I have before," Aloe says.

"That's only a temporary solution," Fox says. "You're needed on the Council, and no offense meant, but collecting water is for the young. What if the Scourge doesn't leave this time? Pinion is right. We need a plan."

"The Scourge has always left," Sable says. "It's only a matter of time."

"But what if they don't? Our children are hungry and dirty!" Pinion's two-year-old daughter, Yew, whimpers by her side. Others murmur their agreement.

"They have a point," Bear whispers. "The fleshies aren't showing any signs of clearing out, are they?" I shake my head back and forth against the rock, my eyes still closed. "And it doesn't sound like the Three have another plan."

"The smell in here alone may drive us out, Scourge or no Scourge," I mutter.

Bear snickers. The small room we use as a toileting area is sufficient for short stays, but not for a lengthy imprisonment like this. The odor's creeping through the entire cave system; my sensitive nose has been barraged by it for days. And it's not only the caves. Bear smells like he's been rolling around in the fertilizer pile in the garden. I don't want to know what I smell like.

"Don't go near Moray, whatever you do. He stinks like a flesh-eater," Bear says.

"Are you two getting into it again?" I ask. "Ignore him. He's an overgrown bully." Moray is one of Thistles' three giant sons. Cuda is another, and I can never remember the third one's name.

"Exactly. And bullies need someone to put them in their place."

"Of course that someone's got to be you."

"Give me a break. It's incredibly boring in here, I need a little excitement."

Someone shushes us, and we quiet down in time to hear Bream say, "What about the Hidden Waters?" People murmur at that.

"The Hidden Waters are a legend," Adder says. "We have no proof they exist."

"Let this be the time to find proof, then."

I sit up. The legend of the Hidden Waters is familiar to all of us. The waters are supposed to be safe—safe to drink, and safe from the Scourge. It's said they can be found by journeying through the caves, but no one knows where or how long it might take to get to them. Groundlings have searched for the Waters before. They returned disappointed, or not at all. We pretended to search, too, as children, playing in the caves while the Scourge was here.

Adder's laughter is harsh, like the meeting of a switch and a bare backside. "It's a fairytale, Bream! We don't have the slightest idea where to look for the Waters, if they exist at all."

Fox speaks up. "If we had another source of water we could move to, then we wouldn't be at the flesh-eaters' mercy when they come." *Or the Lofties',* he doesn't say. "Even if we don't find the Hidden Waters, maybe we'll find another source."

"Are you volunteering to go, Fox?" Adder asks.

"Yes, if need be."

"No, Fox–" Calli's mother, Acacia, says.

"Who will go, then? Who will search for the Hidden Waters?" Pinion calls out, excitement in her voice.

Sable speaks. "Patience—it is no simple matter to look for the Waters. The Council must discuss the idea before any decision is made. Let us meet in private, and we will speak again this evening."

The meeting ends, and is followed by whispered conversations in the crowd.

Bear rips into some dried meat, and talks with his mouth full. "People must be feeling desperate, to want to search for the Hidden Waters again."

"Can't you feel it?" I ask, listening to the low, uneasy voices around us.

"What?"

"The desperation."

"All I feel is my empty stomach and my dry throat," Bear complains. "Oh, sorry, Fenn. I know you're doing your best." He must have looked at my face.

"It's okay." I stand up, brushing crumbs of bread from my lap.

He grabs my arm. "Really, I'm sorry."

"I know." I pull away, and hear him curse under his breath.

I'm not angry with him—it's not the first time I've heard someone complain of their hunger and thirst—but I'm discouraged. Despite all my efforts to stock the caves with food when the flesh-eaters aren't here, and collect the water when they are, there isn't enough of either. I'm weary, body and spirit, from doing my duty, while the people still suffer from deprivation. I slouch toward the passageway. No one notices when I come and go now. Except Eland.

He stops me at the entrance to the tunnel. "Here, take some bread and dried meat with you."

"I'm not taking your ration," I say, "and anyway, I'm not hungry." *Unlike everyone else.*

"Mother's worried about you. She said you're losing weight."

"You still need it more than I do." I squeeze his hand. It's covered in grime. "Ugh, Eland, you're filthy. Why don't you wash up?"

He hesitates before he answers. "No water."

My melancholy deepens.

I trudge up the path to the clearing, six sacks of water safely ensconced in the trees. Peree follows above my head, stopping often to shoot at the most insistent of the flesh-eaters. He's quiet again today, but the creatures aren't. They crowd around me, shrieking and moaning in my ears. I'm too tired to react. I think about the Hidden Waters as I work—if the legend is true; where the Waters might be; if someone will search for them; and if so, who?

"Peree?" I call. "How are your people doing?"

"What do you mean?"

"I mean, how are they feeling?"

"Angry, afraid, wondering when the fleshies will leave."

"Really? I guess I didn't think the Scourge would affect you so much." The flesh-eaters seemed kind of unimportant when I was up in the trees, like so much background noise.

"Of course we're affected. We're used to having water when we need it, like you are."

"But what are you afraid of?"

"Dehydration. Becoming permanent prisoners in the trees. More Groundling fires. And you."

I stop short, then flinch, worried the creatures will run into me. "You're afraid of *me?*"

"Afraid *for* you, really. That the Water Bearer won't be able to keep up this pace."

"My people are worried about the same thing. So am I, for that matter." I start walking along the path again, trying to stick to the shade. It's sizzling today, even under the sprawling canopy of greenheart branches. "Have you heard of the Hidden Waters?" He says he hasn't. "What? I finally get to tell you a story?" I tease, and then I tell him what I know. "Someone suggested we look for the Waters again," I say in conclusion.

"And?"

"And I'm thinking about volunteering." He doesn't respond. "What do you think?"

He swings between walkways before answering. "I think you've lost your mind."

I bristle. "Why, because I want to help my people? What if the Scourge doesn't leave this time? What kind of future will we have if we don't find another source of water?"

"Why does it have to be you? You already stock the caves and collect the water. Why can't someone else do this? And I hate to point out the obvious, but your Sightlessness might be a bit of a disadvantage when you're searching for something and don't know where to look."

"My Sightlessness is my *only* advantage! How long do you think a sighted person will last, wandering through the caves with no light and precious little sense of direction? And if the caves ever end, the fleshies will be there. What good would their sight be then?" The creatures let loose raw howls of longing and need. They repulse me. "What, do you think I want to leave my home, my family, to search for some mythical water?"

"No," Peree says, keeping his voice even. "But I think you'd do anything, go anywhere, not to have to do this anymore." He pauses. "I would, too, if I were you."

My anger fizzles. He's right.

"Promise me you'll think this through," he says. "What you face in the caves could be worse than the Scourge, much worse." I don't see how that's possible, but I promise anyway. I've reached the caves, but I hesitate before going in.

"I know I don't get a say, but I don't like this," Peree says.

"We have to try something."

"There has to be another way. Let me think about it. Give me a day."

"The community's meeting tonight to hear the Three's decision. If I do go, I'll probably leave tomorrow. Aloe said she would collect the water … so, I might not see you for a few days." I want to tell him I'm scared. I want to tell him I'll miss him. But of course I don't. *Coward.* "Be well, Peree." I sidle into the cave mouth.

"Fenn, please don't go."

To my horror I feel tears welling, so I hurry into the gloom of the tunnel. Later, I realize those were the words the hunter used as the cassowary woman flew away.

The decision is made. The Council will allow a volunteer to search for the Hidden Waters. We listen as Sable tells us what the lucky person will be in for.

"Don't underestimate the caves. They were forged long ago by natural forces as powerful and as inevitable as time. The caves are free of the Scourge, but the cold and the lack of light can be equally unforgiving. Your torch may not last more than a few days, and the passages are deceptive. Some lead away from a cavern only to return to it, with you none the wiser. Others end, forcing you to backtrack. And still others grow smaller and smaller until you can go no further. People have been known to wander for days only to find they've barely journeyed beyond their starting point. And if you do find an exit, the Scourge may be there."

"So what's the downside?" Bear asks, to nervous chuckles.

"This is serious," Aloe says. "If someone chooses to look for the Hidden Waters, they need to know exactly what they can expect." I feel like she's speaking to me, like somehow she knows what I'm contemplating.

"You must take adequate food and water, and leave a trail for yourself," Sable continues. "It will help you if you get lost, and if the waters are found you can then make your way back quickly."

I remember a story, from the old days, about two children who enter the dark forest, dropping bread crumbs along the path so they can find their way back home. Animals eat the crumbs, and the children become lost. Nothing edible to mark my trail, then.

"Is there a volunteer?" Adder says.

I take a deep breath and … Fox speaks. "I volunteer."

I can't decide if I'm relieved or disappointed.

"Fox–" Acacia pleads.

"Daddy, don't," Calli says. I haven't heard her call him Daddy since she fell off a rock and broke her wrist a few years ago.

"Someone must go," he tells them, his voice gentle.

"But it doesn't have to be you," Acacia says. She sounds a lot like Peree did.

"I'm afraid they're right, Fox. We need you here," Aloe says.

I'm not surprised. If the Three serve as the brain of the community, Fox is our heart. His optimism and good humor is infectious, even in the cheerless caves.

"Is anyone else willing to go?" Aloe asks.

No one speaks. I stand up, my heart hammering. "I'll go." The crowd murmurs, sounding dubious. "I work in the caves; I'm comfortable here. I've spent as much time exploring them as the oldest among us. I have as good a chance of finding the Waters as any."

Sable says, "Child, thank you for your willingness to serve the community, but you must stay and collect the water."

"Aloe can collect the water. She said so this morning."

"But, Fenn, how will you find your way?" Calli asks timidly. She's not used to speaking in front of the community.

"How will *anyone* find their way? Like Sable said, the torches won't stay lit forever. I'm not afraid of moving in the dark, and when the caves end I can leave without fear of the Scourge."

"And what then? Will you smell your way to the water?" Adder asks, his voice as irritating as a bee sting.

"If I have to," I say.

"I'll go with Fennel," Bear says. "I'll serve as her eyes."

There are several outbursts, but the voice I hear is Thistle's. "That's outrageous! An unpartnered boy and girl traveling together?"

Aloe says, "Thank you for offering to assist my daughter, Bear. But as her mother, I cannot allow it."

"Better luck next time, hero," someone mock-whispers nearby.

"Shut up, Moray," Bear mutters.

"I'll go with Fennel!" Eland calls out from across the room.

"No!" Aloe and I say together.

"But–"

"No!"

After a moment's pause, I hear him sit down again. I face the community, clasping my hands together in front of me to keep from squirming.

Sable says, "Fennel, are you willing to go alone?" I nod. "Aloe, are you willing to collect the water while she's gone?"

"I'll do what's needed for the community, but I'd like a word with Fennel—in private—before this is decided."

"Of course," Sable agrees.

"Come with me," Aloe says.

I pick my way across the main cave, listening to the hushed conversations of the people. I can't tell if they're for or against the idea of me going. Maybe they're just relieved it won't be them. I won't say it out loud, but Adder is right. I don't know what I'll do when I leave the parts of the caves I know well. I remember how vulnerable I felt in the trees, without a map in my head to move by. My chest tightens, and I swallow hard.

Aloe chooses the tunnel where I met with the Three, the night Rose and Jack died. I realize we haven't really talked since then. When I'm not collecting water, I can usually be found curled up in a dark corner, sleeping. Aloe's been busy with Council work, keeping the community organized while trying to dampen discontent. I have no idea if she's still angry about my disobedience of the Council's orders.

I follow the rhythmic sound of her stick, and stop when she does. I feel the absolute silence of the vast, black caves beyond us. It's sobering. I brace myself for a lecture, but instead Aloe hugs me. She smells as unwashed as any of us, but underneath that I can still smell her particular scent of herbs and iron. Her hands clench my arms, reminding me how strong she is. "Are you sure you want to do this?" she asks.

"I'm sure."

"Why?" She sounds curious, not challenging.

"I want to help the community however I can. If the Scourge doesn't leave, then *we* may have to. We'll need a source of water."

"Fennel," Aloe says in the clipped tone she uses when she's about to call Eland out for some transgression or another, "I'm your mother. I know when you're not telling me everything, and I want to know what it is before I agree to let you disappear alone into these caves." She pauses. "Does this sudden desire to find the Hidden Waters have anything to do with Peree?"

I'm surprised, but I try not to show it. "No, why?"

"You spent the night in the trees with him." It's a statement, not a question.

Shock shoots through my belly. "How did you find out?"

Aloe chuckles. "We weren't born yesterday, child. Shrike saw you leaving the trees that morning. He questioned Peree, then informed their Council. We still have to communicate with the Lofties at times, even while we're in the caves."

"Why wasn't I punished?"

"Peree explained how the flesh-eaters behaved when you fell asleep. Sable and I agreed you'd been punished enough, given the circumstances." I notice she didn't say Adder agreed. He probably wanted to banish me.

"Peree didn't tell me you knew."

"The Lofties keep their own secrets, don't forget," Aloe says.

"So he told them I was bitten?"

She gasps. "No, I didn't know you were ... are you all right? Where were you bitten?"

I put her hand over the bite mark on my arm. "It didn't break the skin. I think it's healed now. It doesn't hurt anymore, anyway." I hesitate. "Did you know our protection fails when we fall asleep?"

"Of course not, or I never would have agreed to the punishment." I feel a rush of relief, and realize I'd been wondering all this time if Aloe knowingly allowed the Three to put me in danger. "The Lofty Council told us you thought you heard one of the creatures speak, and that it sounded like ... someone you knew."

More relief. I've wanted to tell someone for days, but I didn't want to make anything worse. "It sounded so much like Rose, but I was so tired, I couldn't be sure. Did anything like that ever happen to you?"

Aloe doesn't answer for a moment. "There were times when I thought I heard something that might have been words."

"Did you tell the Council?"

"Yes. There were no secrets between us. Unlike between you and me these days."

I hang my head. "I'm sorry I didn't tell you about disobeying the Council orders, and about Rose, and the bite, and staying in the trees. But since you joined the Three–" I stop, losing courage, but she waits for me to finish. "I haven't been sure, when I talk to you, whether I'm talking to my mother, or reporting to the Council."

She takes my hands in hers. "Fennel, I'd hoped that we'd have more time to talk after I joined the Three, and before the Scourge came. You've had to bear more than your share of hardship—the Scourge only stayed two days my first time collecting the water."

I think about Aloe at my age, and wonder how much stronger than me, how much braver, she must have been.

"There are many things you need to know," she continues, "but now isn't the time. So I'll say this: you've come to the point in your life when what's best for you won't always be what's best for me, or even for the community. You must decide on the right course for yourself now. But no matter what you do, or what I do, know this—I love you, always." She kisses the back of my hand; her chapped lips are warm against my skin. "That said, I still need to know why you have this sudden desire to search for the Hidden Waters."

I frown. Aloe's words confused me. I'm happy she's not angry with me, but I'm even less sure than before how much to confide in her. What I want to tell her is that knowing Peree makes me think the Lofties may not be as terrible as we've been told, that maybe they're more like us than I've ever imagined. And if they're more like us, then a time might come when there won't need to be a division between us—when we aren't confined to the ground or the trees; when we can raise our own babies; when we can fight the Scourge side by side. A time when Peree and I might stand together as equals, not as Lofty and Groundling. But I don't dare go so far. Those ideas would be considered scandalous.

"I want to help," I repeat. That's the truth, too, if not the whole truth. "Aloe, why does Adder seem to hate the Lofties so much, even more than anyone else? Why does he want to pick fights with them?"

She sighs. "He does have his reasons. Did you know he was intended once?"

I grimace, repelled by the thought of partnering with Adder. "To *who?*"

"Her name was Peony. She was very sweet, and the sighted raved about her beauty. She adored Adder."

"Was she all right in the head?" I ask.

Aloe laughs again. "Adder was brave and clever, and he loved Peony. But he was reckless in those days, and he never knew when to stop his tongue. One day he was showing off for some friends, taunting a Lofty, and the Lofty shot at him. I think it was meant only as a warning. Adder jumped out of the way, and the arrow hit Peony. She died a few days later." She taps her cane on the rock floor. "People change, Fennel, and not always for the better. Adder became increasingly bitter, more hateful toward the Lofties. I suspect he even has a prejudice against Lofty children given to us in the Exchange."

"Well, that would explain why he seems to hate me," I say.

"He doesn't seem to like either of us, it's true," Aloe admits. "Adder can be stubborn, difficult. But he serves our community well, and he's committed to the well-being of the people. We owe him a great deal for his service. People have faults, daughter, and we must try to forgive them as much as we can. Now, enough about the past." Her voice is all business again. "Are you sure you understand the dangers of this search?"

I tell her I do.

"You'll only be able to carry about three days' worth of drinking water. If you've found no sign of the Hidden Waters after two days, you must return. Promise me you will, and you have my permission to go."

"I promise."

"Fennel, think about this while you're gone: I can tell you have feelings for Peree, feelings of friendship, maybe more. But even if he shares your feelings, you'll always be less than human in the eyes of his people, little better than a flesh-eater. And he'd be hardly better in the eyes of yours. Your feelings can only lead to despair."

I nod again. I know she's right, but a part of me—an increasingly stubborn part—wishes she wasn't.

By morning I'm ready to go, at least physically. I have a pack stuffed with food, water, extra clothing, and a bag of herbs from Majoram in case of minor illness or injury. Eland insisted I take his warmer bedroll, and Calli gave me her extra dress for layering in the cold. Bear made sure I packed the rabbit's foot. "Just in case," he said.

I also have my "breadcrumbs:" a pouch stuffed with foul-smelling crampberries. I had the idea to smear them along the walls of the cave every so often as I walked. Their potent scent lasts for weeks when crushed. I should have no problem following my nose back home, and I'm pretty sure *nothing* will be tempted to eat the nasty things.

I've said my good-byes to Aloe, Eland, and Calli. Others come by to wish me luck. Bear asks if he can walk with me to the end of the first passageway. I'm surprised, but I agree. He plucks my pack off my shoulder and slings it over his own.

We walk in uncomfortable silence through the short tunnel, the crackling of his torch the only sound. I'm stiff with fear, thinking about what I'm about to do. I take a few deep breaths to calm myself, and the acrid smoke makes me cough. We reach the fork in the tunnel. To the right is the cave mouth and the forest. To the left is the passage I'll take that leads deeper into the caves, and another, mostly unused passageway that eventually opens to the outside. Bear hands me my pack.

"I wish I could go with you," he says, his voice uncharacteristically hesitant. "I don't like you wandering in the caves all alone, any more than when you're outside with … them."

"I'll be all right." I would've welcomed Bear's company—any company—on my journey, but I wonder how he would've managed in the ceaseless dark of the caves, after the torch went out.

"I know you can handle yourself. It's me. I want to protect you. Do you remember during the fever a few years ago, when I was so sick?" It would be hard to forget the fever. Many people died, and almost everyone else fell ill. I was one of the fortunate ones who recovered quickly. "You mended my shirt, and stitched a bear on it to help me feel better."

I laugh nervously. "I remember. You said it looked like a fleshie. I think that was the last time I was asked to help with the mending. I was terrible."

"I only said that because I was afraid, afraid you'd be able to tell how much I liked it. How much I liked you. I wore out that shirt years ago, but I kept the bear you stitched." He puts a piece of fabric in my hand. "Here it is. I want you to take it, since I can't go with you." He speaks quickly now. "I wish I could've danced with you at the Solstice. I'd been planning to ask you all year, did you know?"

My stomach clenches. "No, I didn't."

"If the fleshies hadn't come, would you have danced with me?"

I don't know how to answer him. The Summer Solstice feels like one of my dreams, not real life. Real life now is the Scourge, hunger and thirst, uncertainty. I can't tell him the truth—I'd chosen to ask a Lofty to dance. But the truth is I'll never dance with a Lofty, because Groundlings and Lofties don't dance together. Peree said so himself. So I say what Bear wants to hear.

"Yes, I would have."

I'm totally unprepared when he pulls me to him and presses his mouth hard against mine. His cracked lips sweep across my forehead and cheeks, and he kisses my lips again, gently this time. Then he's gone.

I lean against the wall in the inky blackness, trying to catch my breath, and a hand clamps over my mouth.

CHAPTER SEVEN

The hand smothers my screams. I claw at it, then stop struggling a few seconds later when I realize large calluses sprawl over the ends of the fingers. Peree.

"What are you doing here?" I hiss.

"I'm going with you," he whispers.

"What? How did you know I was going for sure?" What I really want to know is what he heard, and saw.

"Aloe told Shrike, in confidence."

"I didn't know you would be here–"

"Clearly." His voice is frosty.

"Peree, Bear is an old friend."

"It's none of my business," he says. "We'd better get moving. Is this the passage we take?"

"Yes, but–"

A torch flames to life, and he strides away. I pull on my pack and run my fingers along the walls, hurrying to catch up with him. My insides, which weren't doing very well to begin with, are completely tangled now.

"Your Council let you come?" I ask.

"No. I didn't tell anyone I was leaving."

I grab his arm. "Peree! You have to go back, you can't come with me!"

He shakes me off. "Why? Your friend back there won't like it?" He laughs, but there's no humor in it.

"That's not what I meant and you know it. You'll be in terrible trouble when they find out!"

"Not necessarily. You Groundlings aren't the only ones who would benefit from finding another source of water."

I slow my steps. So he only came to find the Hidden Waters for the Lofties. It didn't have anything to do with me.

"And anyway, isn't it my *duty*, as your Keeper?" His voice is a sneer.

His duty. That isn't any better. Anger at his attitude, and shame that he saw me kissing Bear, get the best of my temper. "Feel free to go back if you're going to act like this. It's not like I asked for your help."

"How could I resist such gratitude?"

"Why are you being such a boar's back end?" I yell.

"Why can't you just say you're happy I'm here?" he yells back.

"Fine! I'm happy you're here!"

It takes a minute, but we both snort with laughter.

"A boar's back end? Really?" he says.

"That's sort of the milder form of the insult. Lofties don't say that one?"

"No, we call people other things."

"Like what?"

"Like, *uh*, bird-waste-for-brains."

We both laugh again, then walk on. Things aren't completely right between us, but the tension is broken. Somehow in the span of five minutes everything changed. I was kissed for the first time, and the last person I would want to know about it was watching. I went from searching for the Waters alone, to being accompanied by the person I would choose above all others—when he's not acting like the back end of a boar, that is.

We enter a cavern smaller than the enormous space we use as shelter when the Scourge comes, but still expansive. The sounds of our movements reverberate far in front of us, and well above our heads. Peree whistles softly.

"What?" I ask.

"The size of this place, and the strange formations." I forgot he's never been in the caves before.

"I've heard they're beautiful," I say, not bothering to hide the envy in my voice. I take a few cautious steps in, arms outstretched, feeling for the columns and curtains of rock I know are there. I find a pillar and walk around it, smoothing the cool surface with my hand.

"They're unbelievable," he says, "like drops of rain frozen while falling. Others splash up from the ground, or fan out like a palm frond. Some are bright white. Some have colors shot through them. You heard right: they're beautiful."

No one ever described the formations to me before. I can't picture them, but I know what falling rain and palm fronds feel like, and it adds depth and dimension to the rock beneath my hand. I make my way through the space to the other side of the cavern, sweeping my arms in front of me, as he looks around. I'm trying to find the passage on the other side.

Peree comes toward me, pausing a few feet away. "Will you let me help you if I offer, or bite my head off, like in the forest?" His voice is still chilly, but I hear a note of teasing behind his words.

"Ask me and find out."

He takes my hand. "May I be of assistance?"

"Yes, please."

As I would with Eland, I automatically slide my hand up to grip his arm more securely in case I stumble. He tenses. Embarrassed, I keep my hand still. He guides me in silence into the next passage, then walks away.

I grope around in my pack for the pouch of crampberries and pull it out. Holding my breath, I crush a few and rub them on the stony wall to mark the entrance.

Peree makes a gagging noise. "What's that smell?"

"Crampberries," I say. "I thought I'd use them to mark my route."

"Good idea," he says, his voice returning to the flatness I already despise. "Ready to go?"

I slide my fingers along the rock as we walk, missing the warmth of his skin.

"So what's your plan for finding the Waters?" he asks.

"I'm not sure it's a plan, exactly. I thought I'd go farther into the caves than I have before, listening for water."

"You're right, that's not much of a plan."

"Well, no one else had a better one. No one else even volunteered. At least, no one the Three were willing to part with. So it's just me."

"Us," he amends quietly.

We spend the next several hours moving through passages that lead to caverns, smaller caves, and ever more passages, trailing foul-smelling crampberries behind us. We stop for a few minutes to rest and eat. Then Peree puts his torch out to save the light for when we reach parts of the caves I'm unfamiliar with. I have a good idea where I'm going for now. I've explored the passages off our main cave many times, although never beyond a day's walk. But Peree stumbles often in the dark, so I keep our pace slow. We walk mostly in silence. Lulled by the quiet, I jump when he suddenly swears.

"How do you stand this? The dark, and the quiet? Talk to me, will you? I can't listen to my own thoughts another minute."

"What do you want to talk about?" I ask.

"Anything, as long as I can hear your voice."

"Can I ask you questions? About your life?" I don't wait for him to say no. "What do you do when the Scourge isn't here? Like, I work in the caves. What's your duty?"

When he speaks again, he sounds closer to normal than he has all day. "I'm a lookout. I walk the perimeter and watch for signs of the flesh-eaters. I also do a little trapping and hunting while I'm out, and I look for parts of the walkways that need repair. I fix them myself if I can, but sometimes a woodworker's needed, so my cousin Petrel comes with me."

"You have a cousin?" Peree's never mentioned family other than his parents before.

"Cousin, and best friend."

"He's your age?"

"Two years older. He partnered last year. Moonlight finally realized he wasn't joking every time he told her he worshipped her. She's expecting now."

"*Moonlight?*" I try—too late—not to snicker.

"Yes, *Fennel.*"

"I'm sorry, but it sounds strange to me."

"Your names sound strange to us too."

I shrug. "They're having a baby? When?"

"Late fall. Petrel's thrilled."

"I wouldn't be," I say, thinking of Rose. I crush more berries as we enter a new passage.

"Why? You're good with children."

I stop mid-smear. "How do you know?" I can't think of a time we even talked about children.

"I just think you would be. Why don't you want them?"

I wipe the remains of the berries from my hand along the wall. "It's not that I don't want them, so much as I don't want to go through the Exchange." I've listened to the sobs of too many mothers night after night for months—years—after having to give up their babies to the Lofties at the

Winter Solstice. Why would I put myself through that? "But plenty of people still seem willing to take their chances, so I don't think the community will miss having one less mother. Do you want children?"

"I don't know, I think so."

"Are you intended?" I blurt the question, but now I'm not sure I want to hear the answer.

"No."

I release the breath I didn't know I was holding. Then I almost choke when I hear what he says next.

"She's too young. We don't partner until the girl is at least eighteen." Suddenly I don't want to know any more about Peree's love life.

We enter a new cave that sits along the fuzzy edge of the map in my head. The churning of my stomach tells me it's almost dinnertime, and my throbbing shoulders and legs insist it's time to stop for the day.

"Should we make camp?" I ask. "This is almost as far as I've explored. We'll have to decide which direction to go from here."

"Better to decide after we've slept," he agrees. "I'll make a fire."

I dump my pack and rub my stiff, aching shoulders with my stiff, aching hands, still brooding about what he said. Why did he touch me that morning in the trees, when he has a partner all picked out? Maybe I completely misinterpreted his touch. Maybe he was just being friendly. I think about his warm hands covering mine, and heat spreads over my body like a liquid blanket. I yank one of the oilskin sacks of water out of my pack, much smaller than the ones I fill at the water hole. It's almost empty.

We share a meal of bread, berries, and a little cured possum meat in front of a welcome fire. It's not much food. My stomach still grumbles as we clean up. Peree's hunger must be even worse, but neither of us bothers to complain. I hear him searching through his pack, and a minute later, there's a sharp scraping sound.

"What are you doing?" I ask.

"Carving."

"Carving what?"

He hands me a smooth piece of wood, about the size of a greenheart seed pod. I touch it, and feel the contours of a perfectly shaped little bird, from its beak and wings right down to tiny wooden feet.

"That's amazing. How did you learn?" I ask.

"My grandfather, Shrike's father. He was a woodworker, like Petrel. If you like it, you can have it when it's finished." I thank him, and hand the bird back. The scraping continues. "Grandfather wouldn't have liked it here, in the caves. He always said the trees are our caretakers. They provide our shelter, our safety, our food, our amusement. It's so strange to be away from them. And I've never slept with more than a wooden roof over my head, much less solid rock."

"What are your homes like?" I ask. As far as I know, no Groundling has ever had more than a glimpse. The platform we spent the night on in the trees was a glorified walkway, according to Peree.

"They're made of wood, like yours, but they're circular, and built around the trunks of the trees. The ones on the perimeter are pretty basic, only good for one person. That's where I stay when I'm on lookout. Others are large enough for extended families."

"How many families are there?"

"I don't know, I haven't counted them," he says, his voice guarded again. What does he think, that I'm gathering intelligence about the Lofties? Maybe he does. "You haven't told me much about *your* friends," he says. "What are they like?"

I tell him about Eland, Calli, and, after a moment's pause, Bear.

"Is he the one from the passageway, the one you're intended to?" he asks casually.

"We're just friends," I mutter.

"Looked to me like he wants to be more than that."

"Maybe so, but we're not intended, and I don't … intend … to be intended." My face is burning. "It's hard to even think about partnering, or having a family, with the Scourge around."

I sit and listen to the fire as he works. Then I pull out my bedroll, and wince. My fingers are chafed from running them along the wall all day.

"Let me see your hands." He takes my fingers in his. "I have a salve that might help. Frond, our healer, mixed it up for me before I left." He rummages around in his pack again, then spreads a thick paste on my fingers. It's cool, and has a pleasant tingly effect on my skin. He wraps cloths around each of my hands and ties them off. I sigh.

"Better?" he says.

"Much, thank you."

I lie back on my bedroll as the fire begins to sputter and die. Peree lies back too. The feeling of utter nothingness surrounding our little camp is oppressive.

"Fennel," he whispers after a few minutes. "Are you awake?"

"Yes."

"What will your Council do if we find the Hidden Waters?"

I hesitate before answering. We played a game as children called Snake in the Grass. Two teams try to steal a small sack of water from each other, while defending their own water at the same time. What makes it interesting is that before the game starts, one person from each side is secretly chosen to be the Snake, who waits for the chance to sneak away with their own side's water and win for the other side. We would be ready to grab our opponents' water for the win, when the Snake would suddenly slip from behind us, carrying our sack for the enemy. Calli was a surprisingly good Snake. No one ever remembered to suspect her. I heard Adder was the best Snake of his generation, hands down.

I want to trust Peree. He acts like he's on my team. But he's a Lofty—and he might be a snake in the grass.

I answer him. "We didn't discuss it. I don't think they believe I'll find the waters. What do you think your Council will do?"

"Thank me for being the brave, selfless sort who would venture through enemy territory to help my people. After punishing me for sneaking off."

"Do you have a Council of Three, like us?"

"No, ours is different."

"How?"

He hesitates. "We all make decisions together."

"Really?" I curl on my side, pulling my bedroll up to my ears. "I never knew that. And it works?" We wouldn't get anything done if we made decisions as a group.

"Most of the time," he says.

It's fascinating to hear about the Lofties. They're like the tree-tops themselves—always nearby, part of our lives—but entirely a mystery. I shiver as the frigid air creeps through my bedroll.

"Cold?" Peree asks.

"Freezing. You?"

"Can't feel much below my elbows and knees. How about another bedtime story, to take your mind off it?"

My face is too stiff to smile. "Please."

"This is the story of how the world was created—according to my mother, anyway ... In the time before time, when all was darkness and silence on the earth, the ancestors lived in caves underground, like this one. One day they got tired of the dark and the cold, and they broke through to the surface, and created the sun to warm and light the world. They made water, air, fire, mountains, rivers, deserts; they created the people, plants, and all the different animals. When the ancestors were tired, they returned under the earth to rest, but they left their spirits in all living things, to bind us together."

I think about that. "Did the ancestors create the Scourge?"

"I don't know. The Scourge isn't part of the story."

"They never are, are they? Like there are no new stories since the Scourge came, none worth telling, anyway." I blow warm air into my curled palms. "I wish we had stories about where they came from, and why. Maybe if we knew, we could find a way to stop them."

"Defeating the flesh-eaters. That would be a good story," he agrees. "Sometimes, when I watch them, I wonder if some part of the people they were is still there, like they aren't willing to let go completely, even if it means living like that. It would make sense, given what you thought you heard."

I think of the people I've known who were dying. They do cling to life, despite the suffering. I shiver again, as darkness swallows the last pinpoint of fire. "Thank you for coming with me, Peree."

"I'm your Keeper; where else would I be?"

"Let's see, at home in the trees by a warm fire, eating a meal with Shrike; or in a little shelter on the perimeter, watching the sun set over the forest–"

He laughs. "Okay, okay, don't remind me."

I laugh, too. Then I turn over and try to sleep. As unsettling dreams beckon me, I think I hear him murmur, "Anyway I'd be watching the Scourge, not the sunset, and wondering where you were. I'd just as soon be here."

His words warm my heart, while every other part of my body ices over in the never-ending night of the caves.

We wake early. It's too bitterly cold to sleep any longer. I jump up and down, trying to encourage my feet to come back to the world of the living. The pounding noise is earsplitting after the silence.

"I'll make a fire again, to warm us up for a few minutes," Peree says, his voice hoarse from sleeping. The sound of it gives me the odd feeling of fingers tickling me on the inside.

"Let's pack up and get moving. Walking will warm us up."

He agrees, and lights a torch to see by while we gather our things. A few minutes later, packs on our protesting backs, we're ready to go.

He tugs my sleeve. "Which way then, fearless leader?"

"You're asking me? I'm Sightless, remember?"

"Hasn't stopped you yet. I trust your judgment."

"I'm really not sure," I say. "This is as far as I've been."

"Then pick a direction."

"Okay." I spin around twice and point. "That way."

"*Um,* that's the way we came," he says.

"Well, I told you not to ask me!"

"Just kidding … that way looks good."

"Bird-waste-for-brains," I mutter, smiling.

He takes my still-wrapped hand and puts it on his arm, then leads me in the direction I pointed. I try to spread more crampberries around the entrance of the passage, but he pulls me back and takes the pouch out of my hand.

"My turn today," he says.

"I don't mind doing it."

"You'd cheat me out of my chance to smell them up close?" His voice droops with mock sadness.

I laugh, and hand him the bag. "Have it your way, then."

He smears the berries, grousing the whole time, then he wraps my hand back around his arm.

"I can manage on my own. The salve you put on my fingers helped a lot," I tell him.

"But I'm scared," he says in an exaggerated whisper. "I don't want to get separated."

I shake my head. "You're impossible."

"Yeah, I've heard that before."

Our laughter doesn't last. The passage is particularly lengthy, and it leads us to another cavern, larger than any we've been through yet. It takes almost an hour to traverse, even with the torch lighting the way. Gaping cavities in the floor make me very glad one of us can see where we're going. We get to the far side without finding another passage to take.

"It's a dead end." Peree kicks at the ground. Small rocks skitter away from his foot.

"It can't be," I say.

"There's no other exit. What would you call it?"

"There's got to be another way out."

"Except there isn't."

I sigh. "Let's go back toward the passage we came in, but around the outside this time. Maybe we missed it."

"Fine, let's go then, before we freeze to death."

He leads me along the edge of the cavern, and our moods blacken as another hour passes and there's still no passage. When I start to smell the crampberries again, I want to scream.

"We're back to where we started!" I say, jamming my fingers into my hair.

He takes a few steps away, then says, "Hold on, I'll be right back."

Minutes pass, or maybe it's only seconds, it's hard to tell. He doesn't return. A shiver wriggles down my spine, and not from the cold.

"Peree?" My voice rings out across the cavern. No answer. "Peree!" I shout. Suddenly I feel more alone than I've ever felt in my life, even more alone than when I took my first steps among the Scourge. "Peree, where are you?"

The echo dies away. I want to run after him, but I wouldn't know where to go. Frozen like one of the formations, terror steals through me.

Suddenly crampberries fill my nose again. *I'm not helpless*, I think, as I inhale the horrible smell. *I can follow the crampberries.* I take a few wobbly steps—and something grabs me.

I shriek.

"Fenn, it's me!" Peree says. "Come on, I think I found another way out."

He drags me forward, but I jerk him to a stop. "Don't leave me like that! I kept calling, but you didn't hear, and I … sort of panicked." My voice trembles.

He pulls me into his chest. I'm rigid with fear, but I quickly melt into the warmth of his body. "I'm sorry. I didn't think it would bother you to be left alone for a minute."

"Well, it did. From now on we stay together, okay?"

"Okay." He squeezes me gently, then puts my hand on his arm. "There's another passageway, right next to the one we took to get here. It goes back in the direction we came." I groan. "Don't worry, it curves off. I followed it for a while, that's why I didn't hear you call."

The passage does bend, seeming to lead us in a different direction from the one we used to enter the cavern. We walk for an age, before coming to a fork.

"Which way? Your choice this time," I say. He picks one, smearing berries before we enter. "How many do we have left?"

"Don't ask," he says darkly.

I frown as we walk. He's only using one or two to mark the entrances as it is. If we run out of crampberries we'll be forced to go back. We've made so many turns by now there's no way we could keep track without the smell to follow. We'd have to start leaving other supplies to mark our trail, and we can't afford to give up what little we have.

"There's another problem, too," he says. "The torch is getting low."

We haven't used it in the enclosed passages, but crossing the caverns takes much less time with light, and it's safer. Formations thrust out of the ground unexpectedly, or dangle dangerously down at face level. Without light we'd have to slow to a crawl to avoid them, not to mention the fathomless trenches in the ground.

I shake my shrinking second oilskin sack. I have one more, but I'll need it for the return trip. "And we're running out of water." I sniff the air as we enter a new cavern. "Peree, did you smear more berries?"

"No, why?"

"I smell them again."

He lights the torch, and swears. "This is where we spent the night!"

"Are you sure?"

"I can see the ashes of the fire. I'm sure." He sounds like he's gritting his teeth.

I remember Sable's warnings about the passages doubling back on themselves. "What time do you think it is?"

"Midday, maybe."

"Aloe told me to stop searching if I hadn't found any sign of the waters at the end of two days. What do we do?"

He takes a deep breath, obviously trying to calm himself. "Take a different passage. Come on."

We trudge back to the fork and follow the other passageway, then another, and another, winding our way through a dizzying maze of new tunnels. My shoulders slump under my pack and my walk slows. We don't say it, but we both know we'll have to turn back soon. We don't say much at all, buried in our own gloomy thoughts. It takes me a little while to realize something feels different.

"Have you noticed we're heading uphill now?" I ask.

"No, I've been distracted by something else."

"What?"

"I can see light."

We walk faster, and hope breaks over me. "I see it, too!"

"You *see* it?" He sounds mystified.

"I mean the darkness isn't as dark now. It must be a way out!"

"Hold on–" He stops, and shifts his pack around to reach something.

"What?"

"I'm getting my bow. We don't know what might be out there." In my excitement I forgot about the fleshies. "Stay behind me."

I do what he says, touched by his protectiveness. But really he's the one that needs shielding from the Scourge, not me. I tense anyway, ready to help in whatever way I can. We move forward, with Peree leading. After a sharp curve in the passage, the space in front of us seems to open up. The air is warmer, thanks to sunlight surging into the cave.

Then I hear a series of guttural snarls, very near. I've never heard the Scourge make these sounds.

"Unbelievable," Peree says.

"What is it, flesh-eaters?"

"No."

"What, then?"

"I think it's ... a tiger."

CHAPTER EIGHT

Peree backs up. I move, too, one hand on his back.

"A tiger? Are you sure?" I whisper.

"Do you remember the story? It's a big animal, yellowish-orange with black markings on its body. What else can it be?"

"What's it doing?" Before he can answer, I hear other sounds. Whimpering and mewling. "Peree, it has babies!"

"I think that's the problem."

"You can't kill their mother, they'll die, too!" So few large animals are left. The idea of killing one—especially an unknown one, maybe even a tiger—and leaving her offspring to die feels very wrong. "Can we go around her and still get outside?"

"The fleshies are out there." His voice is dipped in dread. Now I hear the moans of the creatures beyond the cave mouth. "We're trapping the tiger between us and them. There's another passage, but she's blocking the way to it."

"Let's go back," I say.

The animal's scream rips through the passageway.

"She's coming this way," he says. "Go back down the tunnel—now."

"No. I'm staying with you."

"Don't argue! I'll be right behind you."

"Peree—" The animal's claws scrabble on the rock, maybe five paces away.

"Run!" he yells. My heart spasms with fear, but I don't move, unwilling to leave him. "Get moving, Fenn!" He pushes me backward, and I finally run.

The animal snarls again, and Peree cries out. I clatter to a stop, unsure if I should keep going or try to help him. An arrow springs off the bow. The tiger whimpers. I take a few steps back the way I came, calling to Peree.

"Here," he says, his voice strained.

"What is it? What's wrong? Did you shoot her?" I hear the tiger whining, not far away. Her young still cry, and the flesh-eaters howl.

"Had to," he says through clenched teeth. "She attacked me."

I kneel down beside him. "Where are you hurt?"

He places my hand on the outside of his thigh. Blood slicks my fingers as I probe the wound. It's shallow but wide, with ragged edges. I pull out the pouch Marjoram sent with me, squeezing and sniffing each smaller pack inside until I find the paste of agrimony and yarrow leaves. Peree hisses as I mop the blood and pat the mixture into place.

"This is my fault," I whisper. "If I hadn't said not to kill her, if you hadn't had to push me away, you wouldn't have been hurt."

"Not your fault," he says. "Should've … focused on my target."

"That's my point, you were focused on me, and you shouldn't have had to be." I dig Calli's extra dress out of my pack and tear the bottom into strips. Fumbling with the cloth, I wrap it around his leg and tie it off. He moans, his body shaking. I hold his hand, wishing there was more I could do.

"Can you walk?" I ask, when the shudders begin to slow.

"One way to find out." He makes a move to stand, and I put my arm around him to help. He limps forward a few steps. "I'll manage."

I listen for the animal, but I can't hear her ragged breath anymore. "Is she dead?"

"I think so."

I bend down to find the body, and stroke her coarse fur. She smells of dust and scrubland, but of something far wilder, too. Where did she come from, and how did she survive the flesh-eaters and still feed her litter?

"Do you really think she's a tiger?" I stand, supporting him again. He lays his arm across my shoulders.

"I've never seen anything like her."

"What do we do about the young?"

"If we leave them, they'll starve." He pauses. "We could give them to … "

The flesh-eaters groan, like they know his thoughts. I tense. "No."

"Starvation isn't any kinder," he says.

"No! The Scourge has taken enough. We're not giving them this, too."

He squeezes my shoulders. "Okay, then. Why don't you go on? I'll take care of them."

I shake my head. "I'll stay. We're not separating anymore, remember?"

We walk toward the yipping babies. I know touching them will make what we have to do even harder, but I can't help myself. I reach out and find a tiny warm body, cradling it to my chest. Its teeth prick my fingers like tiny sewing needles.

Tears fill my eyes. "Peree … "

"We can't leave them," he says, "and we can't take them with us. We barely have enough food between us."

I place the baby back with its littermates and stumble down the passage. Sliding to the floor, I press my hands over my ears. A few minutes later, Peree leans against the wall next to me. His breathing is uneven.

"I'm sorry," I mumble. "I couldn't do it."

He doesn't speak for a minute. "When I was first learning to hunt, Shrike and I came across a possum. He wanted me to shoot it. I couldn't. I was ashamed, but he hugged me and said, 'Never confuse compassion with weakness.' I haven't forgotten his words." He shifts his pack onto his back. "We'd better get moving. I don't know how long I'm good for."

I wipe my eyes on my sleeve, and jump up. "We should go back."

"I'll be all right."

"Even if we find the Waters soon, which isn't likely, we still have a long walk back."

"Exactly, so let's see if we can find something before we have to turn around."

"Peree, I don't–"

He limps away. I catch up and put my shoulder under his arm to support him. The groans fade behind us. Loathing for the Scourge leaves me trembling.

"I hate them. They ruin everything," I say.

"I know."

"I can't help wishing … "

"What?"

"Nothing," I mutter.

He turns to me, his lips near my ear. "Tell me."

I shrug, covering the little shiver that moved down my body. "Do you ever think about how things would be different without them? I know it's pointless, but I can't help picturing what it would be like if we could live wherever we wanted. Groundlings and Lofties, I mean. We could all live on the ground, or in the trees."

"Would your people want to? Live with us, I mean?"

I consider his question. Some might be willing. Fox and Acacia. Bream, maybe even Aloe. Then I think of Adder or Thistle living side by side with Lofties, and I sigh. "Some would, some wouldn't. There's a lot of distrust."

"What about you? Do you trust me?"

I hesitate. "I think so."

He chuckles. "Honesty. Another quality I admire." He stumbles, and grunts in pain.

"Are you okay? Do you need to stop?"

"I'm fine." His teeth are clenched again.

"Oh, I can trust you? Really? You're lying already! We should go back." I pull him to a stop. He doesn't argue this time. I'm about to turn us around when I hear something, something barely audible. Peree starts to speak, but I quiet him and focus on the sound.

"I think I hear water!" I say. "Can you hear it?"

"No, but your hearing is better than mine. Let's try to follow it."

"What about your leg?"

"Come on, Fenn, the Waters have to lead outside. And we've got to be close if you can hear it!"

Except we aren't close. Hours, many winding passages, and a cavern later, and the sound of the water is still no stronger than a trickle. I can understand why no one has found the waters before. I have better-than-average hearing, but I can't seem to get a consistent fix on the sound. It teases me, sometimes growing, sometimes almost fading altogether. Peree sits with his back against the wall of the tunnel. He's had to rest often, and he isn't even trying to hide the pain in his voice anymore. I sit beside him.

"What do you want to do?" I ask.

"Keep going."

"Peree–"

"We keep going."

"Has anyone ever told you you're stubborn?"

He sips from his oilskin, and passes it to me. "Once or twice."

"We're running out of water, the torch is almost gone, and we don't seem like we're getting any closer. We've got to get you back."

He doesn't speak right away. "I'm not going back."

I listen for the playful note in his voice, but it's not there. "What do you mean? Is your leg worse?"

"I don't think it was too good to begin with, but yeah, it's worse."

"Let me feel." The cloth covering the wound is swamped with fresh blood, and the skin around it feels like a sun-baked rock. The back of my neck prickles. "We have to get you back."

He speaks deliberately, like he's explaining something to a child. "Fenn, I can't. Even right after the tiger attacked me, I was pretty sure I wasn't going to be able to walk two days back."

"Don't say that … please, don't say it." My eyes fill with tears for the second time today.

"Okay, let's keep going as long as we can. If worse comes to worst, you can carry me."

Joking again. "This isn't funny."

"I know." He strokes my hand. "It's okay, really."

I explode. "What exactly about any of this is at all okay? You're injured, we're over two days into the caves, we can't find the Hidden Waters, and we're running out of supplies!"

"At least we're together. It would be much worse to be in here alone, not finding the Waters, running out of supplies, and injured."

I swipe at my face. "There's a limit to my ability to look on the bright side."

He pulls himself to his feet. I jump up to help him. "Come on, it's not getting any brighter sitting around here."

We walk on and on through the absolute blackness, saving the bit of torch we have left. The passages have been subtly sloping down, tunneling into the belly of the earth, or so it seems. I would have turned around long before, but Peree insists we keep going. I only agree because the sound of the water is stronger now, too. The trickle has become a stream, enticing us on.

I increasingly hold his weight as he weakens. I feel so guilty. Guilty for leading him on this wild-goose chase; guilty that he's in the caves at all, instead of in his trees. A hard voice in my head whispers that none of us would be in the caves if it wasn't for the Scourge and the Lofties, but I dismiss it impatiently.

We camp for the night in an unremarkable cave, much smaller than the massive caverns we've been passing through. I change the dressing on his wound, and he falls asleep the minute we finish our scanty meal. I lay awake, wondering what I'll do when he can no longer walk.

I'm being consumed by the Scourge, torn apart slowly, every fiber of my body screaming in torment. The creatures pant around me, their fetid breath sickening me, as I finally succumb to them.

I wake, shuddering in terror, and realize the panting is real.

"Peree?" I whisper.

"Here." His voice is slurred.

I crawl to him and feel his forehead. "How are you?"

"Nice and warm."

I sigh. He can't be too bad if he still has a sense of humor. My relief shatters when I touch his leg. It's scorching.

"I was dreaming," he says, "about swimming in the water hole. The water was warm, no flesh-eaters. You were there."

"You swim?" I've never heard of a Lofty swimming before.

"Always wanted to. I watched you swimming with the others, wished I could, too."

"The others?"

"You and your friends. Swim, work, cook, play, dance, argue, joke. Everything you did. Watching you for years."

I'm stunned into silence. He's quiet too, except for his labored breathing. When he speaks again, he sounds more lucid. "Years ago, you were lost in the woods. Do you remember?"

"That wasn't exactly an uncommon thing for me," I say warily.

"Your friends were looking for you. A boar charged you."

I tense. "How do you know about that?"

"I was there, in the trees. I shot it."

"I've always wondered … I should've died."

"After that I watched you. Watched after you. I was the lookout, for the Scourge, for you."

I think back to all the times I heard movement in the trees and knew a Lofty was there. It happened so often I took it for granted we were being watched, but "we" being the key word—not just me.

"Why did you watch me?"

"Curious at first, about you, your Sightlessness. How you managed." He moves his leg, and moans. I want to comfort him, but I'm literally frozen. "After the boar, I felt responsible for you, worked hard at archery, hoping to be your Keeper. I wanted to protect you, even if we were separated by the trees."

"I … I didn't know."

He takes my hand, fumbling for it in the dark. "Didn't want you to know. I wouldn't have told you, except it doesn't matter now."

"I'm not letting you die here."

"Who said anything about dying?" His voice cracks in an attempt to laugh.

"I'm finding a way out." I crawl to my pack, and pull it over to him. Then I tuck my bedroll around him, and situate my last oilskin sack and the rest of the food by his side.

"Fenn. No use."

"Don't say that. It's not too late." I take out the pouch of crampberries, weighing it in my hand. It's almost empty. "I'm leaving my pack; I need to move quickly. Here's the torch." I place the piece of wood in his hand. "You saved my life once, Peree. Let me save yours. Please."

He presses my cold knuckles to his lips. "If you insist."

I allow myself to do something I've wanted to do since our night in the trees. I touch his face, exploring his features. I trace the ridged arches of his eyebrows with my fingertips, smooth his eyelids with my thumbs, and follow the firm line of his jaw. His cheeks and chin are forested in stubble. I memorize his face, both the beauty and the small imperfections, like a scar along one cheekbone where his beard doesn't grow, a small lump across the bridge of his nose, as if it had been broken. He lies still, his breathing becoming more even with my touch. I smooth his hair back from his face, and find the feathers Calli said he wore.

I kiss his cheek, and whisper in his ear. "I'll be back."

"I'll try not to wander off," he whispers back. "Be safe."

Safe. All this time he was worrying about me, wanting to protect me. Now it's my turn. I only hope I'm not too late.

CHAPTER NINE

I rush through the passages, running my hand along the freezing, jagged rock walls, listening for the water with every step. I try not to think of Peree lying alone in the dark, his leg burning like a lightless torch. I try not to think about what he told me, and what it means. And most of all I try not to think about what will happen to him. I focus on the water.

I have a theory. I remember Willow telling us the legend of the Hidden Waters as we dozed around the fire as children. She said the waters bubble up from underground, like rainwater seeping from saturated earth. Only this water isn't muddy, it's clean, pure—and most important—safe. Protected. It's what makes me so sure the source is somewhere in the caves. Where else would water be safe from the Scourge?

Willow told us something else. I remember her words clearly, as if she's whispering them to me now. She said the water came from underground and pooled in a water hole. A water hole *as warm as the air in summer.* If the water was really that warm, then it must be outside. Because nothing in these caves could be described as warm.

And if the water can find its way outside, so can we. I hope.

The smell of the caves is changing. It's musty, like Eland's shirt when he comes in from the rain, and every so often I feel a little moisture under my hand. I press on through the dark, willing water to appear.

Miraculously, it does. The roar of a rushing stream grows in my ears and the passage broadens in front of me. I step more gingerly, feeling the ground with my feet before I put my weight down. I can't tell where the rock ends and the water begins with all the echoing noise. When I do find the drop-off, I fall to my knees and plunge my hands into the stream.

I clean my hands and scrub my face, shivering as the frigid water slips down my neck and chest. Then I drink. It tastes very clean, like sipping pure air, but with a slight metallic tang. I want to know where the underground river goes, if there might be a way to follow it outside, but all I can tell is there's no more light here than in the passages behind me. The darkness is complete.

It's not warm, but this has to be it, the Hidden Waters. It has to be.

I don't have time to debate about it. Our water will be gone within the day, and it will be a long, hard walk for Peree to get here, if he can make it at all. I hurry back down the tunnel, berating myself for not bringing one of the empty water sacks to fill for him. I remember the crampberry pouch stuffed in my pocket. I shake out the last one or two berries, and rush back to the stream to fill the empty pouch. The water may not smell so good when he gets it, but it's better than none.

I follow the foul smell of the berries back the way I came, letting my nose guide me this time instead of my ears. As the sound of the water diminishes little by little, my anxiety grows. Will Peree still be conscious? Will he even be alive? By the time I enter the cavern where I left him, the third one I passed through—I made sure to count them—I'm in agony. I stop and listen for his breathing.

"Peree?" His name taunts me, bouncing around the room.

"I'm here," he finally answers, his voice weak. I allow myself to breathe again.

I kneel next to him and hold the pouch of sloshing water to his lips. "Here, drink."

"Mmm, crampberries." He tries to laugh, but ends up choking. I fumble around in the dark, repacking the torch, the untouched food, and the oilskin of water that I left for him. Then I search his pack. There's no way he'll be able to carry it or his bow and quiver of arrows now. I shove his remaining provisions, the medicine pouch, his knife, and the little carved bird into my pack and hoist it up, ignoring the throbbing of my shoulders.

"Come on, we've got to get you moving," I say.

"Can't do it," he whispers.

"We agreed to stay together, remember?" He tries to speak, but I can't make out what he says. "Please, Peree. Try."

A moment passes, then I feel him lift his neck. I support his shoulders as he struggles to a sitting position.

"So dizzy."

I cup his cheeks with my hands, like I used to with Eland when I really wanted him to listen. "Do you remember my first day with the Scourge, when I collapsed with the flesh-eaters all around me? I was terrified, and I wanted to give up, but you made me believe I could do it. Well, I believe you can do this. Find the strength."

He leans back, like he's going to lie down again, but instead he puts his hands under him and, gasping, pushes himself to his feet. I take as much of his weight onto my shoulder as I can.

"One step at a time," I say. "Take it one step at a time."

I sing to him as we shuffle forward, any song I can think of. Songs I haven't sung since I was young; songs Aloe sang when I was frightened or upset. Peree doesn't speak. His rasping breath and the movement of his feet are the only signs he's still conscious. A few times he wavers, like he's about to faint, and I wedge him between my body and the wall, trying to keep him upright.

When I run out of songs I talk to him. I tell him things I've never told anyone, like how frightening Sightlessness can be sometimes, and how exhausting it is to try to be brave, to do for myself, to not ask for help, to be more like Aloe. I tell him how I sometimes envy the sighted so much it hurts. And other times I'm so fiercely proud of my self-sufficiency, I wouldn't be sighted if I had the choice. I tell him how much it meant to have him as my Keeper, to know he was there in the trees, watching over me. He doesn't respond. I'm not sure he can hear me anymore, but I sing and I talk until I'm hoarse, and still we walk toward the water.

I lose track of time and distance again, thanks to the fatigue from carrying my pack and much of Peree's weight, and the constant fear that he'll pass out. I try to remember how many caverns we've passed through, but all the caves and passages we traversed in the last two and a half days blend in my memory. The days since I became the Water Bearer feel like one long, dark passage, with no end. In the blackest moments, my entire life feels that way.

The sound of rushing water brings me to my senses again. Fighting to hold Peree up, I focus the rest of my energy on reaching it. When I can feel the spray of water on my legs, I lower him to the rock floor.

I fill a water sack and hold his head up so he can drink. Most of the water slides down his face, but he swallows a little, and coughs. I cushion his head with a balled-up extra dress, and inch the dry, blood-crusted bandages off his leg. The swelling and heat beneath is appalling. I clean the wound with water until I can feel no more dirt or dried blood, then I squeeze more agrimony and yarrow paste from my medicine pouch and rewrap it. He doesn't stir; I think he's unconscious. When I finish, I wait. Wait for him to wake up, or to die.

I listen to the water rush by. It sounds like it emerges from the rock itself, and disappears back into it, dampening my hope that we might find a way out. Exhausted and dispirited, I curl up beside Peree, my hand on his chest to reassure myself that he's breathing. Lulled by the constant stream of water, I sleep.

When I wake, the first thing I'm aware of is relief. Peree's hand is on top of mine now, and it's still warm, which means he's still alive. I lean closer to listen to him breathe. He croaks, making me jump. I fill the sack, and hold his head again while he drinks.

"Thank you," he whispers.

I lay my hand against his cheek. "How do you feel?"

He shakes his head slightly. "Where are we?"

"The Hidden Waters. We walked here, do you remember?"

"I thought I was dead ... dreamed I was a flesh-eater."

"You're alive."

"I was only sure when I felt you next to me." He presses his cheek into my palm. "Where's the torch? I ... want to see what we came all this way for."

It's hard to find in my pack, there's so little of it left. He struggles up, then helps me light it with shaking hands. The torch crackles to life, and the darkness fades a bit. Peree says nothing.

"What does it look like?" I ask.

"Like a cave. With water."

"Where does the water go? Can you tell?"

"Through an opening in the rock on the far wall."

"Do you see any light beyond, like the stream might go outside from here, or another way out?"

He doesn't answer. The torch almost singes my hand before sputtering out, and the last of my hope goes with it. I have no idea what to do now. I can't get Peree back home in his condition. There's maybe enough food to last one more day. The water might keep him alive for a few days while I go back for help ... unless the infection from his wound kills him first. Despair caresses me with frost-tipped fingers.

"Fennel?"

"I'm here." I take his hands.

"Have you ever heard the story of how the first fish were created?" He sounds different. Resigned.

I fight to keep my voice even. "Maybe you should rest."

"I will soon. Come lie next to me; you're freezing." I pull my bedroll over us and lay with my head on his chest. His voice echoes in my ear. "You know about fish, right? They swam in the waters."

I had heard of fish. A few of the elders ate them when they were children, but the last of the fish died out over a generation ago. No one knew why.

"Long ago there were no fish; every animal lived on the land. The people had plenty, and were satisfied. Everyone—except one boy. He'd loved one of the girls of a nearby community since childhood, and she loved him, but her father didn't want them to be together. The boy was different, an outsider. So the boy gave up, and wandered through the forest for a time.

"He returned several years later, determined to ask the girl to be his partner. He found that although she still loved him, she was intended to another, a commitment she had to honor, according to the community's laws. The boy wanted to fight for her, but the girl told him no. Instead, she would run away with him that night.

"When the sun left the sky, she stole away from her home and met the boy in the forest. They ran and ran, as fast and as far as they could. They ran so far they came to the edge of a vast water hole, where they spent the rest of the night, exhausted, but happy to be together.

"The couple woke at first light and, using driftwood, they made arrows and spears to defend themselves, knowing they would be pursued. Sure enough, men appeared at the water hole soon after. The girl continued to make weapons while the boy shot the arrows and threw the spears with such accuracy that the men had to hide. They held them off this way for a long time, but then they ran out of wood.

"As the boy held the last arrow to his bow, the girl told him she would go back with the men so he could escape. 'No,' he said, 'we must stay together, whatever happens. If we can't live together on land, then we must go into the water.' She agreed, he shot his last arrow, and the boy and girl slipped into the water. The men ran down, throwing their spears at them, and the spears stuck, becoming fins. They swam away, the first fish. And they never again left the water, because to do so would mean certain death."

Peree shifts his weight, and moans. My hands fly to his face, powerless to do anything else to help. After a minute, he speaks again.

"My mother said there were people who believed underground rivers were the boundaries between our world and the afterworld. They thought people crossed the river when they died. I don't want to cross this one. I don't want to stay in the cold and the dark forever." Silent tears slip down his face. "Will you be sure I don't? Let the river wash what's left of me outside, into the sunlight." I want to say he's not going to die here, but I can't lie, so I say nothing. "When you go back, tell Shrike ... tell him he was a good father. He worried about that, since my mother left. And tell Petrel he won. He'll know what it means."

"I will. Is there anyone else you want me to give a message to? Other friends?"

"No other friends."

"But, there must be others you were close to." I hesitate. "What about ... the girl? The one you told me wasn't old enough to partner with yet."

"There's no one. No Lofty girl, at least." He pauses, and when he speaks again his voice is even more hollow than it was before. "We had the same fever you did, and many died. Our numbers were already dwindling before the fever. Now we don't have enough people to do everything that needs to be done. Hunt, gather food and wood, be the lookouts, watch the remaining children. That's why we make decisions together; we don't need a separate Council."

I sift through the little information I have about the Lofties. "Not many of you came to the last few Summer Solstices. We thought you didn't want to celebrate with us, but really there were less of you?"

"For generations we've given up more babies in the Exchange than we've received. Dark coloring seems to be more common than light. It's ironic—our ancestors drove yours out of the trees and created the Exchange to protect our resources. Now we're dying out, thanks to their narrow minds and our own fear and pride."

"Does anyone else know about this? Aloe? The Three?"

"No," Peree says. "It's forbidden to speak to Groundlings about, but I don't think they'll get here in time to punish me."

I can't stand it. "Don't say that, you're not—"

He stops my lips with his fingers. "I want to tell truths now. Something has to change, and soon. My people are afraid, but we'll have to strike some kind of bargain with your people, or we won't survive. Do something for me, when you go back—tell Aloe what I told you. Persuade your Council to help."

"Come back with me and tell them yourself," I plead.

"Does your Sightlessness give you the power to cheat death?"

I shake my head, frustration and helplessness strangling me. "Only to walk among it."

We lie in silence then. Numb with grief, I listen to his slow breathing. For a moment I consider giving up, staying here with Peree next to the Hidden Waters. But voices drift to me through the caves like the whispers of ghosts. The voices of my people, beseeching me to return with some hopeful news. And I have the Lofties to consider now, slowly dying out in the trees over our heads.

Can I do this? Can I go back and shake the foundation of what my people believe: that the Lofties keep us subservient? Would it change anything? I don't know, but I have to find out. I make up my mind. I'll stay with him as long as I can. Then I'll go back.

I try to stay awake, but I'm depleted, body and spirit. I doze off, and I'm the girl from the story, my back to the edge of the water, my hair lashing around me in the gusting wind. I hand Peree the last arrow I've made, knowing the men are coming for us. I tell him I'll go back with them. *No, we stay together*, he reminds me.

And suddenly I know what I have to do.

I try to wake Peree, to tell him my plan, but he doesn't stir. So I stuff what I can into an empty water sack: food, the diminished medicine pouch, the scrap of fabric and the rabbit's foot Bear gave me, Peree's knife, and the little wooden bird. I secure the sack to my body. I don't think about what might happen, or I won't have the courage to do this.

I wrap my arms around Peree, and whisper in his ear. Then I roll us over the edge into the river.

CHAPTER TEN

The water is unbelievably cold. It takes my breath away.

I hold Peree under the arms, feet downstream. He flails as we sweep through the cave. I try to come up for air, but my head meets solid rock, my face still underwater. Panic smothers me—I fight it.

The water throws us into the rock walls. Peree slumps in my arms. We hit an outcropping and pain explodes through my side.

Sliding downwards. The water levels out, dragging us. My ribs are in agony, my lungs exploding. I clear the surface and gasp for breath.

My forehead slams into a rock and water dashes down my throat. I gasp and choke; I'm drowning.

Suddenly, light bursts around us. We plunge into a roaring, plummeting wall of water. Peree's head ricochets against my brow. Stunned, I cling to him like a raft.

And as swiftly as it began, the terrifying ride is over. Calmer water surrounds us. *Warm* water. I try to hold Peree's face above the surface, but his weight pushes me under. My hand brushes against something slimy, slender, and plant-like. I seize it. It's attached to solid ground. I pull myself, and Peree's body, as far up as I can and collapse. Darkness overtakes me.

I wake to the faint sound of birdsong and the rusty taste of blood in my mouth. The water careening down nearby masks any other noise. It's bright, too bright even for me, after so many days in the dark caves. Hazily, I realize we must be outside. I say a quick thanks.

I stretch my arms and legs. Pain greets every small movement. My forehead throbs and it hurts to breathe—the ribs on my left side crackle like a handful of kindling. Raising my head prompts a wave of nausea, so I stay low. I feel like I was thoroughly beaten, which isn't far from the truth.

I hear a low moan, and I panic. *Where's Peree?* If the Scourge is here, he could be gone already. We can't have come this far for him to be taken by flesh-eaters. Battling the pain and nausea, I grope around my body, my hands sliding through mud and grass. I only breathe again when I realize Peree's the one doing the moaning. He's alive. I lie next to him, holding his hand.

Time passes. I drift in and out, only aware of his body next to mine. The light's gone when I come to again. For a moment I think we're back in the caves, but I smell the organic, peaty soil and the bitter nip of the greenheart trees, so much stronger now that I haven't smelled them in days. We're outside, I remember.

I push myself up to my knees with one arm, allowing the other to curl around my injured ribs. I probe my forehead gently. An enormous knot squats on my brow, crusted with hardened blood and mud. Every movement of my head creates fresh fault lines. I lean over Peree, listening for the sound of his breath. It's there, weak but consistent. I'm grateful, and astonished. Truthfully, I wasn't expecting to survive myself.

I wish I could tell where we are. I can hear a few insects in the vegetation around us, but not much else, thanks to what must be the waterfall that spit us out here. Beyond that I'm terrifyingly ignorant. What if the Scourge does come?

I transfer our few belongings to my pockets, then crawl to the water hole and fill the sack. The water tastes pure, like its source, the Hidden Waters. As I pour a tiny stream into Peree's mouth, I hear a new sound—shuffling feet. I freeze, my hands poised over his body, ready to pull him into the water and away from the creatures, but the shuffling is all I hear. Whatever it is, it sounds much smaller than one of the creatures.

An animal? Maybe a possum, or a squirrel? My stomach snarls. I imagine Peree waking to the mouthwatering smell of freshly cooked meat … as if I could catch an animal and make a fire with a bunch of broken ribs. The animal does mean one good thing—the Scourge must not be near. In our part of the forest the animals are indicators of how close the flesh-eaters are. They take to the trees or burrow under the earth at the first sign of the creatures.

I think about the tiger, or whatever she was. How long had she been hiding from the creatures in the entrance to that cave? She must have been desperate. Hatred for the Scourge boils in me again.

The animal moves off, having drunk its fill. We must look and smell half dead, for it to have come so close to us. I take Peree's limp hand and, ribs screaming at the movement, I lie back in the scrubby grass.

When I wake again the air is cool, but carries the promise of warmth as the sun sheds its first light. I get to my feet, wincing at the hammering in my head, and refill the sack for Peree. There's no change in his condition, as far as I can tell. I wonder if he hit his head as many times as I did in the underground river. I wonder if he'll ever wake again.

The forest sounds are louder now. Magpies hop around us, their screeches audible over the crashing water. I sit on the bank and think about slipping in to wash the grime off my body, but I can't find the energy.

I try to form a plan, but what can I do? I doubt I can carry Peree when I'm fresh and uninjured, much less now. I can try to get help, but I have no idea which way to walk. I didn't think about how I'd get home when I slid into the Hidden Waters. I wanted to get Peree out of the caves he hated, to let him die under the sun. Now it looks like that's exactly what he's going to do.

I can't think about the things he said in the caves. It hurts too much, more painful than the aching in my body. I feel like I'm back in the freezing river, being swept away by the events of the last few weeks, no sense of direction in my own life. I'm at the mercy of the water, as I've always been. As we all have been.

Footsteps behind me—this is no possum. I stay very still, afraid to move in case it draws the flesh-eater's attention. I'm about four or five paces from where Peree lies, too far to reach him and drag him into the water to safety. If I can't run, I'll fight. I clutch my side, ready to jump to my feet. I don't know why the creature hasn't already attacked.

"She's here," Peree murmurs. Relief shoots through me at the sound of his voice, followed by dread at his words. He recognizes one of the fleshies? "She'll take you home."

"I'm not leaving you," I hiss.

"Go ... please." The sadness, the futility in his voice tears at my heart. I wait, and listen.

A high-pitched, human voice breaks the silence. It sounds like a child, a little girl, but I can't understand her. *What's she doing out here by herself?* She pauses, then speaks again. This time I recognize the words.

"You aren't one of them, are you?" the girl says.

"One of who?" I ask.

"*Runa.* Sick one."

"No, I'm not sick."

"But there's blood on you, and you're dirty, like them."

"I know, I'm sorry if I scared you. I've been traveling a long time and I'm injured. I won't hurt you." I stand gingerly, and face her. "What's your name?"

"Kora."

"That's pretty. My name's Fennel."

"You can't see, can you?" she asks.

"No."

"Why not?"

"I was born this way."

She considers my words. "So, you can't see what I'm doing right now?"

"No—what are you doing?" I ask warily.

"Waving at you."

I smile, and wave back to her. "Are you here all alone? Where are your parents?"

"In the village. I'm getting water for my mother."

My heart thumps in my chest. "How far is your village?"

"Not far. I can skip all the way there if I want to." She sounds proud.

"Can you take me there?"

"Do you want to skip with me?"

I cringe at the idea. My head is already splitting. "Maybe later. Can we walk fast instead?"

"Okay. Is your friend hurt, too?"

"Yes. Do you think we can get help for him in your village?"

"Sure, come on."

I don't want to leave Peree alone. What if the Scourge comes? But I don't think I have a choice. I try to tell him I'll be back, but he doesn't respond. I think he's unconscious again. I step toward Kora, and she puts her small hand in mine, leading me away from the sound of the waterfall.

I want to interrogate her as we walk: where are we; who are her people; why do they allow a small child to wander through the forest on her own?

But I'm afraid of frightening her, so I stumble along silently, barely able to contain my impatience. The sound of the water fades behind us, replaced by our footsteps and the busy noises of birds. No vegetation touches me as we walk; it must be a cleared path.

"Why are you holding your side like that?" Kora asks.

"I hurt my ribs."

"You should see Nerang, he'll help you. He can help your friend too."

"Is he your herbalist?"

"What's an herbalist?" She pronounces the word *herb-list*.

"Someone who helps people who are sick, or hurt."

"Oh yes, he's our healer, but he helps well people, too. He makes funny faces and tells me stories when I'm sad, and I feel better."

I hear faint voices ahead of us. I imagine what my people would do if a bloody, filthy stranger came out of the forest holding the hand of one of our children, looking for all the world like one of the flesh-eaters. I stiffen, and pray that Kora's people are different.

"It's okay," she says, concern in her voice. "Nerang will help you feel better, too."

"I know." I smile for her.

I try to notice as much as I can about where I am before we're spotted. The sun isn't as bright as by the water hole, but I can feel it on my shoulders. I hear the wind pushing the leaves around far above. The voices sound like they're coming from all around me—the ground and the trees. Bread is baking somewhere nearby. The delicious scent makes my empty stomach contract. I smell freshly cut wood, turned soil, and among it all, the pervasive greenheart trees. My guess is I'm in a community similar to ours at home, but larger, from the sound of it.

"Kora?" A man shouts from across the clearing. "Kora!"

More worried voices call out, and I hear people running toward us. I hold the little girl's hand loosely, ready to drop it in case I'm grabbed or dragged off. A woman speaks, very near to us. Her words are foreign to me, but I hear her fear.

Kora stays close by my side. "Mama, this is my friend Fennel. She speaks the second language. She's not *runa*, but she's hurt. She needs Nerang."

"Where did you come from? How did you get here?" A man asks me angrily.

"Please, I need help." I touch my forehead, assuming it must look as bad as it feels. Pain grips my ribs when I move, and I grimace. I want to ask the people to help Peree, but first I need to figure out if they'll help us or kill us.

"Your head looks like the sky before a storm," a second man says with concern. "What happened to you?"

"I came from the caves, through the river. I hit a few rocks before I landed in your water hole," I say.

Several people mutter. The first woman, who I assume is Kora's mother, asks, "You came from the Dark Place? By yourself?" Her voice is soft.

I make an effort to smile. "I'm pretty much always in a dark place."

"We should take her to Wirrim," the angry man says. "He should know about this."

Kora speaks up again, her small voice determined. "Nerang first."

"The child is right," a new man says. His voice is gentle with what I can only describe as an undertone of suppressed laughter. "The girl is injured, she needs our help. Have we lost our ability to be hospitable?"

"Wirrim should know that a *lorinya* is here, claiming she came from the Dark Place," the angry man says.

"Then go tell him. In the meantime, I will offer our visitor what aid I can. Come with me, young one." The laughing man puts my hand on his arm and guides me away from the others. His skin is smooth; it feels younger than his voice sounds.

"Thank you, Kora," I say over my shoulder.

"Don't forget you promised to skip with me, when you feel better."

"I won't forget."

I hear groups of people talking about me in hushed voices as we walk. It's clear I've drawn a crowd. The man leading me seems oblivious.

"I am Nerang," he says.

"I'm Fennel."

"You have no sight," he remarks casually. "You must be brave, to have journeyed through the Dark Place all alone."

I hesitate, wondering if I can trust him. I already want to. His voice is calming and familiar, as if I've known it all my life. Or maybe it's that he smells of rosemary, like Aloe.

"I wasn't alone."

Nerang pauses. His voice is sharper than before, but still kind. "There are others?"

"Just one." I think of the heat of the wound in Peree's leg, and his last words, pleading with me to go. My words come out in a rush. "And he's hurt far worse than me. He's no danger to anyone, truly, he can't even walk. Please, please help my friend. He's at the water hole."

Friend—the word doesn't seem sufficient somehow. My heart will break if Peree dies, as surely as it would if Eland or Aloe died. It's already splintering. After a moment Nerang calls to someone nearby, in the other language. A man answers. Their short exchange sounds like birds bickering over a meal.

"Our men will go to the water hole," Nerang says.

"Thank you," I say breathlessly.

"You and I will go up, into the trees," he tells me.

"Climb?" I ask doubtfully. My ribs are throbbing, and I'm weak as a hatchling.

He chuckles, and gently presses me forward. I step onto what sounds like wooden boards. Reaching out, I feel more wood—a stripped, horizontal tree branch—at about the level of my stomach. Nerang joins me, then says something in the strange tongue again. The boards under my feet lurch, and we rise into the air. I grip the branch, bracing myself.

"Don't worry, young one, you won't fall," he says.

"Where are we going?"

"To my home. My herbs and treatments are there."

"You all live in the trees?"

"In the trees, or on the ground, as each family pleases."

I can't decide if I'm more shocked that the people get to choose, or that some would choose to live on the ground in constant danger from the Scourge. The platform stops. I don't move, afraid to make a misstep.

Nerang takes my arm again. "This way."

I feel like we're very high, higher than when I was in the trees with Peree. A damp, smoky scent, like water poured over a cooking fire, hangs in the air. A few people line up along the walkway, speaking in their language. Their whispering stops as I go by, then restarts after I pass. I hear the word *lorinya* over and over. I keep my head held high, but my grip on Nerang tightens.

"Relax now. We're here," he tells me.

"Here" is a shelter, mostly dark, and a little cramped and boxy from the way our voices sound when we enter. It smells of things both sweet and bitter, some familiar, others very strange. I'm reminded of Marjoram's workroom back home, where all the freshly picked herbs are dried, ground, and stored. I turn my head toward a particularly pungent scent, and sway with the sudden movement.

Nerang steadies me. "Sit," he says firmly.

It's a bed—an incredibly soft, thick bed—that feels like layers and layers of fluffy feathers. Compared to the stone floors I've been sleeping on for days, it's heavenly. I sink down in it. Nerang moves away, and lights something. Soon, the soothing scent of lavender and some other harsher odor fills the cozy shelter. Water splashes in a basin, and a cool, minty-smelling cloth slides across my face and arms, cleaning away the dirt and blood. I relax under Nerang's gentle touch.

"Where did you come from?" he asks.

My mind is fuzzy with fatigue and the strong scent of the burning incense. Sleep is approaching like a powerful storm. I won't be able to avoid it. I don't want to avoid it.

"Caves," I slur.

"And before that?"

"Forest."

His voice is soft, but insistent. "What are your people called?"

Should I tell him? Is it safe? I can't think. I'm half-asleep already. "Groundlings," I mumble.

"Yes," he says.

I ask only one question before I succumb to unconsciousness. "Where am I?"

"Koolkuna. It means, 'place of safety.' Rest now, young one. You are safe."

I sleep. And for the first time since I became the Water Bearer, I don't dream. A welcome cocoon of peace and painlessness wraps around me.

Only a few sensations break through: the potent incense, the nutty taste of a thin gruel, Nerang's voice. He sings to himself in his strange native tongue as he ministers to my injuries. Voices call to each other outside, the wind taps the door against its frame over and over, a persistent visitor. I don't answer.

But a thought begins to prick at the edges of my consciousness. At first I try to ignore it, like I ignore the sun that tugs on my eyelids in the morning when I'm trying to sleep. But the thought gets louder and louder, repeating itself, forcing me to pay attention. There's something important I need to know.

Peree. Did they find him? Does he live? I try to ask Nerang, but the words tangle up together in my mouth. So I give up and allow myself to drift again, idly wondering what kind of incense keeps me in this dream state.

At first, there's only faint light kissing the darkness of the shelter. The moon? Someone's sleeping nearby, breathing deeply.

I take stock of myself. I'm still in the feathery bed. My chest is wrapped in a tight binding. There's a dull ache in my ribs, and I have a mild headache and a nagging itch on my forehead. I test my body, stretching it bit by bit. I'm tender almost everywhere, but I've had enough injuries to know what healing fractures and bruises feel like.

I sit up cautiously, slide my legs off the side of the bed, and stand. The wooden boards creak, but the breathing doesn't change, so I take a few steps toward the source of the light. A faint breeze blows into my face. It must be a window.

Nerang speaks, making me jump. "How do you feel?"

"Much better, thanks to you. You must have strong healing powers."

"It helps to have a strong patient. Several ribs were broken, and you had a nasty blow to the head, but you're mending nicely." He stands and pours something. "Here, drink."

The water's warm, but tastes bright and clean, like the Hidden Waters. "My friend ... did they find him?" I ask.

"Yes, he's here. He's alive."

My body tingles with relief. "Then I owe you much more than thanks. Where is he, will you take me to him?"

"In the morning. He's on the ground. He couldn't be moved to the trees in his condition."

I frown. "The ground? What about the Scourge?"

"Your friend is safe, I promise you."

I hear the low hoot of an owl outside. The forest sounds quiet and peaceful—safe—like Nerang said. "How do you protect yourselves from them? Why do you allow your children to wander by themselves? Aren't you afraid for their safety?"

He laughs. "There's much for you to learn about Koolkuna, young one, but now is not the time. You need to rest, your body is still healing. And I'm an old man, I need my sleep."

"You don't seem old."

"And you don't seem like you have no sight," he says gently. "Things are not always as they seem. Sleep now. Your questions will be answered."

I climb back into bed. "Peree's really all right?"

"Yes. Sleep." His tone is soothing, but I hear something in his voice, a hesitation. That pause keeps me awake long after I hear his breathing slow again, and after the owl tucks its beak into its wing and sleeps.

I'm still awake, worrying about Peree and wondering about Koolkuna, as the moonlight gives way to the first timid rays of the sun.

CHAPTER ELEVEN

Laughter drifts through the window on the breeze, waking me. It's been morning for some time, judging from the light. The little room is cooler and more pleasant than I would have thought possible in the middle of summer.

I sit up and adjust my sleep-twisted dress around me. I didn't notice what I was wearing the night before, but the dress smells clean and feels unfamiliar. Someone must have changed my clothes. I stand and grope my way around the shelter, memorizing it. It doesn't take long. Two beds, a wash stand with a clay pitcher and basin, and a set of rough shelves with an assortment of clay pots and small leather pouches. I pick up a palm-sized wooden container and smell the contents. Sage, good for seasoning meat. Who knows what Nerang uses it for? The water in the pitcher smells and tastes clean, so I drink. I pour some in the basin, and wash my face.

I pause at the closed door, my hand resting on the wood, trying to slow my heart. There are people out there who are probably very unhappy that I wandered into their village. Imagining again how my community would react to a stranger, I almost go back to bed. But I think of Peree, and step outside.

A hammer beats a staccato rhythm somewhere down below, and the smoke from a cooking fire reminds me I'm starving. Women chatter, their voices drifting through the trees. They sound like they're working. I wish I could tell what they're saying.

"Fennel!" a familiar voice yelps.

"Kora?"

"I've been waiting for you! Every day I asked Nerang if you were awake, and every day he said you were still sleeping. Then this morning he finally said I could visit you! I've been waiting for you to come out since breakfast." She takes my hand. "You look like you smeared berries all over your face, but you don't look as much like a *runa* anymore."

I laugh. "Good … I think. How long have I been here?"

Kora considers. "Three sleeps, maybe?" *Three days!* Fear for Peree washes over me again. "Will you skip with me now?"

"I think I should take things slow. Walk with me instead?"

"Okay. Where do you want to go?"

"To Nerang. Do you know where he is?"

"I think he's with your friend."

"Take me to him?"

"Sure, let's use the ropes." She tugs me forward and I tense, expecting the movement to hurt my ribs, but it doesn't.

"The ropes?" I ask.

"To get down."

I don't know "the ropes," but I'm relieved we're going down. I'm not at all comfortable up here. I stiffen every time a branch creaks or the trees sway. Kora still holds my hand, but I feel around for something else to hold onto. Another tree branch sits waist-high above the walkway, forming a barrier. I run my other hand along it gratefully. We pass a shelter, and I hear a woman singing inside.

"Does your family live in the trees, or on the ground?" I ask Kora.

"The ground," she says, as if that should be obvious. "My brother Darel's only four, he isn't old enough to live in the trees yet. It's not safe for the little ones—they can fall."

Her tone makes it clear she doesn't consider herself part of any group that could do something so careless. I smile to myself, but wonder how dangerous the possibility of a fall is, compared to the constant threat of the Scourge.

"How old are you?" I ask.

"Six. Mama made me a new doll for my birthday. I named her Bega, because she's beautiful. Do you want to meet her?"

I wasn't sure if she meant her Mama or her doll. "I'd love to, after I talk to my friend. I want you to meet him, too."

"He's not awake yet."

I frown. "He's not?"

"He was hurt really bad. Nerang's been with him even more than with you. Mama said your friend's lucky the men found him when they did." Kora lets go of my hand. "We're here—ready to go down?"

"What do I do?"

"Hold the ropes with your hands. Step on the board. Don't let go." She sounds like she's repeating directives she's heard many times before.

I reach out and grab two ropes Kora is holding for me. "What will happen when I step on the board?"

"The rock will go up, and you'll go down," she says. I must have looked less than enthusiastic, because she added, "Don't worry, I'll be right next to you."

Okay, if a six-year-old can do this, so can I. My feet find the board and I step onto it, hands trembling. I begin to fall, but falling isn't as quick or terrifying as I thought it would be.

"See?" Kora says when we reach the ground. "It's not scary."

"You're right, it's not," I agree, but I'm still happy to be standing on the earth again.

"Watch out, here comes the rock."

I jump back, and hear a thud as the weight that provided my controlled descent crashes to the ground. I can feel the impact in my feet. Overall, the platform ride with Nerang seemed a lot safer.

Kora takes my hand again, but we don't get far.

"Hello ... where are you taking our guest?" a woman says. I don't recognize her voice, but she sounds friendly.

"To Nerang."

"Your mother's looking for you. Why don't you find her and tell her where you are? Then you can go to Nerang," the woman says.

"Okay," Kora says. "I'll be right back!"

"I hope I haven't caused trouble with her family," I say, listening to her small feet slap against the ground as she runs off.

"We don't have many strangers here, it's true. But Nerang felt you could be trusted, and his opinion goes a long way with the people."

"I'm Fennel." I hold out my hand.

She shakes it. "My name is Kadee. How are you feeling?"

"Very well. You're lucky to have Nerang as a healer." I say, remembering what Kora called him.

"Yes, he's very gifted. Every family in the village owes him at least one life." She pauses. "When you're ready, the *anuna* would like to talk with you. We have many questions."

"What's the *anuna*?"

"The people. That's what we call ourselves in Koolkuna."

"Can I go to my friend first?" I have questions for the people, too, but Peree is my first priority.

"Of course. Ask Kora to bring you to the *allawah*, the gathering place, afterward. You must be hungry. We'll eat, and we'll talk."

Kora arrives breathlessly back at my side. "I told Mama I'm taking you to Nerang ... are you ready?"

Kadee laughs. "I'll see you soon."

I say good-bye, and Kora leads me on through Koolkuna. Deciphering the layout of the village is surprisingly easy, thanks to Kora's ceaseless commentary. Koolkuna's central clearing is roughly circular, like ours at home. There are work places: a spacious cooking shelter with two large fire pits for boiling water and preparing meals, a place where the launderers clean and mend the clothes, a workshop for the builders—the clattering coming from inside gave me a clue on that one—and a large storage shelter where food and supplies are kept. The gathering place Kadee mentioned is an enormous rectangular shelter used for meetings and feasts, large enough to fit the whole community.

"From the trees," Kora says, "the village looks like a face." She draws a circle around my palm with her finger, then jabs inside it. "The kitchen and laundry for eyes, the workshop for a nose, and the *allawah* is a mouth." I chuckle. Only a child would notice that.

The arrangement of homes in Koolkuna is different, too. Our shelters huddle together around the clearing, but here they range out into the trees, providing more space and privacy for each family, although little security. From the noise of the village, it seems that people are doing exactly what we'd be doing at home—working and talking. We walk by a group of women who were chatting together a moment before. Now they're whispering. They don't sound suspicious so much as curious.

"They're talking about you," Kora informs me.

"I thought so," I say, smiling at her honesty. "Tell me, what does *lorinya* mean? I keep hearing that word."

"It means stranger. That's what they call you, but I don't. You're not a stranger. You're my friend."

"Thanks, I can use one right now."

I'm glad I can't see their stares. Hearing their whispers is bad enough. I don't like being the center of attention even among friends, and right now my friends consist of exactly one six-year-old girl.

We skirt the bustling center of the village, making our way to a quieter spot. The light is dimmer here, as if we're under a thick awning of trees. I ask Kora if there's a fence around the village, or some other kind of barrier, but she says no, clearly wondering why I'd ask such a silly question. As far as I can tell, no one seems a bit concerned about the Scourge. *What kind of place is this?*

The scent of Nerang's strong incense hovers in the air, so I'm not surprised to hear his voice a moment later. "Hello, Kora, Fennel—I'm pleased to see you up and about. How do you feel today?"

"A little tired and sore, but otherwise well."

"I'm glad to hear it. With rest and a little more time, your body will recover, like the forest after a fire."

"How's Peree? Is he awake?"

"He's resting. You may come in, but use this to cover your mouth and nose." He places a cloth in my hand. "Burning herbs have strong healing powers for the sick or injured, but they can be overpowering for the rest of us. Remain outside, please, Kora."

He takes my arm, and a door scrapes open. I quickly understand why I need the cloth; the air that swirls out is cloying. Nerang takes me a few steps inside, and places my hand on what feels like a bed. I feel around until I find Peree's arm. I kneel beside him.

"He's so thin," I whisper. Skeletal is more like it.

"He's rarely awake long enough to eat, but he has been drinking more, and the infection is gone."

My fingers take stock of his face. His eyes are closed over his now-prominent cheekbones, and his beard has grown, but his temperature feels normal. His breathing is slow and regular.

Nerang pats my shoulder. "Try not to worry. He *is* improving."

"What about his leg?" I search for the cloth-covered wound on Peree's thigh, and swallow hard. A large part of the muscle is missing.

"There was a severe infection," Nerang says quietly. "I had to remove some of the tissue, to save his life."

"Will he be able to walk?"

"We must wait and see. It was the only option, young one. If the infection had spread any further, I would have had to remove his entire leg."

I grasp Peree's hand again, bringing it to my lips. What if he can't walk? How will he survive? I should have encouraged him to shoot the tiger. I shouldn't have distracted him when he was taking aim. I should have taken better care of the wound, kept it cleaner. I shouldn't have let him come with me to begin with. If I had done even one of those things, Peree would still be whole.

"This is my fault," I mumble.

"Blaming yourself will not help him heal."

"What will?"

"Your support, your encouragement, and your wisdom."

I raise my head. "Wisdom?"

"Is not having the use of a limb so different from not having one's sight?" Nerang asks. "Let's not get ahead of ourselves. Your friend may walk again. Much depends on his will power."

I touch Peree's face, silently begging him for forgiveness, then Nerang takes me back outside. Suddenly dizzy, I sit down hard and cough as dust floats around me.

Kora sits, too, and pats my face. "Are you all right?"

"She will be," Nerang assures her.

Her hair, coarse and curly, rubs against my cheek as she nestles into my side. She hands me something, a flower, with velvety, oblong petals. "Tell her a story, Nerang, to help her feel better."

"Which one should I tell?"

Kora thinks for a moment. "The legend of the flowers?"

"A good choice." He settles down next to us. "In the time before time, the Creator left the earth to return home to the Sacred Mountain. Before long, all the beautiful flowers that grew around the water holes, in the trees, and in the rocky crevices, began to die. The earth was colorless and barren, the bees were gone, and there was no honey. The people were sad, so they traveled to the Sacred Mountain to plead with the Creator. Everywhere they looked, there was an abundance of flowers, more and more, strewn joyfully around the camp. They cried that they had lost this, the beauty of the flowers, and the Creator took pity on them. She told them to gather as many armfuls of flowers as they could hold, and to return to earth to sprinkle them on the land. She promised them that the earth would never again be barren.

"The people did as they were instructed. Suddenly the land, the trees, and the rocky crevices were covered with beautiful blooms. And from then on, when the flowers died, the people did not fret, for they remembered the promise that was made to them by the Creator. Always, always, no matter how harsh the summer sun, or how biting the winter wind—the flowers will return." Nerang pauses. "There's always hope, young one. Renewal is all around us, every minute of every day. It's the gift of the Creator."

I try to look appreciative, but his story hits too close to home, reminding me of Peree's tales. I want to cry, but now isn't the time. I need information and a plan, so I'm prepared when Peree wakes. "I met a woman, Kadee, on my way here," I say. "She asked me to come to the–" I stumble over the word, "*allawah?* ... after I saw Peree."

"I'm not surprised. The *anuna* have been chittering about you for days. I imagine they want to find out who you are and where you came from. Kora, will you take her? I must stay with my patient."

I take his hand. "Thank you, Nerang. I know you've done all you can for him."

"There's always more to do, young one. Remember what I said. Your friend will need you, when the time comes."

Kora and I walk back to the village. Apparently word got out that I was coming. People are milling around the gathering place, talking, but they grow silent as we approach. My fingers flutter nervously over my hair and dress.

"Mama!" Kora cries. "This is Fennel." She presents me proudly.

Someone comes closer. Her voice is barely louder than a whisper when she speaks. "I am Arika."

"Thank you for allowing Kora to show me around. I have a younger brother, and I know how hard it would be to trust him with a stranger." I try to smile.

"What's hard is stopping Kora from doing what she wants." Arika sounds like she's smiling, too. "I think she's decided that since she found you, you're hers now."

"I'm happy to have a friend," I say.

"Welcome, Fennel," Kadee says from somewhere nearby. "Come in."

Following her voice, I step inside the shelter. The space feels open and airy, as if the roof is high above our heads. There's a fire lit in the center, where something tantalizing is cooking. Kadee helps me find a spot to sit as others come in, taking seats around the fire. My stomach rumbles as a plate of food is placed in front of me.

"Rabbit stew, with fresh bread," Kadee says.

I want to attack it, but at home we wait until all are seated with their meals before we eat. From the sounds around me, people are still getting settled. I clench my hands together in my lap.

"In Koolkuna, it's customary to wait for the guest to begin eating, before we start," Kadee says in a low voice.

Thankful for that particular convention, I take a bite of the stew. It's hot and delicious. The rabbit meat is succulent, cooked in a rich, spicy gravy stuffed with potatoes, carrots, and onion. After days of cured meat, the simple, nourishing meal is more than satisfying. I don't refuse seconds.

I listen to the conversations around me while I eat. I can't understand them, but from the tone of their voices I figure they're speculating about me. I hear *lorinya* often.

Their questions will start soon. I'm afraid to tell them what they'll want to know—that is, everything about me and Peree, and how we came here. But we need the help of these people, and so far they've given it freely. So I eat, building the courage to be honest in the face of uncertainty.

I sop up the last of the gravy with my final bite of bread and put my bowl down. As I do, the conversations around me die. The logs settling into the flames are the loudest sound in the room.

"I'd like to tell you the story of the *anuna*," a man says from the other side of the fire. His voice brings to mind an ancient tree, stooped and covered in folds of wrinkled bark and wispy leaves, but still holding its branches proudly.

Kadee says, "This is Wirrim, our Memory Keeper. He remembers and passes on the stories of the people."

When Wirrim speaks again, his voice has changed. It has a clear, ringing authority to it, like Willow's voice did, like the voices of all gifted storytellers. "Before the time of the sick ones, our people lived far apart from each other. Few spoke the first language, our native tongue, anymore. Most spoke the second language—your language. We gathered from time to time to celebrate, and to pass the stories of the *anuna* to the young ones. It was during one of these celebrations that we received the news that the *runa*, the sick ones, were coming. The world fell into chaos—homes burning, families torn apart—and everywhere, the sick ones roamed. Death surrounded us. We lost many. The *anuna* were frightened, but together we found our way here, to our ancestral home of Koolkuna.

"Here we have lived for generations. We renewed our use of the first language, as a bond between our people, while keeping our knowledge of the second language. We live in peace and safety, taking care of each other with sustenance from the forest and the Myuna—our water hole. Through the years, *lorinyas* have come to Koolkuna. Some stay, grateful to have found a place of safety. Others leave again, haunted by memories of lost loved ones. Now you have come to Koolkuna, and we ask ourselves: will she stay? Or will she leave? What is she searching for?" He pauses, obviously waiting for an answer.

My mouth is dry despite the cool water Kadee gave me with my meal. "I search for … hope. Hope for my people. I came from the forest, some days' walk away. We live on the forest floor, where we grow our food and hunt what we can. But we must hide from the Scourge, what you call the *runa*. When they come we hide in caves until they leave again. We can't leave the forest because we need the water from our water hole. I came in search of a new source of water, to give my people a chance for freedom from the Scourge."

"And your friend?" Wirrim asks.

"His name is Peree. His people live in the trees above us. They depend on the water, too, and he came for the same reason, to find a place where his people can live free from fear."

"You came from the Dark Place?"

"Our legends tell of water in the caves that's protected from the creatures. Peree and I searched for days. We found it, the underground river that feeds your water hole, but he was injured, so we couldn't go back home to tell our people."

"How was he injured?" Kadee asks.

"He was attacked by an animal we came across in the caves." The listening people murmur at that. "She was trapped between us and the sick ones. She protected her young, and Peree protected me." I swallow again, thinking about what it cost him.

"What kind of animal?" a woman asks.

"We thought it might be a tiger."

"Tiger? There are no tigers here," a man says.

"Peree wasn't sure. He'd never seen one before. He said the animal was big and yellowish, with black markings on its body." There are more excited murmurs. I hear the words *lynx* and *cougar*, but they must be the first language because I don't know what they mean. "The wound became infected, and Peree was suffering terribly. We couldn't go back. He didn't want to die in the dark, so I took a chance on the river, hoping to find the sun. Luckily, the sun found us—Kora." I smile toward where I think Arika is sitting. "And … you know the rest."

"I am sorry your friend was injured, but it is good news that you came across a big cat. Very good news," Wirrim says. "The predators are returning."

I hope they won't mind if I ask a few questions now. "What about the sick ones? Where do you hide when they come? The trees?"

"Hiding is not necessary in Koolkuna," Wirrim says. "It is protected."

It takes a moment for the significance of his words to sink in. A whole *village* protected from the Scourge? None of our stories tell of such a possibility.

"How?" I ask.

"As I said, *lorinyas* have found their way to Koolkuna through the years, and like you, they want to understand how we are protected. We find it easier to show them than to tell them. We will show you, too, when the time comes."

I'm not sure what he means by *show* me, but from his tone of voice I sense I won't get any other answers now.

"You and your friend may stay until he recovers. Perhaps tonight you'd like to stay on the ground, closer to him? Nerang says you are healing well." I agree, and Wirrim addresses the group. "Will any of the *anuna* take in our guest?"

Kadee speaks. "She may stay with me."

I'm relieved. As fascinating as the trees are, being up in them makes me queasy.

"Then that is settled. Welcome to Koolkuna, Fennel."

People begin to file out, conferring in low voices. Some greet me with shy words of welcome. Kadee comes to me, and Kora skids up a moment later.

"Thank you for taking me in," I say to Kadee.

"I welcome your company," she replies. "Kora, when you two tire of exploring, bring her to my home."

"Fennel, do you want to meet Bega?" Kora hops up and down in excitement. "She's waiting for us."

"Yes, but on one condition," I say, my voice grave.

"What?"

I muss her hair. "Call me Fenn, as my friends do."

CHAPTER TWELVE

I spend the afternoon wandering around Koolkuna with Kora and Bega. The doll knows an astonishing amount about the people in the village. She tells me all about them as we pass homes and workplaces, and I'm struck by how familiar the stories sound. She could be talking about our community, with one glaring exception: at home our conversations all come around to fleshies eventually, but Kora rarely mentions them.

I catch myself listening for the alarm calls, warnings that the Scourge is coming, as I would have at home. What Wirrim told me is still almost impossible to believe. I'm tempted to ask Kora if she knows how Koolkuna is protected, but it seems devious to interrogate a child.

People seem friendlier after the gathering. They speak to us as we go by, calling me by name. I meet some girls who sound about my age by the storehouse. They are curious, especially about my home, and what it's like to be Sightless. We chat for a few minutes, answering each other's questions. But one of them, Kaiya—Kora calls her Kai—doesn't speak, even to say hello. Bega tells me later that she keeps to herself, but the doll won't say more. It's uncharacteristic for Bega.

Kora leads me to check on Peree late in the afternoon. I sit by his side, holding his hand. I long to tell him about Koolkuna: about the people and how they can live in the trees *or* on the ground, and most of all, how they're protected from the Scourge. But he doesn't stir, and I can only stay a few minutes in the heavily incensed room before I start to feel drowsy and a little sick to my stomach.

Nerang sits outside. The smell of something—cloves?—drifts around my head. I laugh. "You could just go breathe the air in in there for a few minutes, instead of smoking out here."

"A good pipe is one of the pleasures of an old man," he says. "How do you find your friend?"

I frown. "The same."

"Try not to worry." He inhales and releases a slow puff of smoke. "I hear you will stay with Kadee now? I'll take you there. Kora was called home for her dinner."

We stroll through the trees while the sun sinks lower, as if sitting down to its evening meal as well. I hear the rattle of wooden dishes, and the low murmur of conversation. It sounds like home.

"Do you have a family, Nerang?"

He stops to empty his pipe, tapping it against a tree. I hear him crush the remains of the herbs and spices into the dry ground. Very dry, now that I think about it. I can't remember the last time it rained.

"A grave illness swept through the *anuna* years ago. Many were sick, and many died. Despite my efforts, my partner, Yindi, was among them." His voice sounds more resigned than sad. "Her name meant 'sun' in our language. My son is Konol, 'sky.' Yindi and Konol—my sun and my sky. Konol's grown now, a few years older than you."

"I'm sorry about Yindi."

"As am I. But like the legend of the flowers, life goes on and hope blooms again." We walk a little farther among the trees and pause in front of what must be Kadee's home. The door squeaks as it opens, and the aroma of cooking food greets us. "I've brought Fennel to you, Kadee."

"Would you like to stay for dinner, Nerang?"

"Thank you, no. I need to speak with Konol before he leaves with the hunting party. There's much to do to prepare for the Feast of Deliverance." Then he says to me, "I'll be checking on your friend in the morning, if you'd like to visit him again?"

"I'll bring her," Kadee offers.

"That's okay, I think I can find it myself," I say, not wanting to create work for her.

"After only one day?" Nerang says. "Impressive. I'm beginning to understand how you found your way through the Dark Place."

"Oh, Peree helped. He had torches, and we used crampberries to mark our path–"

114

"I meant your tenacity, young one," he says, and shuts the door. I turn to Kadee, smiling self-consciously after Nerang's compliment.

"Would you like me to show you around my home, so you know where things are?" she asks.

I accept her offer. Her home has smooth dirt floors and wooden walls, like ours, but it's larger. It has two rooms: a sleeping room, and the sitting area, situated around a small fire pit. I wash my hands in the basin against the wall as Kadee ladles our dinners onto plates. We take them outside to eat.

"I hope you'll be comfortable here," she says, when we're settled.

"I already am. It reminds me of home."

"And you miss your home, no doubt. Will you tell me about it?"

I describe our part of the forest. I tell her about Aloe, Eland, and my friends. I tell her of the freedom of summer afternoons swimming in the water hole, my love of dancing and baking bread, the expectant silence of the caves that makes me feel they're only quiet when no one is around to hear their hushed conversations. Conjuring my home helps me feel less homesick. The pungent scent of the greenhearts and the breeze tousling the leaves overhead almost convince me I'm there.

"It sounds like a peaceful place," she says.

"It could be, without the Sc—the sick ones." *Or the Lofties*, I almost say, before thinking of Peree. I take another bite instead. Leftover rabbit stew, and it's still delicious. "So, what's the Feast of Deliverance that Nerang mentioned?"

"Every summer the *anuna* celebrate the anniversary of finding Koolkuna, and deliverance from the fate of the sick ones. The hunting party will gather enough meat for all, and we'll harvest the first summer crops in preparation."

I swat at a mosquito buzzing close to my ear. "When is it?"

"At the next full moon, and we have much to do before then, as Nerang said. Would you like to come to the gardens with me tomorrow? We can certainly use your help."

"I'd love to, after I check on Peree." We laugh, because she said, "After you visit your friend, of course," at the same time.

We talk through the cool evening, until the mosquitos' persistent questing drives us indoors. Kadee is a good listener, quiet, but with a surprisingly exuberant laugh. I like her. As I fall asleep I realize I did most of the talking; she said very little about herself.

The incense is almost gone when I visit Peree the next morning. Nerang says the fresh air should encourage him to wake. He tells me he'll send someone to find me when he does, so I go to the gardens with Kadee.

I enjoy wandering through the rows, handling and sniffing each plant as we tend them. Many of the herbs and vegetables are familiar, like the carrots and potatoes in the stew; others are foreign to me. Kadee tells me their names and uses. I try the leaf of something called a turnip, and make a face at the bitter taste. She assures me the roots are delicious when cooked, and I tell her I'll take her word for it. At one point I smell rosemary, and I can almost hear Aloe scolding Eland for throwing clods of dirt at his friends in the next row. Homesickness backhands me, leaving me off-balance the rest of the morning.

Kora finds me in the gardens and invites me to their home for lunch. I meet her little brother, Darel, and Arika's partner, Derain. Derain has a big booming voice. He sounds huge, but somehow he's not intimidating. I like him right away; he reminds me of Bear. Derain, Kora, and Darel wrestle after we eat. The children giggle as their father pretends to be felled like a tree by their punches. Kora and Arika ask if I'd like to help them with the laundry duties. I agree—reluctantly—when I learn the *anuna* hang the wet laundry to dry up in the sunlit trees.

We take the ascending platform, and they lead me to a wide, sunny area wedged between the triangular points of three sturdy trees. Somehow it feels safer than the narrow walkways, and I relax. Ropes crisscross the space, giving me something to hang onto. My ribs barely ache now as I raise my arms to hang clothes over the ropes to dry. Other men and women join us, sharing news about their families as they work. They steer the conversation to other topics when I ask about the sick ones, but there's no undercurrent of fear as there is at home. I'm struck by how easily the people of Koolkuna live.

Later, Kadee and I sit by the fire and eat our dinner. I tell her about my day, and that I'm worried I haven't heard anything about Peree.

"You said he's not one of your people, that he belongs to the other group. Yet you clearly have a connection with him."

"I thought I'd hate him, before I met him. I *wanted* to hate him. Everyone despises the Lofties. But," I struggle to put my feelings into words, "I feel different about him now, and different about the Lofties *because* of him."

"I see," she says, in a way that tells me she understands more than I'm saying, maybe more than I know myself. It makes me want to change the subject.

"So I've told you all about my family, but you haven't mentioned yours." I'm surprised she lives alone. She sounds younger than Aloe, but certainly old enough to have a partner, and children.

"I did have a family once, but I ... lost them." She hesitates. "You see, I haven't always—"

The door bangs open, making us both jump.

"What is it, Kai?" Kadee says.

The girl speaks in a flat, clipped voice, the words spilling out like dried beans from a sack. "Nerang sent me to tell the *lorinya* to come quickly. Her friend is awake."

I hurry through the night, not waiting for Kai to guide me, trusting my sense of direction. When I reach the shelter I shove open the door without knocking. I can still smell a trace of the burning herbs.

"Peree? Nerang, is he okay?"

"Yes, young one, come in. I hope Kai didn't alarm you. I wasn't sure how long your friend would be awake. As it turns out, he's refusing to ever sleep again until he sees you."

"Fenn." Peree's voice is raspy, but lucid. I rush over to him. My fingers flutter over his face and smooth his hair. I blink back tears of relief. He catches my hand and pulls it to his lips.

"Well," Nerang says with a small cough, "I'll be outside if I'm needed." He closes the door as he leaves.

"How are you?" I ask, pressing my hand to Peree's cheek.

"Never better," he croaks.

I kneel next to the bed, and feel him stiffen. "Who did that to your face?"

I sigh. "I did."

He touches my forehead. "You look terrible."

"And that's a terrible thing to say to a girl."

He chuckles. "You're really here? I'm not dreaming?"

"Not unless I'm dreaming, too," I say.

He shifts his body, and sucks in a breath through clenched teeth. "I sincerely hope your dreams aren't this painful."

My smile vanishes. "I'm sorry. What can I do?"

"Nothing. Reminds me I'm still alive … because of you."

"Nerang saved your life, not me."

"Who is Nerang? And where the hell are we?" Peree whispers.

"He's an herbalist. Wait until you hear about Koolkuna, you won't believe it. It's protected. I don't know how yet, but Wirrim said he'd show us soon."

"Back up—who are Koolkuna and Wirrim? Start at the beginning. The caves are the last thing I remember. My head feels like it's crammed with dandelion fluff."

"I'll tell you as much as I can, but we may not have much time. Nerang is big on resting."

I describe our short, treacherous ride in the underground river—"Part water dragon, like I said," Peree teases—and how Kora found us. I tell him the story of the *anuna*. He's as astonished as I was to hear that Koolkuna is safe from the Scourge, and that the people live wherever they choose.

"Where are you staying, then?" he asks.

"On the ground, at Kadee's. I hate to admit it, but I don't think I like being in the trees. It scares me."

"Something scares you? I don't believe it."

"What really scared me was thinking that you weren't going to make it," I whisper. Tears threaten to flow again.

"Fenn, we're out of the caves. We're alive. We're okay." He tries to push himself up, but falls back, stifling a groan.

I wince. "I'm so sorry. I wish I'd done so many things differently. Maybe this wouldn't have happened. You might not have been hurt at all, if it wasn't for me."

He smoothes away a tear. "I didn't know you were such a martyr. Please stop blaming yourself."

"Who can I blame, then?"

"How about that Nerang guy? Let's blame him."

"Peree!"

The door opens. "I hate to interrupt, but I must change his bandages. And he needs his rest."

I flash a grin at Peree, and mutter, "Told you."

118

He takes my hand again. "Come back soon? I'll need someone to show me around when I get on my feet."

I grimace at him. "Go easy. You've been unconscious for days."

"And I'm not going to waste any more time lying around." He sounds so confident; I can't help smiling again.

I squeeze Nerang's arm as he walks me out. "You're wonderful, Nerang."

"I thought you might be surprised at how well he sounds."

I nudge him. "Maybe he won't need my strength after all."

"Don't be too sure," he says, suddenly serious.

I want to ask what he means, but he steps back inside, leaving me standing alone in the soft spotlight of the moon.

I wake early the next morning, and slip out to check on Peree. He's asleep, but Nerang's there, mixing up a batch of the paste of calendula and comfrey he's been applying to the wound. Considering all the fuss the man makes about people resting, he doesn't seem to get much sleep himself. He promises to send for me when Peree wakes.

Dew wets my feet as I walk back to Kadee's. She stayed up waiting for me the night before, to hear how Peree was doing. I appreciate her concern. And she's the only one who calls Peree by name, instead of by "your friend."

Kadee and I are cleaning our breakfast dishes when Kai comes again, to tell me Peree's awake. I wonder why she's Nerang's messenger. Maybe they're related, or she's his apprentice or something.

"Your friend certainly has his appetite back," Nerang says as I duck into Peree's shelter a few minutes later. "This is thirds, is it not?"

"You said I needed to eat to get my strength back. How else can I do it?" Peree mumbles from the corner of his mouth.

"I said get your strength back, not make yourself sick," Nerang says.

"Right now I'm only sick of being an invalid. It's time for me to get up."

"Are you sure you're ready?" I ask.

"Give yourself time," Nerang urges.

"I still have one good leg. The other one will have to find a way to keep up with it." I hear him set the dish down and push himself off the bed.

I step closer. "Peree, maybe you should—" Too late. He collapses, and shrugs away from my hands. "Will you stop being such an idiot? Let me help you!"

I put my shoulder under his like I did in the caves, and we stagger around the shelter. I can hear his teeth grinding in pain, but he refuses to stop until we've made a complete circle back to the bed. After a minute of rest, he's up again. The second time around seems a little easier for him. As we walk, I notice a few little differences, like his shirt. It's clean, for one thing. He must have had a change of clothes. He's too thin, but he smells really good—his familiar honeyed scent mingled with mint. Nerang probably used the same wash that he used to clean me up. I lean in a little closer, inhaling it.

After a few more laps around the cramped room, Nerang insists Peree rest. Peree insists he rest outside. "I need some fresh air after all that incense," he mutters.

"Pigheaded, isn't he?" Nerang says to me.

"You have no idea."

Nerang leaves us with a warning that he'll be back soon to wrestle Peree to bed if necessary. We sit down outside, our backs against the trunk of an impossibly wide, furrowed greenheart tree. He describes how the village looks from here.

"Petrel would love to see this," he says. "Those platforms they use to carry people up and down, the intricacy of their walkways—it's spectacular."

"So are their gardens," I say. "They're so much more developed than ours! They have all the vegetables and flowers we do, and more. Then again, they don't have to abandon their crops every time the sick ones—I mean the flesh-eaters—come."

"Sick ones? Is that what they call them?"

"*Runa*, in their language. And they call the caves the Dark Place."

"They got that right." A bird screeches, and Peree startles. "I can't relax, stuck on the ground and barely able to walk. My ears kind of tingle all the time, listening for the Scourge."

My mouth curls with the irony of a Lofty experiencing for the first time what all Groundlings feel, practically from infancy. "I know what you mean."

"I guess you would." His voice is tinged with apology.

We listen as people walk by, chattering to each other in the first language, followed by a group of children, playing some kind of chase game. Their excited screams remind me of the night of the Summer Solstice. It seems like seasons have gone by since then.

"So, how are people treating you?" Peree asks. "When he's not babying me, or trying to suffocate me with incense, Nerang seems nice enough."

I jab him with my elbow. "Peree! Nerang's been amazing! Neither of us were in great shape when we got here, and now look at us."

He snorts, and a second later I get the joke. My head is still horribly bruised, my ribs are wrapped, and part of his leg is missing.

"Yeah, we look great, like a couple of patched-up corpses." He presses his shoulder to mine. "But I'm grateful to him for taking care of you, when I couldn't."

I flush. "Really, everyone's been wonderful. Kora and her family, and especially Kadee. I want you to meet them. You'll like them."

"Sure," he says absentmindedly. "The people here—they're different."

"What do you mean?"

"The way they sound. How they look," he says.

The people do sound different, because of their accents, but I wasn't aware they looked any different. I ask him what he means.

"Some look like me," he explains, "with fair hair and light eyes, light skin. Others are darker like you. Some have dark skin and light hair. Some have skin as black as the night sky."

"I guess it doesn't surprise me. Wirrim said plenty of *lor–*, I mean strangers, have come over the years. And if the Exchange proves anything, it's that children don't always look like their parents."

"It's a lot to take in," he says. "One minute I'm pretty damn sure I'm about to die, the next I wake up in a village of survivors, and they're protected, and they're living here like one big happy family. I don't know what I expected when I came with you to find the Waters, but it wasn't this."

I hesitate, chewing on my lip. I'm not sure this is the right time to bring this up. "Peree? Do you remember how you told me in the caves, that there are less of you?" I remember what else he told me in the caves, about watching me, and my face heats up again. "It seems like Koolkuna might be what you were looking for, for your people. There's still a lot I don't know about it, but I do know it's safe, and the people are kind."

He nudges me again. "Trying to get rid of us, Groundling?"

I smile. "With you Lofties gone, we could stay in your trees when the Scourge comes, and not have to hide in the caves. Less *accidents* with arrows, too."

"I thought you hated the trees."

"Let's see," I tap my finger to my lips, "stay on the ground with the flesh-eaters and hide in the caves, or live safely in the trees? I think I can get over my fear of heights."

"So you wouldn't mind if I left home for good?" He's still joking, but there's a serious note to his question.

"I'm thinking out loud, that's all."

"Well," he pushes himself to his feet, using the trunk of the tree for support. "I want to take a closer look at the village, especially those walkways. And since that will involve actually being *able* to walk, I'm going back to the shelter, completely unassisted."

"Peree, be careful." I jump up and follow uselessly behind him as he hobbles across the grass.

"I'm good, it's no prob–" He stumbles.

Nerang catches him. "Pigheadedness may help you heal, but stupidity will not. It's time to rest now."

Peree mutters something that sounds like, "I take back the nice part."

We finally get him settled back in bed, grumbling all the way, and he's still asleep when I come back to visit him later that afternoon. Nerang laughs, saying pigheadedness can only take you so far.

CHAPTER THIRTEEN

I mean to get up early the next morning, but Kadee's sitting room is flooded with sunlight when I finally wake. As I near Peree's shelter, I'm surprised to hear a female voice. It's Kai.

"That one rolled!" she says.

"No, it didn't," Peree says.

"It did too, cheater!"

"Are you kidding? I don't have to cheat to win a child's game."

"Cheater," the girl says again, her voice teasing.

"Fine. As proof of my noble nature, I'll take the high road. Take your turn."

"You bet I will."

Somehow I feel like I'm intruding as I step into the doorway.

"Fenn!" Peree sounds startled, and something else … guilty? "Do you know Kai? She was showing me a game they play here. It's called, *uh,* spill sticks."

"And you were cheating," she murmurs to him.

"We met," I say, wrestling a smile onto my face.

"I'm going," she says to him. "You better practice. I won't be so easy on you next time."

Next time?

"See you. Thanks for the game," he says, as she slips almost silently out the door. Like a snake. "So, how'd you sleep?" he asks me.

"Fine. You?" I can't keep the clipped tone out of my voice.

"Great," he says.

I hover near the door, suddenly annoyed. They weren't doing anything suspicious, I tell myself, only playing some kind of kid's game.

Together.

Alone.

Maybe it was that Peree sounded like he was having fun. Have we had fun together? Surviving the Scourge, wandering around in freezing caves, being attacked by animals, and almost dying. Fun? No.

"Oh, hey, guess what? Nerang made me a crutch." I hear him take a few stumping steps. "Let's go for a walk."

I try to shake off my irritation. "Are you sure you're up to it?"

"Absolutely. Plus my warden's letting me out on good behavior."

"I wouldn't go so far as to call your behavior good," I say, and instantly wish I hadn't.

He sighs. "Fenn, Kai was just being nice. I think she's kind of lonely. She's been hanging around here a lot. She's like one of the men—Nerang says she hunts, and she's really good with a spear."

Great—she's lonely, hanging around a lot, and they have hunting in common. Was that supposed to make me feel better? I shake myself again. I'm being ridiculous, and a little mean-spirited. Well, he's not the only one who can take the high road. "No, I'm glad you're making a friend," I say firmly.

"So do you want to take a walk? If so, we better get out of here, before Nerang changes his mind and locks me up again."

I take him on a quick tour of the village, pointing out the gardens, the workspaces, and the *allawah*. I share what I know about the people, too, which is a lot, thanks to Kora and Bega. Then we take a ride into the trees on the magical flying platform. It's not quite as bad this time, but I'm still nauseatingly attuned to every lurching upward motion. Peree laughs at my queasy expression. We stroll around the walkways, stopping often so he can interrogate carpenters, and examine such fascinating things as bend knots and junctions. It's good to hear him so enthusiastic.

The people don't seem as suspicious of Peree as they did of me. I guess they've gotten the word that the *lorinyas* are harmless. Or maybe it's that Peree probably doesn't look too dangerous while leaning on a crutch with a heavy limp.

The laundry area's deserted today. Peree leads me to the edge of the platform, helping me duck under the rows of empty ropes. He describes the view of the forest, and the nearby hills. Somewhere in there, the Hidden Waters bubble.

"Want to sit for a few minutes?" he asks, his voice a little too innocent.

"Why? Do you need a rest?" I tease.

"Don't tell Nerang." He sits, stretching his legs out in front of him with a contented sigh.

"So what do you think of Koolkuna?" I ask.

"You were right, it's amazing. It reminds me of a story my mother told once about some people who were trying to reach this safe place where they could live, but they had to walk through a valley of death to get there. When they arrived, they found green pastures and calm waters, and all the food they needed—you know, without having to fight each other for it. And something about all the animals living together there, too. The tigers lay down with the sheep, or something like that. I can't remember the details, but it was a good story."

"Speaking of tigers, the *anuna* were pretty excited that we ran across a big animal like that. Although they didn't think it was a tiger," I say.

"All things considered, I wish we hadn't run across her. But she was beautiful …" He sighs. "I wish it could have gone another way."

"Me too." I lie back and fold my hands across my stomach. The wood of the platform is warm, and as smooth as a polished rock. The afternoon sun heats my skin. Peree lies back too, his head close to mine.

"I wonder what everyone at home thinks happened to us," I say.

"Probably that we're in some kind of paradise, toasting our safety with the cool, clean Hidden Waters."

I laugh. "That is pretty much what we're doing."

"We've earned a little downtime, don't you think?"

Eland, my mind whispers. *Aloe, Calli.* "I guess."

We avoid the subject of home from then on, talking instead about Koolkuna. It's peaceful, lying side by side with Peree, enjoying the sun and the cool breeze that crops up, as the afternoon stretches on. It's as close to fun as we've had. And I don't remember ever feeling this … safe. Contentment soaks into places deep inside me, empty places I didn't even know existed.

I'd planned to take Peree by Kadee's house on the way home, but as he drags himself slowly across the dusty ground, it's clear he's overdone it today. We go straight to his shelter instead. By the time we get there, he doesn't even complain about getting into bed.

"How's Peree today?" Kadee asks when I come in a few minutes later. She's preparing our dinner.

I ask for a broom and start sweeping, determined to make myself useful. "Unbelievably well. He's stronger each time I visit him. I never would have thought he'd be able to walk so soon, even with a crutch. Then again, he can be hardheaded when he wants something."

She laughs. "So Nerang said."

I think about his game with Kai. *Yeah, he's getting his strength back all right.* An idea floats into my head, and I stop mid-sweep. "Kadee, Peree told me not long ago that he's always wanted to swim. I thought I might give him a lesson. But is it okay to swim in the water hole? Is it protected?"

"The protection at the Myuna is … strongest, at midday. I'd go then. I'm sure he'll enjoy it. That's very thoughtful of you." I notice her pause, but I don't know what to make of it.

"I owe him," I say. I tell her about the swim he arranged for me.

"It sounds like you're lucky to have each other."

I smile at her. "I'm lucky to have *you* as a friend, too. I know Peree will feel the same way when he meets you."

"I hope so," she says, and she sounds strangely wistful.

The next morning I stop by Peree's shelter on my way to the gardens. He's already outside, practicing with his crutch. He sounds like he's moving well, but I can hear the sharp intakes of breath as he puts weight on his bad leg.

"I have a surprise for you," I tell him.

"What is it?"

"What kind of surprise would it be if I told you? Be ready to take a little walk around lunchtime. Maybe you should res–"

"Don't say it!"

"All right, all right." I laugh. "I'll be back in a few hours."

I spend a contented morning helping to dig up vegetables and listening to people talk about the upcoming Feast of Deliverance. I find myself getting caught up in the excitement. Two younger girls giggle and chatter in the next row. Kadee suddenly laughs beside me.

"What is it?" I ask, struggling with a disobliging carrot.

"They're talking about Peree."

I rub my forehead with the back of my soil-covered hand. The bruise still itches a little. "What about him?"

"They're calling him *Myall*—it means wild boy. Apparently they think he's quite handsome."

I hack at the crumbling earth around the carrot with a stick. *Wonderful.* First Kai, now these two. Aren't there any other eligible men in Koolkuna?

I leave the gardens a little before noon. The wild boy's outside when I arrive. He tries to take the packed lunch Kadee made for us, but I wave him off.

"You just focus on staying upright," I say.

"I'll do my best. So, where are we going?"

"You'll see."

He sighs. "Have I told you I hate surprises?"

I stop walking, worried I'm making a mistake. "Really? We don't have to—"

"Joking, joking ... I just hate waiting."

"Come on, then," I say.

We take a path around the clearing, staying under the shady trees, stopping occasionally to let Peree rest. He transfers the crutch from arm to arm as if it might be bothering him, but he doesn't complain. When we turn away from the village onto the path to the water hole, he hesitates.

"Are you sure about this?" he asks.

"Sure about what?"

"That this way is safe?"

"Kadee said it's protected," I say.

"And you trust her?"

I nod.

"Okay, I guess. It's not like we've seen any sign of the fleshies since we got here." He limps forward again.

"That's true. I wonder when they'll decide to show us how the protection works. Why all the mystery, do you think?" I ask.

"No idea."

"They'll probably want to talk to you soon, now that you're on your feet."

"I don't mind talking to them," he says, "but I hate feeling like I'm on display. Everyone stares at me when we walk around the village."

I grin. "Maybe they can't help themselves. I heard some girls talking about you at the gardens. You should hear your new nickname, it's *wild.*"

"What is it?"

"Wouldn't you like to know," I say.

"No, not really," he says, but he sounds pleased. "So, where are we going again?"

I groan. "Didn't anyone ever tell you patience is a virtue?"

"Yeah, but it didn't sink in."

"Clearly. We should be close." I can hear the waterfall now. "Look for a path that leads to the left."

We take the path, and Peree stops as we near the waterhole. I have to raise my voice to be heard. "Do you remember this place?"

"No, not really, more like I dreamed about it."

"What did you dream?"

He doesn't answer at first. "You'll laugh."

"I won't."

"I was the hunter and you were the cassowary woman. One of your sisters came to bring you home."

I nod. "That must have been when Kora showed up. You told me to go with her." I think back to the moment she found us. It was early, soon after first light. Kadee implied the water hole was less protected at other times of the day. So what was Kora doing here then?

Peree whistles. "That waterfall—I'm feeling even luckier to be alive. The water level looks low, though. Nerang said they haven't had much rain this year."

"I've heard that too. They're trying to conserve water in the garden."

"The rains always come, though, right? There hasn't been a real drought in years," he says.

Willow used to talk about the last drought. She said it was a terrible time. The water hole almost completely dried up, and the people were desperate. The flesh-eaters were especially dangerous then, picking off the people who left the caves mad with thirst.

"So the surprise is a picnic?" he asks, taking the sack from me. "That's great, I'm starving. Plus I was beginning to think you were leading me here as bait for the Scourge."

"It's a picnic, but I also thought …" Suddenly I wonder if it was such a good idea to try to surprise him with a swim lesson. What if he isn't interested? "You know how Nerang said it would be good to soak your leg? And you said you'd always wanted to swim. I thought maybe I'd give you a lesson, if you want."

"Seriously? You will?" He drops his crutch, and I hear him pull off his shirt. I picture his uncovered body, and my body flames. I turn away to hide my embarrassment.

"Your men swim with their shirts off," he says, uncertainty in his voice, "don't they?"

They do, but I never found myself imagining many of them naked. I force myself to sound casual. "All the time." I kick off my shoes. "Come on, last one in is a fleshie!"

We leap in—well, hop is more like it. Peree's cautious because of his leg, and I have to be careful about where I'm jumping. But the water is incredibly refreshing after the heat of the midday sun. I dive under and come up streaming, the slick mud squishing between my toes. I swim toward the center of the pool, smiling as I glide under the surface, thrilled to be in the water again. After a few minutes of splashing around, I wade through the water to him, my dress clinging to my legs like a bashful child.

"Ready for your lesson?" I ask.

"Ready."

"Let's start with floating on your back—that's what all our toddlers learn first thing," I tease.

"Watch it, Groundling, or I'll drag you up into the trees and make you stay there."

I laugh, holding up my hands. "Anything but that! Okay, lie back in the water with your arms and legs out, like this." I demonstrate. "Don't worry, I'll hold you. You won't sink."

I stand to his side and slide my hands under him as he tries it. The lean muscles of his back tense at my touch. "Try to relax."

"Easier said than done," he mutters.

I know what he means. As my fingers slip across his bare skin, heat spreads from the soles of my feet to the roots of my hair like I'm in a pot of boiling water instead of a sun-warmed water hole. By the time Peree stands again, my heart is pumping unevenly, and my legs feel strangely disconnected from the rest of my body.

I struggle to keep my voice normal. "Good job. Now try again, and this time I'll only help if you need me." My hands itch to touch him again as he tries to float on his own, but I rest them on my hips instead. When he stands, water cascades down from his hair and torso. I don't let myself imagine for too long what it might feel like if my arms were around him.

"I can float," he says proudly.

I smile at him. "And now if you get in over your head, you know what to do."

He steps closer. "What if I am already?"

"If you're already what?" I ask.

"In over my head."

My heart thumps again. "Then you, *um*, float, and kick your legs and move your arms, until you reach a safe place."

Another step closer. "But what if I don't want to be safe? What if I want to be reckless?"

"Then you ... drown?"

"Exactly," he murmurs.

We're almost touching, the water trickling down our bodies. My skin explodes in goose bumps, and not from the cold. He slides his hands down my arms from my shoulders to my fingers, smoothing my skin. I can't breathe, fearing what I might do if I gave my hands free reign—and fearing not having the chance again if I don't.

A bird swoops across the water beside us, breaking the spell. I step back. A few moments pass. When Peree speaks again, he sounds almost normal. Almost.

"Let's check out that waterfall. I like to get a good look at the things that almost kill me."

After several deep breaths to compose myself, I follow him. We skirt along the outside of the water hole. It isn't that deep—at least at the edge— or very far to the waterfall. Peree finds a narrow pocket in the wall of rock behind the falls, big enough for two. He climbs in, and helps me up beside him.

The water careens down in front of us, battering the surface of the pool. It's magnetic, exhilarating, undeniably powerful. I lean toward the spray and thrust my hand into the freezing column of water, but it's slapped away. So I reach for Peree's hand instead. He wraps his cold fingers around mine.

I consider all that's happened since we came to Koolkuna. When we survived the waterfall, it was like we emerged into some other world. Somewhere not quite the same as the one we knew before. A magical place, out of one of Peree's mother's tales. The valley of death? I live there. I know all about it. But here I'm a stranger. A *lorinya*. As I hold Peree's hand, I wonder if there's a possibility we could find our own space. Somewhere we both belong. Somewhere between the ground and the trees.

Peree and I make our way back to shore, and lie down in the sun to dry out. Something's changed between us. The air around our bodies feels charged, like the forest before a storm. I'm excruciatingly aware of him: his slow, even breath, his face turning an inch toward the sun, his hand twitching at his side. And I can tell he's equally aware of me. It's stirring … and scary, like the dangerous pull of the waterfall.

I unpack the lunch Kadee made. Peree digs in. I pick at a thick slice of bread.

"Nerang wasn't kidding about your appetite," I say, trying to lighten the mood.

"The food is good. Different, but good. I could get used to it."

"Anything tastes better than days of dried meat." A familiar pang cuts through my chest. What is Eland eating now? Are he and Calli and Bear still in the caves? What challenges is Aloe facing on the Council? I long to hear their voices and know they're safe.

"I wish you could see the color of that water. It's half green and half blue. Beautiful, like …" he thinks about it, "like Moonlight's eyes. Not like our dirty brown water at home."

I'm surprised at the flare of resentment I feel when Peree compares the "beautiful" blue water to another girl's eyes, even if she is pretty much family. Especially considering he also described brown, the color of my eyes, as dirty. I keep my face smooth, to hide my hurt feelings.

I'm still nursing my pride as we finish our picnic lunch and walk back to the village. We stop in front of Kadee's door, and Peree takes my hand.

"Did I do something to make you angry?" he asks.

"No, I'm fine," I say quickly.

"Are you sure?"

"Of course."

"Okay," he says doubtfully. "Thanks for the picnic, and the lesson. Maybe next time I'll be brave enough to put my face in the water."

I force a smile. He pulls me in for a hug … and the hurt feelings dwindle as my body surges with that bewildering energy again. I tighten my arms around him, crutch and all.

Voices come toward us through the trees. Sounds like Nerang and–

"Kadee!" I take his hand, pulling him toward them. "Come meet her …"

I trail off as Peree jerks to a stop beside me.

"I don't believe it," he says.

"What?" I ask.

"It's you."

"Yes, it's me," Kadee says. "Hello, my son."

CHAPTER FOURTEEN

My mind spins. Kadee is Peree's *mother?*

"What are you doing here?" He sounds like he's seeing a ghost. I guess he is.

"This is my home." Kadee's voice is quiet.

"Since when?"

"Since I left the trees."

He doesn't respond for a moment. "All this time you've been here? We thought you were *dead!* Or worse."

"I'm sorry," Kadee says. "I know I have much to explain, but I've been waiting until you were stronger. Will you come in and talk with me now?"

"Oh, is it a convenient time for you, then? Are you sure you don't want to wait a little longer? It's been ten years, what's another day?"

"Please, son–"

"Don't call me that. You gave up that right when you left us." The astonishment in his voice is gone, replaced by a barely controlled rage.

Kadee takes a step toward us. "Peree–"

"You know what, don't bother explaining now. It's too late."

He's gone, into the forest.

"Peree, wait!" I move to follow him, but Nerang touches my shoulder.

"Let him go, young one. He's had a shock. He may need some time."

I turn on him. "You knew about this, didn't you? Why didn't you tell me, so I could prepare him? And Kadee—I thought you were my friend! Were you using me to get information?"

"No!" She sounds miserable. "I planned to tell you both. I was waiting for the right time."

I shake my head. "Well, somehow I don't think this was it."

I wander around for a while in the forest, listening for Peree, but I don't hear him. I literally stumble onto a knee-high, flat rock in a quiet patch of grass, and I stop to sit. A small stream bubbles nearby, but the sounds of the village are faint from here. I'm not sure where else to look for Peree. Maybe Nerang was right; maybe he needs to be alone. Nerang is usually right—except about this. He should have told me about Kadee.

She must have found Koolkuna somehow after she left the forest. But why didn't she go back, or at least let her family know she wasn't dead? I know her well enough to believe she's not cruel or uncaring. She must have had a reason. What could it be? What would drive her to leave her child like that, without a word?

A few nights ago, when Kai came to tell me Peree was awake, Kadee was going to tell me about her family. So maybe she wasn't deliberately trying to keep me in the dark. I guess there isn't a good time to spring something like this on someone. Poor Peree.

When the heat becomes unbearable, I cross to the shaded stream and step in. Flies dance around my head as I wade across the slippery stones. I think about our swim, and touching Peree as he floated in the water. The stream isn't particularly cold, but I shiver. If the recent electrical current between us is permanent, things are going to be a lot more interesting from now on. A stick cracks in the forest in front of me.

"Peree?" I call.

Something—something not human—moans. I clamber back out of the stream and stand on the opposite side from the creature, poised to run.

"Is someone there?" I say, my voice shaking a little. Whatever it is moves through the underbrush toward me. It sounds too heavy to be an animal. I turn and rush back to the village, not waiting to find out if the creature follows.

I'm curled up in a chair in Peree's shelter, shivering in my soaked dress. I wasn't sure where else to go. I've been listening, but everything in the village sounds normal. At one point I heard Kora asking after me, but I didn't go out. I don't want her to see me like this.

I'm not sure why I'm so unsettled. I knew the flesh-eaters were still out there. No one said they weren't. I guess I'd let my guard down a little, stopped listening for them. Hearing one again brought back memories I'd as soon forget. The smell of rotting flesh, and the sound of agonizing hunger. Memories of Rose and Jack and their unborn child. Even after I begin to breathe easier, I stay curled up in a ball. It feels safer this way.

Eventually I hear Peree's uneven steps outside, and Nerang's serene voice. Kai's with them, too. Is she *always* around when I'm not? The door opens and something solid raps my head. I yelp.

"Oh, sorry Fenn, I didn't see you there," Peree says.

I rub my scalp. "What was that?"

"My crutch—I tossed it at the chair when I came in. Are you okay? You look … strange."

I tell him what happened, and he wraps me up in his arms. "I'm sorry you were alone."

"I'm better now," I mumble into his shirt. "How are *you* feeling?"

He flops onto his bed. "Angry. No, furious. I can't decide if I'm angrier that she left, or that she let us think she was dead."

I sit on his bed, too, and gently lift his bad leg onto my lap. "Did you talk to her?"

"Why should I? The situation's pretty clear, isn't it? She left us to come here. What else is there to know?"

"Why she left? She must have had a good reason."

"Like what?"

"You said she was restless in the trees, that she wanted to have more freedom. Maybe she found that here, because Koolkuna's protected."

"We protected her!" For a moment I hear the wounded ten-year-old boy Peree was when his mother disappeared. A moment's enough—it's painful. "She liked it here. She didn't like it at home. Either way, it doesn't change anything. She didn't love us enough to stay." He thumps the wall with his fist. "Whatever. I'll probably find out, whether I want to or not. Nerang says she's all broken up, and I should give her a chance to explain. He wants us to meet them at the water hole at dawn."

"The water hole? Why?"

"Who knows? Something about seeing clearly there. It's Nerang—the man can't just say what he's thinking."

"But the water hole is less protected in the morning."

His laugh is short and sharp, like the rap of a woodpecker. "Maybe they're planning to get rid of us now that we know the truth about her."

"I'm sorry, Peree. I mean, I'm glad she's alive, but I'm sorry you found out the way you did. I don't know if this will help you, but she seems lonely. And I think she was going to tell me about you the night you woke up. I don't think she meant to keep it from you for long." I reach for his hand and find his knuckles are wrapped in cloth. I hold them up. "What happened here?"

"I couldn't see straight for a few minutes after I took off. A couple trees are a little worse for wear."

"I didn't know you had such a bad temper," I say, and I'm only half teasing.

"I don't, usually. I think it's … everything. My leg, Koolkuna, and now my moth– Blaze, Kadee, I don't even know what to call her. But you've been through at least as much as me, and you seem to be handling it a lot better."

I shrug. "I'm a Groundling. We learn to expect change. Especially me, being Sightless. Things surprise me all the time. I'm used to it."

He slides his fingers between mine, braiding them together. "Will you stick with me a little longer, bad temper and all?"

In answer, I brush my lips over his bandaged knuckles. I want to say we'll be like the fish people in his story, and stay together no matter what. But then I think of Aloe's warning before I left home, and I remain silent. If I've learned anything since I became the Water Bearer, it's that what I want and what I have to do rarely coincide.

We spend the afternoon in Peree's shelter, avoiding mothers, healers, and nosy dolls. Hungry and thirsty, we venture out as evening falls, but discover someone left food and water for us outside the door. I wonder if it was Kadee.

While we eat, I think about where I should sleep. I don't feel right going back to Kadee's, considering how Peree feels about her. But picturing spending the night with him makes my stomach clench. Things have evolved between us since that first night in the trees, and the freezing nights in the caves. The swim today only confirmed it.

His thoughts aren't far away. "If you want to stay here tonight, I'll sleep on the floor and you can have the bed."

"Not with your leg," I say. "I'll take the floor."

"I won't be able to sleep, knowing you're uncomfortable."

"I won't stay at all if you don't take the bed."

He chuckles. "Hmm, what to do? I suppose we could share the bed …"

I hesitate. I don't know if there are rules about unpartnered boys and girls spending the night together in Koolkuna, but there sure are at home. I cringe at Thistle's shrill accusations of impropriety, then I push her out of my head and slam the door shut. "We could."

Peree takes his time cleaning our dishes, while I wash my face and hands with the last of the clean water. I try to detangle my hair with my fingers, but I give up halfway through when I realize he's waiting by the bed, probably watching me.

"After you," he says.

Thanking the stars that I'm relatively clean from the swim this morning, I climb in. He joins me, holding his breath as he eases his leg up, and pulls his bedroll over us. We lie on our backs, no part of our bodies touching. Not easy to accomplish in a narrow bed. I don't move a muscle, ultra-aware of the length of his limbs beside me and the rise and fall of his chest as he breathes. Locks of his wavy hair mingle with locks of mine. A hot, prickly feeling slides over my skin.

He snickers. "I don't think I'm going to be able to sleep like this, either."

I laugh too, fighting the urge to giggle like the girls in the garden this morning. Peree turns on his side and gathers me into his body, sending jolts of energy through me again. Surprisingly it feels more natural this way, though—like I belong here. We lie quietly for a few minutes, getting used to the feeling of being together. When he finally speaks, his breath tickles my ear.

"You know the story of the cassowary woman?" I nod. "I think my mother was trying to tell me she was leaving, with that story, without really telling me. And to tell me how she felt." His voice is tight. "I want to hate her for going away. But I can't, not completely. I'm not the little boy anymore; I'm the hunter. And a part of me understands and forgives her, even if the boy doesn't want to."

I hug his arms with my own. He draws me in even closer.

"Sleep well," he murmurs, as if reassuring me he *is* planning to go to sleep. It takes me a long time, but I finally do.

I wake to the sound of scraping. It's early, still dark, and I'm alone in the bed.

"Peree? What are you doing?" I whisper.

"Making a bow. If the flesh-eaters might be at the water hole, then I'm going armed."

I tuck the bedroll around me against the chill, and listen to him work. "Need help?"

"Untie a few feathers from my hair?"

I slide my fingers through his tousled hair and find the sleek feathers. He tells me how to attach them to the sticks he's gathered, while he strings the bow. I do the best I can, but I have him check my work, afraid the arrows won't fly straight if I make an error.

When he finishes, he slings the bow across his back. "I'm going out to practice. Want to come?"

We stumble through the predawn to a nearby clearing. I lean against a tree, shivering in the cold wind that snakes through the branches, while he sets up a target. There's no sign of the sun, and the birds are silent. The air around us feels heavy and tense, as if it's holding its breath.

"A storm is coming," I mutter.

Peree notches the first arrow and releases it. It slices through the air, but skitters across the ground somewhere beyond the target. He adjusts the bow then shoots again, releasing each arrow in turn, making small modifications after every shot. The last few drive into the target. He retrieves the arrows, then stands in front of me and brushes a few wind-blown locks of hair back from my face.

"It's time."

People leave their homes, moving in hushed groups toward the water hole. I hear the platforms drop slowly in the trees, carrying others to the ground. The sun doesn't penetrate what must be dense clouds overhead. My hair flaps around my shoulders, then clings to my face, buffeted by the wind. I wish I had something to tie it back.

Kora slips in next to us, holding my hand as usual. I introduce her to Peree as we follow the path from the village to the water hole. I wonder if I was wrong that this has to do with the Scourge. At home we would never bring children near the flesh-eaters. But nothing in Koolkuna is as I would expect.

We turn toward the water hole, and the roar of the waterfall grows. It's hard to hear the sounds of the forest now. The *anuna* are gathered, and more come. Arika greets us quietly, then speaks to Kora. I hear Kadee and Nerang. People stand in small groups, passing around cups of water from the water hole. We drink, too.

"What's going on?" Peree mutters. "Nerang didn't say this was going to be a public apology."

"It's the offering," Kora says.

"What offering?" I ask.

"To the *runa*."

Peree whispers in my ear. "I don't like this."

I don't either. Huddling closer to Peree, I pull Kora into me. I can't hear the creatures between the waterfall and the wind. I feel horribly exposed.

The trees quiver and shudder, thrashed by the wind. No rain yet. Wirrim's voice suddenly rises above the elements. I didn't think he sounded strong enough to walk all the way here.

"When the *anuna* came to Koolkuna many years ago, we knew it to be our ancestral home. We did not know it would also provide the sanctuary we required, away from the sick ones. We hid in the trees, sending only the quick and the brave to the water hole to gather our life-sustaining water—"

A vicious crack of lightning interrupts him. I shield Kora as well as I can. Then I smell them.

The Scourge is near.

Peree drops his crutch and draws his bow tight. I clutch Kora. Wirrim speaks more urgently.

"When we came to Koolkuna, we were afraid of the *runa*. But quickly we realized they were changing. They were different."

The flesh-eaters are close, in the trees around us. I hear them ... but instead of moans and shrieks, I hear voices. Human voices. Pleading for food, for water. For someone to help them die.

"What's happening?" I ask Peree.

He sounds haunted. "I don't know."

"You do know," Nerang says. "See them. See them as they really are."

"But these creatures limp instead of sprint, their skin is cut and bleeding and bruised. Their hair is dirty and twisted. They look ... ill. What happened to them?"

Nerang answers. "They are the same. *You* are different."

"They can't be the same. I've watched the Scourge tear people limb from limb," Peree says. "I've seen them surge in packs over their prey. These things aren't capable of that."

"What you saw was an illusion. An illusion caused by a strong poison, poison in the water you drink and the meat you eat," Wirrim explains.

"Poison? What are you talking about?" Peree says.

Wirrim's voice is gentle, like he knows this is difficult. "When I was a child, a *lorinya* came to Koolkuna from the City, searching for lost loved ones. Before she moved on she told us many stories, and among them, how the *runa* came to be. In the days before the sick ones, the people of the world were at war. When neither words nor weapons satisfied their hate, they used poison."

Thunder bursts. The creatures almost echo Wirrim, murmuring "war" and "hate."

"She said the poison was created many years before the Fall. It was so dangerous it was locked away, but later it was found by others who thought they could control it. They destroyed their enemies, and our world, in the same damning blow. The poison spread, uncontrolled, through the air and water, settling in the ground and the crops. It killed many people and animals. And it had another devastating effect: It caused people to lose their minds, their understanding—they went mad. No longer able to care for themselves, they became like senseless wild animals, desperate in their hunger and fear. These people joined growing groups of the similarly afflicted, and they became the *runa*. The woman who told us these stories called it a 'madness of many.' They have roamed the earth since that time.

"Pockets of survivors like your people, those who do not die or go mad, are still vulnerable. Instead of seeing the *runa* as ill, you see grotesque, flesh-eating monsters—what you call the Scourge. You kill them, and you separate yourselves from them, in trees or caves, and so you avoid succumbing to the madness yourselves. But you live immersed in your fear, and the poisoned water feeds your illusions—sip by deadly sip."

He's saying we're all *poisoned*? Eland accidentally hit me in the head once with a rock. This sensation is similar, like whatever force keeps me upright and centered just wandered away. I speak for the first time, struggling to be heard over the wind, and the pleas of the creatures.

"Why do they look and sound different to Peree and me now? What protects Koolkuna?"

"When the *anuna* arrived here," Wirrim says, "we drank from the Myuna and we no longer suffered from the madness. We could see the *runa* for what they were—people in great need of help. The Myuna comes from the Dark Place deep beneath the earth. It is pure; the poison did not contaminate it. Now you have drunk from it for many days, and eaten only the meat of animals who drink from it. The poison no longer controls your minds."

The sounds of the Scourge *have* changed. It's as if I should have understood them all along, if I'd only been listening properly. Mesmerized, I take a step toward the creatures.

"Fennel," Peree growls. "Don't."

"It's okay," Kora says, stepping with me.

I stop. Walking into the Scourge myself is one thing, but allowing a child to get any closer is another. I'm about to tell her she can't go, when Wirrim speaks again.

"Bring the offering."

Kora moves forward. I try to pull her back, but Arika touches my arm.

"Please don't worry. She's given the offering before."

"What *is* the offering?" Peree hisses.

"Food for the *runa*."

"Food? You *feed* them?" he asks.

"I'm going with Kora," I say.

The sickening smell grows with each step. That hasn't changed. The instinctive terror from being close to the creatures crashes through me, but Kora and the others don't hesitate. They walk to the edge of the clearing and stop in front of them. Dishes rattle as they're laid on the ground.

One of the *runa* speaks, its voice weak and feeble. "Thank you."

I reach out to it, pity overcoming fear. My trembling hand meets cold flesh for only a moment. It feels human, yet lifeless at the same time. The flesh of a corpse.

"They don't like to be touched," Kora whispers, pulling me back.

The sick ones take up the food. And as they melt back into the trees, every truth my life was built on vanishes with them.

CHAPTER FIFTEEN

People begin to leave the clearing as I make my way back to Peree's side. Many touch me as they go, or speak to me with soft words of encouragement. I'm too stunned to respond. The trees sound like they're being torn to pieces by the whipping wind, and we're being doused with spray from the waterfall, but I barely notice. I don't even hear Kadee move over to us, until she speaks.

"Come to my home if you'd like. I'll make you breakfast, and answer your questions."

I wait for Peree to respond, but he doesn't, and after a moment, she walks away. I touch his arm, and realize his bow is still aimed at the line of trees, as if he thinks the *runa* will turn and charge us at any moment. He releases the arrow. A moment later it strikes a tree.

"I can't believe it. I wouldn't have believed it, if I didn't see them with my own eyes," he whispers.

I can't believe it either. I didn't see them, but I heard, and felt them. And that was enough.

Kora waits on the path, joining us as we walk toward the village in silence. I'm surprised to hear people talking and laughing in normal voices, discussing their day—until I consider that what was earth-shattering to Peree and me is accepted from a very young age by everyone else here. Kora is proof of that.

"Do you want to go to your mother's?" I ask him. I don't know where else to go. Nothing feels real to me, like I'm waking from a nightmare, but only just.

"Don't call her that," he murmurs, sounding as dazed as I feel. "She doesn't deserve it."

"But that *is* her name," Kora says.

"What do you mean?" he asks sharply.

"Mother is what Kadee means in our language."

"Why would she be called that?"

"Mama said it was because her son was all Kadee talked about for so long, when she came to Koolkuna. Mama said she cried for weeks and weeks."

Arika calls to Kora, and she runs off. Peree doesn't speak again, but as we wander through the village, I realize he's leading us to Kadee's home. She welcomes us in right away. The gentle warmth of the fire is a relief after the penetrating chill of the wind, and the shock of what we learned.

"You have questions," Kadee says, as she puts a pot of water on the fire to boil. I wait for Peree to say something, but he stays silent.

"The water hole," I say, "at home. It's been poisoned for years? So when we drink from it, it plays tricks with our minds? Is the Scourge even dangerous at all?"

"They can be. They aren't the horrific creatures the poison creates in your imagination, but they are still hungry and desperate, like Wirrim said. They must feed themselves, as we all must. They eat animals—usually raw, which only makes them sicker—and they've been known to attack people, too, if they're starving. It's probably what led to the first reports that they consume human flesh."

That explains the bite, the night I fell asleep in the forest. The creature must have been hungry enough to take a bite and see if I fought back, like a scavenger animal. Rose's plea echoes through my head. Was she still human at that moment, not yet consumed completely by the madness?

"What happens to their minds?" I ask.

"Our knowledge isn't complete, but they seem to retain their awareness only for a short time. They forget who they were or how to care for themselves. And as far as we can tell, they don't live long. They become ill, weak from exposure to the elements, and they die. They seem to travel in groups to give them an advantage in hunting, and perhaps as some vestige of how they lived before they became *runa*. Their name is derived from two words—*boolkuruna*, which means 'homesick,' and *birruna*, 'dangerous.' The sick ones are both."

She pours us each a cup of tea, and offers fresh bread and berries. I nibble a little, to settle my uneasy stomach. Peree remains mute.

I ask, "What really happens when someone is being consumed, then?"

"It's difficult to understand, but the closer a vulnerable person—someone under the influence of the poisoned water—comes to one of the sick ones, the more likely they will slip into the madness and join the *runa*. It's as if the sight, sound, and smell of the sick ones overwhelms their senses, and completes the illusion."

An unexpected rage floods through me. "This is unbelievable! All these years, all these generations of people, all the fear and pain and devastation—because of some *poison* that makes us believe things that aren't true? Nothing since the Fall has been *real*?"

"What is reality, Fennel?" Kadee asks gently. "It's what we, as a group, believe to be true. If a group, aided by the powerful effect of a poison, believes it's threatened by a mindless pack of monsters, then that *is* what's real.

"Ever since I was a little girl," she continues, "I only saw the sick ones, never the Scourge. The creatures have always looked and sounded to me as they did to you today. I was more frightened by the violent reactions they caused in others than I was of them. When I tried to tell my parents what I saw, they seemed wary, fearful. They told me not to speak of it. So I never did. But it didn't change what I experienced. It didn't change my reality."

Peree grew still beside me as Kadee spoke.

"Why are you different?" I ask.

"Nerang says some people, very few, are unaffected by the poison. He doesn't know why or how. I only know I never saw them as monsters, and the divide between what I saw, and what others believed to be true, only grew with the years. Peree, when you were young, the Council sentenced me to a night on the ground. Do you remember?"

"It's hard to forget your mother disappearing," he says coldly. I touch his arm. When she speaks again, Kadee sounds like she's pleading. Pleading for Peree to understand.

"I wandered for days, frightened and lost, until I found Koolkuna. These people took me in, and showed me for the first time that what I knew in my heart, but never revealed for fear of what others would think, was true. It was very hard to return home, but I couldn't be away from you any longer. I missed you terribly."

Peree doesn't respond.

"I was eager to share my good news with our people, but my hopes were shattered when I told your father. He thought the time I spent on the ground had driven me mad. He said if I told anyone else, he would take you from me. So I tried to forget what I knew, and to carry on with my life, even if it meant living a lie. Eventually, I couldn't do it any longer. I was miserable ... ready to harm myself. The night I left, I told Shrike I was returning to Koolkuna, and I wanted to bring you with me. He flew into a rage, and threatened to kill us both. So I came back alone."

Peree scoffs. "Unbelievable. You blame Father, when you're the one who abandoned us?"

"No, of course not. Your father is a strong-willed, brave man, fiercely loyal to his family and his people–" I can only imagine the look Peree gave Kadee when she spoke of loyalty. "But he's human. I didn't expect him to believe me right away, but I did hope he might trust me enough to come see Koolkuna for himself."

"He wouldn't go?" I ask.

"Like Groundlings, there's little Lofties fear more than exposure to the Scourge. Walking through the forest only on blind faith is a journey not many would be willing to make. Shrike was afraid I would spirit Peree away, take him where he didn't dare follow—here to Koolkuna. No, he wasn't willing to go."

Peree was willing. It was through the caves, not the forest, but he came with me. I didn't consider how daunting it must have been for him to leave the trees.

"Son, to see the man you've become is a joy I didn't think I'd ever have, the answer to my prayers over the last ten years," Kadee continues. "I've been content here, but I wasn't *happy* until the day the men carried you into the village from the Myuna—the day I saw you again. And to know you have a caring, faithful friend is an added blessing." She squeezes my hand, and I smile at her.

"Did you tell anyone else about Koolkuna, before you left?" I ask.

"No, stars forgive me, I didn't have the courage after Shrike's reaction."

"But he knows you're here now, or at least he knows Koolkuna exists," Peree says slowly. "He may have told someone."

I almost choke on my tea. "Do you think he told Aloe? She was more supportive of the idea of me searching for the Hidden Waters than I thought she'd be."

"Shrike and Aloe have always been close," Kadee says, a hint of something unexpected in her voice. Envy? Regret? "Or at least as close as a Groundling and Lofty could be. What did the Council say about you accompanying Fennel?"

Peree snorts. "What Council? We don't have one anymore."

"What? Why not?" She sounds genuinely shocked.

"Not enough of us left to need one."

Haltingly, his voice pitched low, he tells her the story of the fever and its aftermath. As Kadee begins to cry, I excuse myself and slip out, giving them privacy. I need air, and time alone to think. My mind is overloaded with information and my body brims with pent-up emotion.

A steady rain finally falls as I wander toward the clearing where I heard the sick one. Was that only yesterday? I'm just now starting to consider the implications of what we learned. Almost everything about my community, where we live, how we live, is based on the belief that the Scourge is monstrous, existing only to consume us. And the framework of my life as well—the combined gift and curse of my Sightlessness, my responsibilities of stocking the caves and collecting the water—was defined by the flesh-eaters. It collapsed in one morning.

I reach the clearing. I can hear the stream bubbling over the soft thrum of rain on leaves. And I hear something else. Voices singing in the first language of the *anuna*. I stand under the canopy of a tree and listen, strangely soothed by the unfamiliar, discordant tune.

Footsteps approach, followed by the sweet scent of clove blending with the fertile smell of moist earth. I wonder how Nerang keeps his pipe lit in the middle of a rainstorm.

"Come in from the rain, young one."

I don't move. "Why are they singing?"

"It's a song of celebration. The Myuna has not been as plentiful of late. Where is your friend?"

"Talking with Kadee."

"Good, they have much to discuss."

I turn on him. "How long? How long have you known who we were?"

"I suspected where you were from the moment I saw you. You were dressed so similarly to Kadee when she first appeared in Koolkuna. But I didn't know who your friend was until Kadee told me."

"Why didn't you tell me what you knew?" And I don't just mean why didn't he tell me he knew where I was from, or that Peree was Kadee's son, but all of it—all the secrets he'd been keeping. I don't have to say it. He understands exactly what I mean.

"First, because you were close to physical and mental exhaustion when you arrived. You needed time to rest and regain your strength. Second, Kadee needed to be the one to tell you both. How your friend may be related to my friend is not any of our business, despite what Kora's doll might have to say on the matter." I crack a small smile at that. "And third, you weren't ready to hear it. You needed your strength, and you needed your friend to mend first. Those needs coincided with the amount of time required for you to drink from the Myuna before we showed you the nature of Koolkuna's protection."

Protection. The word bounces around inside my head.

"Nerang, what is it about being Sightless that protects me?"

I catch another whiff of the sweet smoke before he speaks. "When Kadee told me about the protection provided by your Sightlessness, I was puzzled. Then the answer became clear. The illusion caused by the poison is powerful, but because you are Sightless, you're less convinced. Your eyes don't deceive you, if you will, as ours do. And, from the beginning you were told you could not be harmed. You *believed* you were protected, as much as others believed they were not. And so it was."

I shake my head, boggled by the idea. "All my life Sightlessness has been celebrated as a gift to myself and my community, something to be grateful for. But it's meaningless. A weakness after all."

"Forgive me for making assumptions, but I suspect it has given you much."

"Like what?" I scoff. "Other than more scars and bruises than I can count."

"Bravery, strength of character, willingness to sacrifice for others. Even wisdom. You may be Sightless, young one, but you have more vision than most your age."

I try to resist, but the corner of my mouth lifts again. "I bet Yindi couldn't stay mad at you either."

Nerang chuckles. "True."

I comb my wet, stringy hair back from my face. "I don't know what to do with all of this. It's too much."

"Give yourself time."

"I don't have time! I need to go home. I'm afraid to think about what's happening back there. And now I somehow have to convince my people that pretty much everything they believe isn't true."

"Faith has been limited since the Fall," he agrees. "At first we tried to simply tell *lorinyas* the truth, but we found we had to prove it to them by having them drink from the Myuna. Yet, you have one advantage we do not."

"What's that?"

"Your people know you, and trust you. You can use that."

I think of Adder and Thistle. "Not all of them."

"I didn't say it would be easy, young one." He puffs on his pipe. "Of course, there is another choice you can make."

I wait, but he doesn't say anything. "What is it?"

"You can stay. Create a life here in Koolkuna, as Kadee did. You would be welcome."

I step back, startled by the powerful yearning his words prompt in me. I can picture it—my life in Koolkuna. Working in the sunny gardens instead of alone in the caves; drying and preparing herbs for Nerang, maybe even learning his healing arts; taking Kora under my wing; getting to know the others who have been so kind to me since I arrived. I want that life badly. The safety and comfort Koolkuna offers is seductive.

And I could have it. I could stay here. I could let people think I died trying to find the Hidden Waters.

Eland, Aloe, Calli, Bear, Fox ... Like a dead roll, I hear the whispered names of the loved ones I'd never be with again if I take that path. I shake my head, and take another step away.

"No."

Nerang's voice is gentle, as if he could hear my thoughts and sympathized with my struggle. "I thought you would say that. Well, then. Before you go we will talk about what might be done to convince your people they need not fear the *runa*."

The singing faded away while we spoke, leaving only the steady tattoo of rain in its absence. A shout rises from the village.

"Ah, the hunting party has returned," Nerang says with relief. "And they've had success, from the sound of it."

The idea of eating freshly cooked game twice in one summer makes my mouth water. "Are there more animals here? Because of the Myuna?"

"The animal populations are returning. It was a good sign that you saw a predator in the Dark Place. The return of the large animals means their food source, the smaller animals, is thriving. They in turn will stay near the Myuna, bolstering our food supply."

I think about the tiger—or whatever she was—and her babies, and the dark, hopeless hours that followed, and I shiver. "You said the Myuna hasn't been as plentiful? What happens if it dries up?"

"It won't, as long as the rains stay," he says, but worry infuses his voice. "I must go and see Konol. Would you like to meet him?"

"Yes, I would … but later."

"As you wish. I hope you'll stay at least until the Feast of Deliverance. The moon is full in two days' time." He grunts. "And it may take us two days to convince your pigheaded friend he's not strong enough to make the journey back with you yet."

I sigh. "I know."

"I could use my incense to drug him again," Nerang says thoughtfully, and I laugh. "But hopefully it won't come to that. Until later, then."

I turn my face to the sky. The rain is diminishing; the clouds have finally wrung themselves out. Individual drops join together and slip away down my nose and cheeks. I find the boulder I sat on before and curl up next to it, ignoring the chill.

I sprint through the forest. Light leaps through gaps in the trees, warming my head and shoulders, then vanishing the next moment. Birds encourage me from their perches. I've never run so freely, so fearlessly. I don't care where I'm going. I just run. The feeling is unforgettable.

"Fenn."

Peree's voice drifts through the trees. I slow my pace, listening for him, unsure if he's there in my dream, or in the rain-soaked reality I've left behind. Could he be in both? I pause, one foot on a firm, sunlit patch, and the other sinking into spongy, wet ground.

"I've been looking all over for you. Are you alright?" He leans over me.

"Yes," I mumble, but I stay still, reluctant to give up the powerful sense of freedom in my dream. Until I realize I can't feel my fingers or toes. "Actually, I'm freezing."

"Let's get you inside." He pulls me to my feet, and wraps his arm around my hunched shoulders. He leans heavily on his crutch as we walk.

"How are you?" I ask.

"Okay, I guess. We both said things that needed to be said." He sounds less angry than I've heard him sound since he found out Kadee was alive. "My grandparents, her parents, died during the fever outbreak. All I have left is my grandmother Breeze, Shrike's mother. Did I tell you that?"

"No—I'm sorry."

"So was Kadee." He's quiet for a moment. "I realized something. She left us … but she didn't really leave us behind."

I consider again how I would feel if I stayed in Koolkuna and never saw Aloe and Eland again. "I can believe that."

He leads me into his shelter and gets to work on the fire. I sink into the chair.

"I'm having a hard time believing any of it," he says. "If I hadn't seen the way the creatures looked …"

"They sounded pitiful. I wanted to help them."

"Yeah," he grumbles, "I wasn't too happy when you touched that one."

I shrink from the memory of its cadaverous skin under my hand. Where are the *runa* now? How do they survive without shelter, extra clothes, a fire? No wonder they don't live very long.

"If you want to change," he says, "your pack is there on the bed. I brought it over … in case you needed anything. "

I pull a cloth out to dry myself, and the extra dress Kadee gave me, but I can't change with Peree three paces away. So I hunch in a chair and listen to him work. He hoots in triumph as flames finally pop and hiss into existence. Then he seems to notice my dilemma.

"Change. I'll go outside."

I dry off and pull Kadee's dress on quickly, then call him back in. "I can turn my back if you want to change," I tell him.

"That's not necessary." He sounds amused. His soggy shirt falls to the floor, and I assume his pants are next. The heat from the fire is suddenly stifling. I shuffle things around inside my pack, trying to look unfazed, but who am I kidding? Every sliver of my attention is focused on him.

"What's that?" he asks.

I realize I'm gripping Peree's knife, the little bird he carved, and the rabbit's foot. They were all rolled up in the fabric remnant Bear gave me. I crumple the cloth bear in my hand to hide it, and hold his knife out to him instead.

"Here, I took this out of your pack when we left the caves."

He takes it from me. "Thanks, I've been missing it. And now I can finish your bird. Is that the foot of a rabbit?"

"It's supposed to be for good luck. A friend gave it to me."

He plucks the fabric from my hand. "And this? It looks like a fleshie."

I shrug. "Sewing isn't exactly a talent of mine. It's an animal, a bear."

I wonder if he remembers Bear was the name of the "friend" he saw kissing me. From his silence, I'm fairly sure he does. He hands it back, and I shove it into my pack.

"Our women wear the carved birds on leather ties around their necks," he says. "I could make a cord for yours, if you want."

I finger the little carving, then hand it to him, too. "Thank you, I'd like that."

We warm our dinner, and sit down to eat. There's a new silence between us that's uncomfortable, but not awkward. It's not like we don't have anything to say, more like we're bursting to say things we know we shouldn't. I push the food around my plate. It's hard to eat with nervous tension like a grasping hand in my gut.

"Your hair's still wet," Peree says. "Come over by the fire and let me dry it."

I scoot closer and turn my back to the flames. He sits to my side, and picks up handfuls of my hair, gently combing his fingers through the damp tangles. He takes his time, working his hands through each section until it dries. I relax slowly, just enjoying the feeling of his hands moving through my hair. After a few minutes, his fingers begin to glide across my shoulders, down my arms, and back up to graze the sensitive skin of my neck, lingering on the bare skin. I tense again. He scoops my hair up and lays it over my shoulder, then traces a looping trail down my back to my waist. The fire feels closer now—like I'm roasting over it.

"I'm going home," I whisper, "after the Feast."

His hand pauses at my hip. "What?"

"I'm going back."

"Fenn, I'm not sure my leg is ready for that kind of walking. Can't we wait for awhile?"

"I can't wait. I need to know what's happening there."

He pulls his hand away. "So I'd just hold you back, is that it?"

"That's not what I mean–"

"That's exactly what you mean," he snaps. "I get it. You have a duty to your family and your people. And *that's* most important."

"Peree–"

"Forget it."

I know what I'm doing. Trying to push him away, afraid of what might happen if I let things go too far. I want to smooth things over, but what can I say? No matter how much I might want to ignore it, I do have a responsibility to my people. I was supposed to try to find the Hidden Waters, and be home within a few days. And I *do* miss my family. This wasn't supposed to be some kind of holiday.

"I'm sorry," I whisper, reaching out toward him. "I have to know if Eland and Aloe are okay."

He exhales slowly, and slides his finger along a particularly deep scar on my hand. "Your commitment to your people and your duty ... it's one of those things I admire about you. I don't expect you to change now."

My willpower falters. I lean forward and touch my forehead to his, breathing in his sweet scent. "Why did you have to be so great? I'm supposed to hate you."

He chuckles in a throaty way that does nothing to dispel the fire raging inside me. "I'll try to be hateful in the future."

He pulls his bedroll down from the bed and wraps us up in it, curling his body around mine again. I hear his breath quicken, but he doesn't touch me any further. I'm relieved—and disappointed. A part of me wants to roll over and face him, let things lead where they may. At the same time I want to jump up and run.

I've never felt this conflicted about someone before.

My relationships with Aloe, Eland, Calli, even Bear, grew out of the close ties of family and friendship, nurtured since childhood. I've never questioned my feelings for them. But with Peree it's different. We were thrown together. I didn't expect to have anything with him at all, apart from the distant relationship of Water Bearer and Keeper. The intensity of our bond confounds me.

I can't deny I have strong feelings for him. But I'm holding back, resisting the growing intimacy. If I let go of my heart, give myself over to him, what will we do when we go back? No Groundling and Lofty ever made a life together. There's no precedent for it. What would our families say? What would the Three do? Where would we even live? I wish I could say it didn't matter to me. But it does. I care for him, but I care about my family and my people too.

So I do nothing, snared in a miserable tangle of desire and caution, longing and fear.

CHAPTER SIXTEEN

I wake early the next morning, and carefully untangle my arms and legs from Peree's. I have to put some distance between us; I can't think with him so close. I go to the only woman in the village I can talk to. It's my bad luck that she also happens to be his mother.

"Fennel, I'm so glad you came." Kadee takes my hands in hers. Her skin feels dusty.

I rub my fingers together and a smile crosses my face. "Flour?"

"I'm doing some baking for the Feast. How are you?"

"Still shocked about everything, I guess."

"And upset with me, for not telling you sooner about Peree."

I shrug. "I was, a little, but I know you had to tell him first."

"He was so badly injured, and then when he woke up, I didn't know how to say the words."

I nod. "I wouldn't know either."

"Somehow I doubt that. You don't seem like you'd shrink from a difficult situation."

My cheeks flame, thinking about the night before. "*Um*, would you like help with the baking?"

"Please—I have so much to do still."

I'm as much of a failure at cooking as I am at sewing, but I do love to bake. When I was about eight, I pestered the baker unmercifully one afternoon until he finally shoved ingredients at me and showed me what to do with them. I fell in love with kneading the dough, feeling the soft mush slowly thicken under my fingers. Over time I learned how dough feels when it's the right consistency, and how bread smells when perfectly baked—spongy and warm inside, crusty outside. I still sometimes join him at the clay oven near the roasting pit when I finish early in the caves.

As Kadee and I work, blending and forming the lumps of dough, my mind wanders back to Peree. Suddenly I realize the dough I'm working with has become more rock than loaf. She takes it from me with a chuckle. "Do you want to talk? You must have a lot on your mind."

"It's about Peree."

"Is he all right?"

"Yes, it's just … I think he wants … more from me than I can give him." I squirm with embarrassment, but I have to talk to someone, or I'm going to explode. "I'm sorry, I know you probably don't want to hear this about your son."

"I want to hear anything you have to tell me, Fennel," she says. "Anyway, I'm not surprised. I won't claim to know Peree or his feelings as I once did, but I do know young men. And the way he looks at you–"

I groan. "Not that again. What does that even *mean*?"

"He watches you. All the time. When you move, he moves. When you smile, he smiles. When you walk away, it seems hard for him not to follow. Clearly he has strong feelings. But do you feel the same way?"

"Does it matter?" I grab my head in frustration, remembering too late that my hands are covered in sticky bits of dough. "No matter how we feel about each other, there's no future for us! Not one I can see, anyway. I'm a Groundling. He's a Lofty. That's not going to change, no matter what happens when we get home."

"The future can be hard to predict," Kadee says. "I certainly never saw Koolkuna in my future, when I was your age. And after I came here, I didn't allow myself to hope I might see my child again, but that too was meant to be. Who knows what might happen to any of us? All we can do is follow our hearts." After a moment she says, "*It is not in the stars to hold our destiny, but in ourselves.*"

"That sounds like something Wirrim would say."

She laughs. "Those words were written long ago, before the Fall."

"Written?" I wonder if that's a Koolkuna word.

"Writing is … marks on a piece of cloth. Marks that can be read and repeated. People used to write down what they thought and said, so that it could be passed on to other people. I can show you what I mean, if you'd like. It won't take long."

155

We clean the dough and flour off our hands and leave the village, walking along the path to the water hole. A bird shrills from a tree beside us and I automatically tense. I wonder if I'll ever quit listening for the Scourge, or if it will always be part of me, as permanent as my Sightlessness.

"When I came to Koolkuna the first time, I was entranced by Wirrim's storytelling," Kadee says. "I was especially intrigued by stories from before the Fall, when the world was a vastly different place. After I went home, I was afraid to tell people the stories, worried they'd ask where I learned them. So I whispered them to Peree at bedtime, night after night."

I smile. "He told me some to distract me as I collected the water."

"They distracted *me*, too, and they helped me remember my time in Koolkuna."

We pass the turn to the water hole. I can hear the crashing waterfall as we go by. I didn't even know the path continued on. "Where are we going?"

"To a special place—for me, at least. The place where I learned many of the tales."

Some minutes later we enter a large clearing that's unimpeded by trees, judging from the bright light. Tall grass sweeps across my legs. It's quiet, except for the chitchat of the birds. They sound like they're gossiping about us.

"When I returned," Kadee says, "Wirrim didn't have enough stories to distract me from my misery over leaving Peree. So he brought me here."

She leads me forward, placing my hand on something solid and rough, like rock, but too even to be natural. It feels man-made, like clay. I explore up, down, and across, but the rock feels the same all over.

"It's an old building, from before the Fall," she says.

Excitement bubbles through me. "Really? An actual pre-Fall building? Our teacher, Bream, talked about them. Is this one as high as the sun?"

Kadee laughs. "No, but it's taller than our homes. There are other buildings here, too. This was a village once, like ours, but larger. When the people arrived in Koolkuna, it was already abandoned—except for the *runa*. Come in, but watch yourself, the building is old. It does its best to crumble while we're not looking."

I immediately notice the smell as I step inside. It's dusty and dank, and makes my nose itch. There's an intriguing odor, like the rows of pouches and pots on the shelves in Nerang's room in the trees. The building is dark, but not pitch black, and the floors are firmer than wood. Something in here absorbs the sound. I stretch out my arm, feeling for anything recognizable.

"What is this place?" I ask.

Kadee places something in my hand. It's rectangular, flat, and smooth—like a piece of sanded wood—but softer, with some weight to it. I explore it with my fingers. The top pulls up, revealing another smooth, featureless surface underneath. And there are more beneath that one. When I move my fingers across their edges, it sounds like a bird fluttering, stretching out its wings to fly.

"What is this?"

"A book. These are called pages." She crinkles one under my fingers. "It has the little markings I told you about. They're called letters. When you know how to read the letters, the pages tell you the stories. This one's called *Viennese Silver: Modern Design 1780–1918.* It has pictures, but not all books do."

"Viennese silver? What's that?"

"I don't know, I haven't read this one. The room is full of books and I've only read a fraction of them. Here, feel this stack." She guides my hand to more of the books, piled on top of each other. "There are hundreds like it." I take a few steps forward, moving my hand from place to place, and everywhere I find more piles.

"How did you learn to–" I yelp. A book fell on my foot. A hefty one, judging from the throbbing in my toes.

"How did I learn to read them?" Kadee guesses, after checking to see if I was okay. "Do you remember Wirrim told you about the woman who explained the significance of the Myuna to us? She arrived weak and sick, like you and Peree, only she wasn't so young as you. She stayed for some time recuperating."

"Wirrim said she came from the City?"

"Yes, or what was left of the City after the Fall. Her people survived by hiding in small groups, mostly underground. It was very difficult. There were more *runa* in the City—many more, and it was hard to hide from them—but there were also more survivors. They helped each other. The woman called this a library. People came here to read books for knowledge, and to entertain themselves. Her people remembered and passed down the ability to read, and she taught Wirrim while she was here. When he saw my interest, Wirrim taught me."

I'm fascinated. Until a few days ago I didn't know there was a way to live other than how we did. To find Koolkuna, with people like ours, yet so unlike them too, and now to hear about other survivors from the City … it's like one of Peree's stories. Too fantastical to be true.

Kadee continues, "Reading has been my love and my duty ever since, along with working in the gardens. I read as much as I can about the world before the Fall, the world this building was once a part of. And when Wirrim goes on, I'll become the Memory Keeper for the people."

"Really? I didn't know that." I try to hide it, but I'm surprised. While Wirrim doesn't seem to be a leader in the way the Three are, he's obviously a well-respected member of the community, sought after for his opinion. For the *anuna* to allow a *lorinya* not only to stay, but to inherit a position of honor, only highlights how different Koolkuna is from home.

Kadee wanders through the room. "The first book I ever read on my own was a collection of simple children's tales called *Animal Fables and Stories from Around the World.* I heard Wirrim tell the people stories from it when I was first here, then I told them to Peree." I smile. So that's where the stories about tigers, the cassowary woman, and the first fish came from. "I'm using the book now to teach Kora and a few of the other children to read. Some of their parents don't see the need, but they humor me."

I set down the book about modern silver, whatever that is, and trail my hand along the piles. The dust makes them feel like they're coated in flour.

"Come over here, there's something else I want to show you," Kadee says. I make my way, cautiously this time, around the stacks to where she stands. She hands me an open book. "Feel this one."

I run my fingertips across the surface of the page. "It's bumpy."

"I found it a while ago, and remembered it when I met you. It's a book for the Sightless. You read it by feeling the raised dots. There are others like it."

I can almost feel a pattern to the raised portions of the page. Recurring patterns, although I have no idea what they might mean. A meaning just beyond my touch that unlocks a world of stories. "I want to learn," I whisper.

"Maybe you can."

"How?"

"You create your destiny, remember?"

I think about everything that's happened since I became the Water Bearer. *Not so far, I don't.*

We wander through the piles a few minutes more, as Kadee tells me about books she's read and others she wants to. I like this peaceful, disorderly place with its musty smell. I'll miss it when I leave, like so many other things about Koolkuna.

I find Peree at the *allawah* deep in debate with Konol. Nerang introduced them earlier in the day, and from the sound of it, they spent most of the day arguing about the advantages and disadvantages of bows versus spears for hunting on the ground. Konol's voice is loud and his speech is fiery, nothing like his father's, but I like him.

Peree tells me they still need more meat for the feast. He's going out with a few of the hunters. And Kai's going with them.

"What about your leg?" I ask, keeping my voice low. I don't want to embarrass him in front of his new friend.

He picks a bit of dried dough out of my hair. "My warden okayed it. Anyway I've got to start testing it sometime, and we won't go far. We'll camp tonight, and hunt at first light."

Although I'm not thrilled to hear that Kai's part of the hunt, I'm relieved Peree's going. I don't think I can survive another night as tense as a bowstring, pretending to sleep.

I've never slept alone. I don't relish the silence of Peree's empty shelter, so I spend the night at Kadee's. She lights a cheery fire, and reads to Kora and me from *Animal Fables and Legends*. I dream of chimerical talking animals.

The next day the village hums with activity, as the people get ready for the Feast of Deliverance. I help Arika, Kora, and some others repair woven baskets to carry food in. They tell me about the feast as we work. It's held by the water hole. Offerings are made to the *runa* to start. Wirrim and Kadee tell the story of the people, and all the babies born over the past year are blessed. Then the feasting and dancing begins. "And it may not end," Arika adds, laughing.

The people tell stories from past feasts—like how one man drank so much plum wine he passed out stuck in the mud around the water hole and had to be pulled out the next morning. Or the time some of the children accidentally set fire to the feast table and charred a week's worth of food.

Their laughter is infectious. I'm as excited as anyone in Koolkuna by the time I bathe and change into one of Kadee's freshly laundered dresses.

Peree returned in early afternoon. As I passed through the clearing on an errand for Arika, I found him giving Kai an archery lesson. They were teasing each other and laughing, like before. Having fun. Kai slipped away again, barely taking the time to greet me. *I really don't think I like that girl,* I thought to myself. Peree and I talked briefly, then he left to help Konol prepare the clutch of rabbits and several possums they shot. He sounded tired but content, more like himself.

I feel more like myself, too, as Kadee and I follow the path to the water hole, carrying baskets stuffed with fresh bread and newly harvested vegetables from the garden. Kora skips beside me, and before I know it, I'm skipping, too.

"Finally!" she crows. We skip madly, until we collapse in a giggling pile of arms, legs, and stray lettuce leaves.

We arrive at the water hole, and I help Arika prepare food for the sick ones. Feeding the Scourge is still such a bizarre idea, not to mention that in Koolkuna they make them *part* of the celebration. Nerang finds me as I work, and asks if I'd like to have a chat. We stroll along the edge of the water, toward the waterfall, and sit on a downed tree trunk.

He sighs. "Ah, it's good for an old man to rest after being on his feet all day."

I shake my head and smile. "You make it sound like you have one foot in the grave, but you never even seem to sleep. How old are you, anyway?"

"To tell you the truth, I'm not sure. But complaining about my infirmity prompts regular dinner invitations from the widows."

"Nerang! You're terrible!"

He's unapologetic. "I never learned to cook. I have to beg for my meals."

"I doubt Konol lets you go hungry."

"He is a good son, if a bit reckless at times. He and Myall appear to have much in common."

Wild boy. I snort. "Peree seemed happier today after hunting with Konol." *And Kai.*

"He is improving quickly, but he's too thin and easily winded. He tries to hide it, but I think his wound continues to cause him pain. Still, I doubt I'll be able to keep him here for long once you leave." He mutters about pigheadedness. "It will be quieter, when you go. Your presence in the village caused quite a stir."

"I appreciate all that the *anuna*—and especially you—have done for us. I'm sorry if we created any problems by being here."

He pats my arm. "Causing a stir doesn't necessarily equate to a problem. The presence of *lorinyas* over the years has not always been easy, but we learn from the experience. We learn more about the world beyond Koolkuna, and about ourselves, reflected in the gaze of an outsider. Tell me, what do you think of us?"

I think for a moment, then answer honestly. "I think you're people who live peacefully with each other, who welcome strangers, who care for the creatures that could be their worst enemies. You embrace kindness and cooperation. Koolkuna is what I'd like my community to become."

Nerang chuckles. "We hide our blemishes well, then. It's not always as idyllic as you give us credit for, but we do strive for peace and kindness."

"Have you had any brilliant ideas about how to convince my people the water is poisoned?" I ask hopefully.

"Without the Myuna to clear their minds, it will be difficult. Even if they trust you, their fear of the *runa* will be strong. You can't bring the Myuna to them, so perhaps the only solution is to bring them to the Myuna."

"What do you mean?"

"I spoke to the *anuna*. You may bring your people here to take the waters. Those who wish to may stay. The same offer will be extended to Kadee and Myall's people."

"But there are so many of us. And I know you're worried about a drought."

"We've always been provided for," Nerang says. "There's no reason to think we won't be now."

"It's too much to ask. You can't–"

He quiets me. "We've enjoyed good fortune. We would like to share it with others."

I'm humbled by the generosity of the offer. It's everything I'd been hoping for, but didn't dare admit. To know my family and people are safe, and not under the influence of the poison, to not have to hide in the caves, to choose to live on the ground or in the trees—it's a stunning vision.

Would the Three even consider it? I think about it. They would have to be persuaded to allow me to lead everyone through days in the dark caves, culminating with a suicidal swim. All to convince them that the reality they've always known *isn't* real. It's ludicrous.

I shake my head. "They'll never do it."

Nerang is quiet for a moment. "Did you not walk among the creatures, trusting the assurances of your people that you would be safe?"

"That was different."

"Why? Don't discount your authority so easily, young one."

I fling out my hands. "Young one! That's my point! I'm not one of the Three, or one of the elders. I'm not even an adult yet. No one will listen to me."

"They trusted you to collect their water, and to search for the Myuna."

They didn't have a choice. "Thank you, Nerang, truly. I'll present your offer to my people. But I don't even know how I'm going to get home yet." I gesture to the plummeting waterfall. "Is there another way into the Dark Place? I don't think I can get in the way I got out."

"Kadee knows the way through the forest. She agreed to guide you."

"Really? She's willing to go back?" I ask.

"It surprised me as well."

While we talked, the last of the light faded from the sky, and was replaced only by the brighter, more focused glow of the bonfire. A babble of voices was audible over the waterfall before, but now I only hear two.

"Well," Nerang says, standing, "we've successfully avoided the last of the preparations for the Feast. Shall we return and enjoy the fruits of their labor?"

"You really are terrible, aren't you?"

"No, I'm hungry." He takes my arm, and his voice is abruptly serious again. "Be cautious when you return home, young one. Change can be frightening, and fear makes people dangerous."

We walk back along the edge of the water hole, and the two voices grow clearer. Wirrim and Kadee are telling a longer, more detailed version of the story of Koolkuna that I heard when I arrived. We stand at the perimeter of the circle of light and listen.

"Where were you?" Peree whispers in my ear, startling me.

"Talking with Nerang," I whisper back. "Did I miss the offering?"

"Yeah. Lucky you." He pauses. "I don't know, feeding the Scourge. It's disturbing."

"I know."

"You missed the blessing of the children, too," he says. "They call them *gurus*, or something. It was strange, sort of the opposite of the Exchange." One more difference between here and home.

I have renewed admiration for Wirrim and Kadee's gifts as they tell the story of the early days of Koolkuna. I can feel the terror of the *anuna* as they escape the City and make the dangerous journey to their ancestral home, their fear slowly changing to relief as they realize what they've found in the Myuna: refuge, salvation, deliverance.

Peree slides his arm around my waist. Standing in the glow of the fire, with the soothing flow of the waterfall, surrounded by people who accept me despite my being a *lorinya,* and held by someone who cares for me, I feel secure. Not a common feeling for any Groundling. I want this for Calli, for Eland, for all my people.

Wirrim blesses the Feast, and a few moments later the music starts. The instruments and rhythms sound similar, but not quite the same as our own. All around us people begin to pair up.

Peree takes my hand. When he speaks, his voice is formal. "Fennel, would you like to dance?"

I smirk, and lower my voice, trying to imitate his melodic voice. "Groundlings and Lofties don't dance together."

"Why not?"

"Tradition, I guess."

He pulls me close, his hands spread against my back, and he whispers in my ear. "To hell with tradition."

Then he kisses me. A brief touch of his lips against mine, but enough to send lightning bolts streaking across my body. Before I can react, he spins me around and we're off. I didn't know the Lofties danced much, up in the tops of the greenhearts, but Peree clearly learned somewhere.

I can't stop grinning. I finally got my dance.

CHAPTER SEVENTEEN

Later, we escape the noise and the warm crush of twirling bodies. I barely had a break, dancing with Peree, Kora and Bega, even Konol and Nerang. My head spins a little from the wine, but otherwise I'm euphoric, holding Peree's hand as he guides me out of the crowd.

"Take a walk with me?" he asks, when we reach the cooler air close to the water. I don't care where we go, as long as it's not to sleep. I don't want the night to end. He whistles to the music as we stroll through the trees that surround the water hole. After passing a few other couples seeking solitude in the darkness, we're alone.

"Nerang's quite the dancer," Peree says. "He's full of surprises, isn't he?"

I laugh, thinking about how he gets his meals. "Yeah, he is."

"So what did you two talk about for so long?"

I hesitate. I don't want to ruin the mood. "Tomorrow."

"What's the plan?" he asks casually.

I fill him in on my conversation with Nerang. His offer surprises Peree, too, but the news that Kadee will take me back doesn't.

"I asked her to be your guide," he says.

"You did?"

"What did you think, that I'd let you go by yourself? Wandering through the caves or the forest all alone, when she knows exactly how to get there? What kind of Keeper do you think I am?"

"A devious one."

"Well, you're still going to have a tough job once you get there. Koolkuna will be about as real to our people as camels and cassowaries. But Nerang's offer is generous."

We amble down the path to the village, our hands still linked.

"Dark out here," Peree says. He pulls me to a stop. "Wait, I want to try something."

"What?"

"I want to feel what it's like to be Sightless."

"Close your eyes and you pretty much have it," I joke.

"No, really. I'm going to walk for a while without looking where I'm going."

"But you can open your eyes any time. That makes it different."

"I promise I won't for at least thirty paces. Would that be more real?"

Nope, I think. But I don't say it out loud. I'm touched that he's trying to empathize.

"Okay, here goes," he says. I hear him limp away several paces, already veering off the path. "*Ugh*, reminds me of being in the caves."

"Be careful. Your leg—"

Sure enough, he stumbles over something, cursing. Well, he wanted to know what being Sightless feels like. Injuries go with the territory. I go to him, but he shrugs me off.

"Hang on, I still have twenty-four more paces to go."

"I think you got the idea."

He's already walking again, straying even farther away from the path. A bruised shin, scraped hands, and two more heartfelt curses later, he returns, grumbling. We skirt the village, heading in the direction of the little clearing where he found me the other day.

"Well, what did you think?" I ask, trying not to sound amused.

"I think I wouldn't last long if I was Sightless. Do you ever wish you could see?"

His question surprises me. "Of course, all the time, but it's sort of pointless. Like wishing to be taller, or to have blonde hair, or to be able to fly. Why do you ask?"

"You almost never want to know what things look like, so I wasn't sure."

"I can't always picture it when someone describes something, even if I can touch or hear it too. It's like tasting something when you aren't sure what it is, and no one can confirm that you're eating what you think you're eating."

Peree laughs. "I know what that's like. Shrike's cooking leaves a lot to be desired."

When we reach the clearing, I sit in the grass at the base of the rock and pull my legs into my chest. A warm, dry breeze blows the stray hairs around my face. The nearby stream gurgles like a contented baby.

"I guess I don't like to ask what things look like. It feels weak," I say.

"What's wrong with being weak sometimes?"

"Grow up with Aloe, and you'll know. She's a rock. I only remember her crying once, when my foster father died. I was young; Eland was a baby. I didn't know what to do to comfort her." I smooth my dress over my knees. "I wish she'd open up to me more."

"Yeah … I know the feeling."

I wait, but he doesn't elaborate. "Okay, what's that supposed to mean?"

"Open. Not a word I'd use to describe *you,* either."

"What word would you use?"

"I have a few."

"Like what?"

"Like stubborn."

I straighten up, my hair flying around me. "Stubborn? That's my word for *you.* You can't take it."

He scoffs. "You don't think you're stubborn? We wouldn't be out here, days away from home, if you didn't insist on finding the Hidden Waters yourself."

"Who insisted on coming with me? And who insisted we keep going despite a life-threatening injury? And who insisted he get up and walk against the healer's advice? *You're* stubborn," I say.

"Unusually, annoyingly responsible–"

"Grumpy, ungrateful–" I'm about to say something about how two-year-old Groundling children swim better than him, but his next word stops me.

"Beautiful." He slides my hair back over my shoulder. "Especially in the morning sun, or by firelight, when the red in your hair heats up like burning embers."

"And what about my dirty eyes?" The words pop out before I can stop them.

His hand rests on my shoulder. "What?"

"Nothing," I mumble, mentally banging my head against the rock behind me. "Something you said when you were describing our water hole."

"I wasn't talking about your eyes. I'd never describe them as dirty. *Muddy* maybe–"

I choke. "First I'm slimy or scaly or whatever, and now I'm muddy? You have a way with compliments, don't you?"

"I said you were strong, competent, and beautiful. Can I help it if that's not what you heard?"

"Now I don't listen?" I try to look offended.

"Wow, Fenn, you're hard work. Just … shut up for a few minutes. Please. I have a story to tell you."

"I don't know if I'm in the mood," I tease.

"And *I'm* stubborn and grumpy? Listen, I really want you to hear this one."

I settle back against the rock. "All right, I'm listening."

"So, there once was a boy who lived in the forest, high up in the trees. He was devilishly handsome, damn good with a bow and arrow, and better-than-average at storytelling." I groan, and he shushes me. "Okay, okay, he was an *amazing* storyteller—satisfied? So, this boy. He was pretty happy at first, but as he got older, he was lonely. He found himself watching the ground, and not for prey. He was watching a girl. Every day he watched her, hoping he'd have the chance to meet her." He pauses. "I know the boy sounds kind of creepy, but really he's not."

"Oh no, of course not."

"Anyway, one day the boy got lucky. He met the girl, and talked to her. Not only was she beautiful, but she was brave and kind, and yes, a lot like a lizard." I smack his arm. "When he had the chance to go on a long journey with her, he didn't hesitate. But then she dragged him through ominous, pitch-black caves, made him battle wild animals and frostbite, and almost drowned him in a raging river, before they washed up on the shores of a magical village, where an evil old man first tried to suffocate the boy with incense before he finally relented–"

"Peree! That is so unfair!"

"Anyway, the boy recovered, mostly, and together he and the girl learned many strange and wonderful things about the village. And every day the boy spent with the girl, he saw how she was even more incredible than he first thought. He realized she was the most incredible girl he'd ever known, or ever would know."

My heart thrums and heat spreads through my body. I'm giddy from the wine, the dancing, and the turn our conversation is taking.

"The problem is," he says, "I don't know how this story ends. The girl has to go back home to the forest, and the boy can't go with her. And she has obligations at home, to her family, and her friends, and maybe even to another boy. And to make matters worse for our hero, even if he's really, really lucky and the girl feels the same way about him, he's not sure how they can stay together, because their people aren't exactly friendly. But the boy wants to stay with the girl, very much."

"Peree, I–"

He presses his lips to mine, softly, then again, his sweet scent clouding my head even more. Whatever I was going to say drifts away like a dream upon waking. "You don't have to answer now. I know you can't make any promises. But I want you to know what *I* want. And that's you." He traces my collarbone with his fingers. "You're the first thing I think of when I wake up and the last thing when I go to sleep. You're my sun and moon and stars, my past and present—and I hope you'll be my future."

He kisses me then, a real kiss this time—slow, soft, searching—a kiss that asks questions, but without words. His lips are on my lips, his hands on my skin; his body presses mine down into the grass. His freshly shaved cheeks and chin are soft and smooth. I weave my hands through his hair, and pull him closer. To touch someone—him—so freely, calls tears to my eyes.

His voice is hoarse as he murmurs in my ear. "So take that with you tomorrow as you travel home. Know that I love you, and I want you, and I want you to choose me." His lips move against my ear like the wings of a moth. I shiver under him. "No pressure."

I laugh, but his hands and lips and tongue make me forget what I thought was so funny.

We wake early the next morning, our arms and legs jumbled like an unruly ball of thread. I kiss him, and whisper good morning.

"Was it a good night, too?" His voice has that rough edge of disuse that makes my blood dive headlong through my veins. I press my lips to his again in answer. He rolls on top of me, pinning me, and I wrap my legs around him. A little later, he flops onto his back, groaning.

"You can't leave today," he says. "I'm going to be in a very bad mood every minute of every day until I can follow you."

"Nerang will be happy to hear that." I sit up, and try to smooth my frenzied hair. "If it's any consolation, no matter what I find at home, I'll be miserable, too. I'll miss you." I frown, realizing that even when he comes back to the forest I'll still be missing him, separated as we'll be by the trees. "Peree, about what you said last night, what you told me–"

"Don't say anything now. Maybe it doesn't make much sense, but if you want me, too—I mean more than using me for one night–" he laughs at my protests and goes on, "I want to know it's without any strings attached. I need to know you're mine alone and nothing can keep us apart. And you can't honestly tell me that right now. Not without going home first."

He's right, I can't. I reach for his hand, a large lump in my throat. "What did I do to deserve you?"

He kisses me lightly. "Bad luck, I guess."

We walk back to the shelter with our hands locked together, the sun patting our backs. He helps me pack my bag with my few belongings for the trip home. Home. I'll be with Aloe and Eland again by the end of the day. They must have given up on me by now, unless Shrike told Aloe about the possibility of Koolkuna. I hope he did.

"I have something for you," Peree says. He places a heavy object wrapped in cloth in my hand. A knife.

"*Um* … thanks. Is there some reason you think I'll need this?" I ask.

"You never know."

"Don't you need it?"

"I can borrow one from Konol."

I take it reluctantly. The overwhelming longing to stay—in Koolkuna, in safety, in Peree's warm arms—threatens to overcome me again. I swallow hard and run my thumb along the blunt edge of the knife.

"Here, I have something else for you." He walks behind me and puts something around my neck. I feel the weight of the little carved bird against my chest before my fingers confirm that's what it is. The cord feels strange against my neck. I've never worn a necklace before, except the daisy chains Calli and I used to make when we were little.

"Show the bird to Shrike," he says. "Tell him I trust you."

"Come home soon and tell him yourself."

"I will."

I put my arms around him. "Promise?"

He kisses me one last time. A solid, upfront kind of kiss. "I promise."

The sun is too hot as Kadee and I press through the thick forest. Insects hum, but I don't hear a single bird. They must be holed up out of the heat, like any reasonable creatures would be. Sweat spreads under my pack, making my dress itchy and uncomfortable. I'm grateful for the shade of the trees. The heat would be unbearable without it.

We're following the curve of the mountain ridge that contains the cave system. Kadee says if we keep it on our right, we'll eventually get to our part of the forest. We've already been tramping for hours through the gnarled underbrush. I was holding her arm at first, but now the trees are too dense to walk side by side, so I walk behind her. She tries to warn me of obstacles on the ground like stumps and fallen branches, but there are too many. I've tripped several times and bounced off more than one tree. Vegetation yanks my hair and tries to snag my pack. I moved Peree's knife from my pack to my pocket, to cut away the vines and brambles.

Kadee's been quiet since we said our good-byes to the small party who saw us off from Koolkuna. Nerang gave me a small pouch of medicinal herbs for treating bruises and scrapes. "You'll need these, I think," he said cheerfully as he handed them over. Peree's right—the man can be exasperatingly smug sometimes.

Peree promised to follow quickly, and Konol joked that he'd carry him back to get rid of him if he had to. A scuffle ensued, a sure sign of male friendship. Kora sniffled as she and Bega hugged me good-bye. I said I'd be with them again soon. I hope I told the truth.

Peree's knife in my pocket and the bird nestled against my chest are the only physical reminders I carry of him. But I have memories, and the best of them were from last night: dancing and laughing with our friends, then kissing him in the long grass of the moonless clearing. I try not to think about how it could be like that every day—in Koolkuna.

I push a branch out of my way. It slips out of my hand and grazes the side of my face. Kadee checks on me, and I assure her I'm fine for the forty-second time today. An insect buzzes closer to investigate my stinging cheek; I must be bleeding.

Soon after we started out, I asked Kadee how she was feeling about going home.

"Nervous, excited, worried. Mostly nervous, I think," she said.

"What made you decide to go back now?" I'd been wondering about her reasons since Nerang told me she would take me home.

"Other than that you needed a guide?" she said. "When I was younger, people thought my lack of fear of the Scourge was courage. They thought I was brave, and I let them believe it. But I'm not. Not in the ways that count. I knew it was wrong to run away from my family that night, but I didn't have the nerve to tell my people what I saw and accept the consequences. I didn't have the strength to brave Shrike's anger, or to stay with my son who needed me. I think I do now. I'm hoping I can make amends and return to Koolkuna free of the guilt I've held close to me for years."

I think about that as we walk. Do I have the courage now to tell my people what I know about the Scourge, and about Koolkuna? Or will I be like Kadee, and shy away from their anger and fear?

Kadee suggests we take a break. I hunt around for a little shade and dump my pack on the ground, then pull out one of my water sacks. We're each carrying two, enough for a day of walking. After that, we should be home—and drinking the poisoned water again. I wonder how long it will take for the poison to convince me the sick ones are the Scourge again. Will I gradually slip into the madness, or will I wake up with it one morning?

"Are you hungry?" Kadee asks. "Nerang gave me some treats. He dries berries the children collect, pounds them flat, then rolls them into sticks."

"I didn't know he could make anything, he told me he hits up all the widows for dinner!"

"Well, it's no fun cooking for one. I should know. Here, try one."

I take a bite. It's sticky, seedy—and tasty. "He's been holding out on me."

Kadee laughs, and tells me of other people's hidden talents. Amarina, a woman we worked with in the garden with a high, thin voice like birdsong, can coax a fire from a soggy pile of rotting wood. Derain, Kora's father, has a knack for soothing crying babies. Sleep-deprived mothers at their wits' end often call on him in the middle of the night.

"Who knew?" I laugh.

"We all have secrets," she says, and I can tell she means something more than being good with fires or babies. The chorus of insects breaks off, as if to hear what she'll say next. I wait, too, giving her time, while something slithers forebodingly through my gut. "You know Peree came to Shrike and me in the Exchange, don't you? He was such a beautiful baby, strong-willed but smiley, with sparkling green eyes and yellow curls sprouting from his head like forsythia. I thought he might be a new beginning for me:

171

something to care for and love, something to distract me from the misery of not being able to tell anyone what I knew to be true about the Scourge. He was all of that … for a time. But as he grew older, I longed for another child. I thought having a baby with Shrike might bring us closer, strengthen our relationship in ways we hadn't been able to manage ourselves."

Blood pumps in my head, beating out a warning, and my breath speeds up as if I'm in danger. I can't make sense of my body's reaction. It's like I know what she's going to say, and I don't want to hear it.

"I gave birth to a daughter when Peree was two. She was beautiful, like him, but with a full head of gleaming dark hair and watchful brown eyes. We named her Daybreak—hoping, more than believing, that her hair and eyes would lighten, like the sun brightens the night sky."

"You had to give her up in the Exchange?" I whisper.

"To my unending guilt and anguish." Kadee's voice is pitched low. "Shrike told me her foster parents named her for a sweet, delicate herb. Then we never spoke of her again."

I gasp, unable to take a full breath. Suddenly light-headed, I grab a handful of dirt and rub it between my hands, trying to keep myself grounded.

"For several years I didn't know what became of our baby," she continues. "Then I saw her one day, far below, playing near the gardens. She was spinning in the tall grasses, her hands skimming over the tops of the stalks. It had to be her—the same dark hair, the same fine-boned face. My child. I wanted to climb down and swoop her up, tell her I was her mother, and that I loved her. Then, I'll never forget, her foster mother came, calling her name. My daughter touched the woman's face, searching it, feeling her smile … and I realized she couldn't see. Somehow, my child had lost her sight."

I open my mouth to speak, but no sound comes out.

"I was devastated. I couldn't understand how my perfect, healthy baby became Sightless. Was it an illness? An accident? I went to our Council. I asked them to tell me the truth. And nothing was the same for me after that."

I'm stunned. "I can't believe it … *you're* my mother?"

She cups my cheek in her hand. "Yes, love." She speaks to me gently. "And, unfortunately, there's more to tell you."

My head swivels back and forth against her palm, before I realize I'm moving it. "I don't want to know any more. This is enough. I've always wanted to know who my natural mother was, and now I do"

Kadee's voice is gentle. "You need to know the rest and I need to tell you. Not to be cruel or spiteful, but because I won't collude with lies anymore. I can't. You're almost an adult, and you need to hear this before you return home. You should know what they did to you."

"What *who* did?"

"Your people."

My stomach twists like a wrung-out rag. I feel sick. "What did they do?"

Kadee lays her hands across my eyes, and her voice breaks with a soft sob. "Blinded you. My baby girl. They took your sight."

"They wouldn't. Aloe wouldn't let them."

She doesn't speak for a moment. "I'd like to think she didn't have any part of it. After all, the same thing happened to her."

"You mean … they blinded Aloe, too?"

"Do you think Sightlessness is so common that babies would be born without sight, generation after generation? If so, why aren't any Lofties Sightless?"

I can barely catch my breath to speak. I'm breathing hard, and bile fills my mouth. "Why? Why would they do that to us?"

Kadee's words are fissured with grief. "For the good of your community. So you could bear the water when you came of age. And I suppose they thought they were giving the gift of protection from the Scourge."

"But why me?"

"Because you were a Lofty baby." Her voice is suddenly hard, her meaning clear. No Groundling would destroy the sight of their own child.

I scramble around the tree and throw up the berry stick and what's left of my breakfast. I wave Kadee away, but she won't go. She holds my hair back from my face, rubs my back, and tells me how sorry she is. I stay on my hands and knees, panting and spitting, until my stomach is empty.

After a few minutes I crawl back and collapse against the tree again, my head in my hands. I feel like someone placed a rock on my shoulders that's forcing me down, down, down into the ground. I don't know if I can bear up under its weight.

"After I saw what they did to you, the idea of leaving the trees forever took hold of me," Kadee says. "The Exchange was bad enough, but I couldn't stay among people that allowed their children to be maimed, even for the good of all."

I consider her words. What happened to me wasn't Kadee's fault any more than any other parent over the years that cooperated with the Exchange. But she could have said something about what she knew. Did Aloe know I would be blinded, and allow it to happen? Or even suspect? I'm not ready to deal with that possibility yet.

"Does Peree know you're my ... mother? Does Nerang?"

"Both Peree and Nerang know I had to give up a child, but neither know that child was you. When I saw how you and Peree felt about each other, I thought you might want to be the one to tell him."

Peree and I aren't related by blood, but the man and woman who raised him are my natural parents. That's practically family. I think about telling him that, and my stomach twists again. "And Shrike?" I ask.

"He knows. He may have even asked Aloe to foster you. She wanted a child. I've often wondered if you were part of the reason Shrike wouldn't go to Koolkuna. If he left the forest, he'd have to leave *you*, too." She pauses. "Fennel, I'm going back today because I failed as a mother. I failed you when I gave you up in the Exchange, and I failed Peree when I left the trees. It's time for me to stand up, not only for my children, but for all the children of the forest."

I told Peree I expect surprises, that I'm used to them, but nothing could prepare me for all of this. Kadee is my mother, Shrike is my father, and Peree is sort of my brother. My people intentionally blinded me, and Aloe fostered me as some kind of favor. I pitch to the side again, retching.

When my stomach empties, tears well up like blood from a wound. I cry for our world, destroyed by people who recklessly believed they could control a deadly poison. I cry for the sick ones, doomed to walk the earth hungry and wretched, shunned as monsters. I cry for our people, who hide in caves or trees because they can't see the world as it really is. And I cry for myself. Because for no good reason, I can't see at all.

CHAPTER EIGHTEEN

I sit, waiting for my stomach to settle and my legs to stop shaking. Kadee doesn't press me to talk or to keep moving. She waits beside me, a witness. I want to be angry at her for giving me up, and for leaving Peree. Mostly for being weak. But at first all I feel is the dazed, empty sensation that my world was again overturned like a bucket of dirty washing water.

When the rage comes, it snakes through my veins, hardening my resolve. Who did they think they were, treating innocent children this way? All of them—Lofties and Groundlings. Who decided babies could be traded like so much meat or grain? Used to serve their purposes? That people could be separated and kept in their place with threats, brute force, and fear, supported by antiquated traditions?

Kadee. Aloe. Shrike. The Three. Every adult in my life, everyone who ever had the responsibility to protect me, failed me instead. I've spent my life trying to live up to what my family and my people expected me to be. What they *made* me. The Water Bearer. Until now, I didn't allow myself any other choice but to do my duty. Until now.

I stand and wait for the dizziness to pass, then I swing my pack on my back. It's time to go home. And Kadee's right. It's time for the secrets and lies to end.

Clouds wander in front of the sun, dispelling the heat. When the trees thin out, Kadee offers me her arm again. My mother's arm. I pay more attention to it now. It's thin, but not so bony as Aloe's. Her skin is softer, too. I wonder if I look like her at all. No one ever said so, but they wouldn't have unless the resemblance was striking.

There's rustling in the woods, and soft moans. I stiffen.

"Don't worry," Kadee murmurs, catching my hand. "It's only the *runa*."

I clamp my lips together, pushing down the panic. In my seventeen years, no one ever said, "Don't worry, it's only the Scourge." They were too busy running.

I focus on keeping the same steady pace as the creatures draw near us. The stench threatens to gag me again. My throat tightens and the hair bristles along the back of my neck. As more of the sick ones shuffle up, Kadee pulls food from her pack, offering it to them. These creatures don't give thanks, but they do eat. Or try to eat. It sounds like the food dribbles out of some of their mouths. I try to summon any feeling more compassionate than disgust. I fail.

I can't yet forget the horrific stories of the Scourge I grew up hearing, the memories of the many times they pursued us to the caves, or the hordes of them pressing in on me, their tongues worrying the flesh where their lips should be. The foul smell brings the memories back so clearly. I press Peree's little bird against my chest, wishing he was here.

The creatures follow us, muttering and moaning for help. When one of them stumbles toward me I shrink away, trembling with the desire to run. Run anywhere. It doesn't matter which direction, as long as it's away from anything familiar. I want freedom. I want to escape. Like in my dream.

As usual, it's the thought of Eland that keeps me moving forward. Despite everything I learned today, or maybe because of it, I need to know if he's all right.

"How much longer?" I ask, my voice stiff and unrecognizable.

"Not long. I recognize the shape of the hills here. We're close."

That brings a question to mind. "Why don't the *runa* go into the caves? They would at least offer protection from the weather."

"Because of the cold and the dark. They're even less prepared to deal with it than we are. I know it's hard to think of them as people, but that's what they are. Sick, confused, sometimes dangerous, but people."

One of the creatures mimics her, repeating the word *people* several times, like a young child just learning to speak. "Can they ever be brought back? Their minds, I mean?"

"The *anuna* tried caring for a few of the sick ones, to see if they could reverse the process of the poison. It seemed to depend on how long they had been sick." She hesitates. "Kaiya was one of the few successes."

That stuns me. "What?"

"We don't speak of this often," Kadee says. "As a young girl, Kai wandered away from her parents, into the forest. The tracking party found her, but she had become *runa*. In time, Nerang was able to bring her back."

"Is she ... normal, now?"

"Yes. For the most part. But I'm sorry to say she was never quite treated the same after that. People feared her, I think. She's always kept to herself— a loner either by choice or necessity."

"She liked being with Peree."

"He was kind to her. He didn't know about her background. And, well, she's a young girl, and he's a handsome boy."

So I keep hearing. I scowl, feeling the familiar irritation, but it's followed by guilt that I didn't try harder to befriend Kai. I know how isolating it can be to feel different.

Kadee squeezes my hand tentatively. "I don't think you have anything to worry about, when it comes to Peree's feelings about you." She stops, and I hear her drop her pack on the ground. "Take out any food and water you have. We need to leave it here."

"Why?"

"For the *runa*. Otherwise they'll follow us home. Anyone who sees them will think we're in danger of being consumed."

At that, I do what she asked, and we walk away as the sick ones surround the small pile. Lost in my brooding, I start to wonder if we're close enough to home now for me to recognize anything. I'm accustomed to retracing my steps when I'm away from the community, not approaching it from a completely unknown direction. The truth is, I could stumble right into our clearing and not realize it. So I'm not too surprised when that's exactly what happens.

The sun is setting, intensifying the darkness, when Kadee slows again. "Welcome home," she says.

Really? I hurry forward, groping in front of me to find anything that feels familiar. It smells like home, but then again the entire greenheart forest smells like home. There are no voices, or sounds of fires being kindled, or smells of food being prepared. I only hear a few plaintive bird calls from the trees. My heart sinks. Everyone must still be in the caves. But why? The Scourge isn't here.

"The shelters look like they haven't been used," Kadee says. She sounds worried. "Fennel, perhaps we should–"

An arrow slices the air beside my ear. Another divides the narrow space between us.

"Stop right there," a man says from the trees. "Unless you want to be under the ground by morning."

We freeze. A moment later, someone snickers.

"Then they'd be Undergroundlings, Petrel," a boy says.

"Quiet," the man mutters.

"Petrel? Is that you?" Kadee calls.

The leaves above us tremble as someone moves closer, following a walkway. "Who's there?"

"It's your Aunt Blaze," Kadee says. "And Fennel, the Water Bearer."

"Try again," he says bitterly. "Blaze is dead, and so is the Water Bearer."

"No, we're alive … and Peree, too," I say. "He was injured, but he's recovering."

"Peree's alive? Where is he?" the boy chirps. He sounds younger than Eland. *Why is a young boy armed and shooting at Groundlings?*

"Thrush, go find Shrike," Petrel says. The boy runs off, skittering down the walkway like a squirrel. I hear Petrel pull an arrow from his quiver to reload his bow.

"Trusting, isn't he?" I whisper.

"He used to be," Kadee says sadly.

"What's going on?" I whisper. "Where do you think everyone is?"

"I don't know." She takes a shaky breath, and I realize how hard this must be for her—coming home, preparing to see the partner and the people she left years ago. I wish I could muster more sympathy.

"It'll be okay, Kadee," I say. But they're just words. Something is very wrong, I can feel it.

"Best to call me Blaze for now. They won't know my new name."

Heavier, slower footsteps move through the trees, stopping above us.

"Blaze."

It's Shrike. And right then I know Kadee was telling the truth about him. Peree couldn't have sounded more shocked when he saw his mother for the first time in Koolkuna. Shrike sounds resigned, like he knew this day might come.

"I brought our daughter home," she says. Shrike's silent for a long time. Then a rope ladder clatters down a few feet away from us.

"Don't go down there, Shrike," Thrush pleads.

"It's all right. This is my *family*." His voice is harsh, and I feel Kadee stiffen next to me.

"But one's a Groundling, and I've never seen the other one before," the boy says.

Petrel shushes him. The ladder squeaks under Shrike's weight as he climbs. If we're standing where I think we're standing, this is the same place the Lofties dropped down to the clearing during the Summer Solstice celebration, and the ladder they used to escape when the Scourge came. When they left us to fend for ourselves. Bitterness pecks at me, opening old wounds.

"I am Shrike's partner, but I left the trees," Kadee says to Thrush. "I went to a place called Koolkuna. It's safe there, with plenty of food, water, and no flesh–"

"Stop," Shrike says. He drops down beside us, the solid thump reminding me of the rock falling from the trees to the ground in Koolkuna. "Don't fill his head with lies."

"They aren't lies," Kadee says.

"Forgive me if I don't instantly believe you," Shrike says. "Honesty wasn't your forte, was it?"

"I've been to Koolkuna," I say, "and what she says is true."

A heavy hand lies on my shoulder briefly. "Fennel, I'm glad to know you're safe. But there's a history here that you don't understand."

"I understand enough," I say. "Like that you and Blaze are my natural parents, and Aloe only fostered me because you asked her to."

Shrike chuckles. "Aloe wanted you from the second you were placed in her arms at the Exchange. She adored you ... we all did," Shrike says. Regret is strong in his voice. When he speaks again, his voice has hardened. "Where's Peree?"

"In Koolkuna," Kadee answers. "He's safe."

Shrike must have looked less-than-convinced, because she says sharply, "I'm his mother. Do you think I'd lie about that?" In that moment I can understand how she got her Lofty name.

I step between them. "I don't know if it will help, but Peree told me to show you this."

I pull the bird carving up from under the front of my dress. Petrel whistles softly from the trees. Shrike plucks it from my fingers and examines it.

"It's good work," he grunts.

"He said to tell you he trusts me."

"I guess *so*," Petrel says. He laughs, but I don't get the joke.

"I promise he's okay. He injured his leg, but it's getting stronger every day. He's coming back as soon as he can."

Shrike just stands there, holding the bird.

"I know this isn't easy," I say softly. "It wasn't easy for Peree and me to trust each other either."

He lays the bird back down, and I tuck it away.

"Where are Aloe and the others, Shrike? Are they all right?" I ask.

"They're in the caves."

"Why?" I listen closely, but I can only hear the gentle sounds of the forest. No creatures.

"There's been some trouble."

An uncomfortable prickling starts at my scalp and wriggles down my neck. "What kind?"

"Your people attacked us—they actually came up into the trees." He sounds like he still can't believe it. "We drove them back, killing one. And one of our women was also killed in the crossfire."

"Who?" Kadee and I ask in unison. I don't think we're asking about the same person.

"Glow," he tells Kadee. "She was the lookout that night. I don't know the Groundling's name. Since then, we've kept them confined to the caves."

I gasp. "You can't!"

"No? Why not? We didn't start this."

I'm as shocked by his tone as I am by his words. Peree was clearly regretful when he told me about killing Jackal, so different from the contempt suffusing his father's—my father's—voice.

"They must have been desperate!" I say. "The people don't want a war."

"The Three should have considered that before they made their decision." Now he sounds resentful. As one of the Three, Aloe had to agree to the plan. Why would she do that? Was she outvoted again?

"How long are you planning to hold them hostage?" I ask.

"Until we receive a formal apology, and word that Adder has been replaced on the Council of Three. We think the order came from him."

I shake my head. "He'll never give up being on the Council."

"Then he's condemning your people to death," Shrike says flatly.

I have to find out what's going on in the caves. And quickly. "Shrike, I need to talk to Aloe. Maybe there's something I can do. Will you allow me to collect the water in the morning, so I can talk to you again?"

I imagine something unspoken passing between Kadee and Shrike, but after a moment, he agrees.

"Be careful how much you tell Aloe. She's ... changed," he warns.

His words chill me. I want to question him, but even more I want to get in the caves and find out what's going on for myself.

"Will you be okay?" I ask Kadee, already turning to leave.

"I'll be fine. Go to your family." She sounds wistful.

My family. My natural parents are standing beside me for the first time since I was an infant. But it's not how I imagined it. Not at all.

I pass into the mouth of the cave, leaving behind the last rays of the sun and any hope of warmth for the near future. As I trail my fingers along the familiar rugged walls of the passageway, I'm slapped by the overpowering stench of human waste. It's not quite as bad as the Scourge, but close.

My chest is tight with anxiety and anticipation. I haven't begun to process all I learned today, and now I'm faced with yet another crisis. I need rest, and time to think, but I don't think I'll get it anytime soon. If Adder won't step down, and the Lofties won't back down, I may have to try to lead everyone through the caves to Koolkuna. If I can persuade them to go. One impossible task after another.

I can sense the wavering light from a torch ahead.

"Hello?" I call. The torch moves closer.

"Fennel? That you?" The man sounds astonished. I better get used to people thinking I've come back from the grave.

"Believe it or not."

He laughs. "I don't."

I struggle to place the voice. "Moray? What are you doing way out here in the passage?"

"Guard duty, watching out for Lofties." I hear the clunk of a spear shaft being leaned against the wall. "So where ya been?"

"You definitely wouldn't believe me if I told you."

"Try me."

"Later, okay? I've been walking all day and I really want to find my family."

"Come on, I'll take you. I'm dead bored anyway. I could use the excitement."

I'd rather go on alone, but I don't want to be rude. Moray strolls next to me, the torch floating at his side. "How are things?" I ask cautiously.

"Could be better," he answers nonchalantly. His tone confuses me.

"Why? What happened since I left?"

"A lot."

"Is everything okay … in here?"

"Sure, why wouldn't it be?"

I give up. Clearly I'm not going to get much out of this one.

We're at the fork. I can hear voices ahead to the left, through the short passage to the main cavern. To the right is the tunnel leading deeper into the caves, where Peree saw me kissing Bear. *Bear.* What am I going to say to him?

"*Ugh*, the smell in here …" I pinch my nose.

"Yeah, it's bad. We all stink like a bunch of fleshies. Hang on for a second."

I'm impatient now that I'm so close, but I wait, listening to him set the torch into a holder on the wall.

"Okay, let's go," he says. I turn toward the cavern, hideous smell and all.

My head jerks back as Moray's hand slams over my mouth. He presses me into his chest.

"Don't fight, sweetheart. I'll just make it harder on you," he whispers, choking me for emphasis.

My heart pounds in my throat as he drags me backward, deeper into the caves. I barely manage to keep my feet under me and breathe.

My nerves are screaming, but I make myself focus on where we're going. Moray pushes me into a new tunnel. I think it's the one that follows close to the outer edge of the caves, eventually exiting into the forest. It's hardly ever used. Moray must want privacy.

He releases my mouth. "Can I trust you to keep quiet? No screaming."

I nod. He moves us down the passage, his arm tight around my neck.

"Why are you doing this? What do you want?" My voice is raspy.

"No questions."

"But–"

"Shut it, or I'm gagging you. You'll figure things out soon enough."

He pushes me along in front of me. I can barely focus through my panic. I'd forgotten how long this passage is, but finally I smell fresh air. We must be near the opening. Moray ties my hands behind me with what feels like a thin but strong piece of rope.

"Please, you don't need to do this," I whisper.

"Yeah, I do, actually. Orders. You're banished for colluding with the enemy, or something like that. Tell you the truth, I wasn't listening all that close." He jerks the knot tight.

"Orders? Whose orders?"

"Who gives all the orders around here? The Three. Now, hold still and keep quiet. Fight me, and I promise I won't be any kind of a gentleman about this."

He pushes me back on the ground, my hands pinned under me. I'm even more confused—for about a second. He kisses me, his lips covering my mouth like slabs of meat. His tongue thrusts into my mouth and I gag. When his hands rove down from my chest to my abdomen, I do the only thing I can think of. I bite down. Hard.

Moray roars and rears back. I turn my face away, expecting the blow, but his fist lands in my stomach instead. Tears leap to my eyes.

He paces around, cursing me, but he can't really form the words. I try very hard not to cry. He leans over me, a revolting mixture of blood and spit dribbling across my face. Then he slaps me.

"You blind bith. I don't want Bear's theconds anyway."

I would laugh if I didn't think he might kill me. He yanks me to my feet and I turn to face him. My next move will be a knee between his legs.

I don't get the chance. Moray pushes me backward out of the cave. Then he spins me around, and herds me into the trees. Branches whip my face and arms, but I don't make a sound, and he sure doesn't stop.

Suddenly the ground drops out from under me. I don't fall far, but there's a sickening pop in my ankle when I hit, and blinding pain. The lower part of my leg shakes with it. I grit my teeth and hold in a moan. I don't want Moray to know how much it hurt. Something falls next to me.

"Thu bad you don't have any food or wather in there." It must be my pack. "Poor Bear, he'th worried about where hith intended got to. But maybe ith better thith way conthidering who you were with, looking for the Wathers." He spits, hitting my bowed back. "Good luck, traither." His footsteps retreat.

I lie on my side, stunned from the blows to my stomach, face, and ankle—not to mention the sudden change in my circumstances. I take slow, deep breaths, controlling the urge to vomit. I don't want to be stuck with a pile of stinking sickness.

When the nausea subsides I try to crawl, hoping to figure out where "here" is. My ankle throbs as I creep around. It's obviously some kind of hole in the ground, roughly circular, and a little more than a man's height in each direction. The floor beneath me is hard-packed dirt. I know I'm not near our clearing, or the Lofty walkways, given where the tunnel we traveled lets out. This is an uninhabited part of the forest.

I stand with effort, keeping most of my weight on my good ankle, and turn my face up to the surface. It's pretty much night now; only a weak, watery light trickles in. I run my bound hands around the smooth sides of the pit. I can't find any rocks, roots, or other signs of vegetation. From what I can tell, the top of the hole is no more than a few feet over my head, but even with two healthy ankles and unbound wrists this probably wouldn't be an easy climb. The pit seems man-made. Was it dug just for me?

I slump back down, minding my aching ankle. How long can I last in here, without food or water, and with no hope of rescue? I'm already thirsty and hungry from walking all day. A dullness steals through my mind and panic scrabbles in my chest, making it hard to breathe or think. I fill my lungs and scream as loud as I can, hoping someone might hear it. Or that it might chase the smothering fear away. My mind clears a bit with the piercing sound, but the tight feeling in my chest doesn't lessen.

The earth around me swallows some of the sound, like our blankets when Eland and I used to giggle into them at night. Eland. I was so close to being with him again. Did *he* think I should be banished? Did everyone? And why would they? I didn't collude with anyone. I didn't even invite Peree to come with me to search for the Waters, although it might look that way. Is this what banishment really means? Binding someone's hands and throwing them in a pit until they die of dehydration? Or was this a special sentence just for me, because I'm protected from the Scourge? Tears run down my cheeks. I can only absorb so many horrible revelations about my community today.

I have no idea why the Three would want to banish me, and I can't believe Aloe would be part of it. Adder yes, Sable maybe, but not Aloe. Something terrible must be going on in the caves. There's no other explanation.

I scream again, louder this time, hoping someone might be able to hear. Someone does, but it's not who I was hoping for. I hear a groan, followed by the scent of death. A large group of the sick ones gather at the edge of the hole. One minute I hear the moans and screams of the Scourge, the next I can make out words—the pleading and pitiful cries. Like there are two different types of creatures above me. I listen, unable to do anything about their misery, or my own.

I lay on my side, the pack beneath my head. It's hard to get comfortable with my hands bound behind me. The earth is cold, and there's little room to move around. The darkness is complete. I curl up, shivering.

One time I left a loaf of bread baking too long in the oven. The gooey, fragrant blob of dough that went in came out an ashy, inedible rock. At this moment it feels like the same thing has happened to me. The people, places, and predictable routines—the flour and shortening of my life—have transformed into something strange and foreign. Something unrecognizable.

Lying in the dark with only the moans and entreaties of the sick ones to listen to, my mind plays tricks on me. The trees overhead whisper and mutter to each other. I hear things I don't think are possible, like soft laughter or singing. I imagine torch light touching the darkness.

A white-hot fury builds in me as I huddle at the bottom of the pit. How did I end up here? I followed Aloe's example, never questioning her commitment to duty. I always assumed being Sightless was the honor people told me it was; an honor that brought certain hardships and specific responsibilities with it. Aloe performed her role as the Water Bearer without complaint, and I accepted that one day it would be my role too. But really I was being used. I was deliberately blinded to provide a service to my community. A service that, it turns out, isn't even really needed or helpful, since it's the poisoned water that created the Scourge and kept us prisoners all these years.

I could have stayed in Koolkuna where I was safe. Instead I returned home to my people. Now, thanks to them, I'm banished without even a chance to defend myself. So where does all that commitment to duty leave me?

Alone. Thirsty, hungry, and in pain, in the bottom of a pit. And growing more furious by the minute. The anger seethes through me, making my arms and legs quiver. I'm angry at the Three; angry at Aloe for not treating me like the adult I was becoming and preparing me for my difficult role; angry at the people who must have turned a blind eye to the things being done in the name of our community.

Surrounded by darkness and silence, anger and fear take on physical forms, and a destructive will of their own. They crouch next to me in the pit with toothy grins and clawed hands, waiting to tear into me. When they begin to pace around and around me in circles like predators stalking prey, I start singing. Like I did when I first faced the Scourge, or when I half-carried, half-dragged Peree to the source of the Hidden Waters.

I sing to keep the darkest thoughts away. The ones that make me wonder if my people are even worth trying to save.

I sing every song I can think of, until I'm out of songs, then I sing them again. The sick ones are quiet, as if listening. When I finally finish I feel hollow and empty, my throat and mouth terribly parched. The simmering rage burns through me like a grass fire.

I close my eyes, and water surrounds me. The hole is filling with water, rushing in from above. I lap it up, tasting earth and salt and rust. But no matter how much I drink, I can't slake my thirst. The water creeps up my chest to my neck. I need to start swimming, but when I try to move my arms and legs in the familiar ways, my limbs don't respond. Panic prickles along my scalp. I'm not going to starve or die of dehydration in here. I'm going to drown.

In the odd way of my dreams, I can see. The sick ones gaze down at me in uncharacteristic silence. Only it's not the sick ones now, it's the Three—Aloe, Sable, and Adder. Others surround the hole, too. Eland, Bear, Calli, Fox and Acacia, Bream, Pinion, Yew. I call to them for help, but they just stare back at me, their faces impassive. Then, one by one, they turn away. Eland is the last to leave. He smiles at me and a tear falls from his eye, joining the deluge. Then he goes away, too, as the water covers my face. It pours into my mouth and nose and throat. I dissolve, not into dust, but into more and more and more water.

CHAPTER NINETEEN

I wake with a start. There's light. Morning. My first feeling is relief that I'm not drowning, but the relief only lasts a moment when I hear a low groan. I realize what woke me—something is in the pit with me. I scramble back until I'm pressed against the wall.

The sick one must have either just jumped in, or fallen. It's not touching me—yet—but with horror I realize that if it's hungry enough, it might attack, like the one that bit me. My hands are bound, and it's only a matter of time before my body shuts down from fatigue, leaving me defenseless. I stay pressed against the dirt wall as the creature paces in the small space in front of me.

I can feel something sharp poking into my leg. Peree's knife. Why didn't I remember it was in my pocket when Moray first grabbed me? I manage to ease my dress far enough around to pull it out. Then I press the rope binding my wrists against its sharp edge. I can't put much pressure on the knife with my hands bound, but I begin to saw as best I can. It's insanely tricky. The knife keeps slipping and twisting. I nick my wrist, and a trickle of blood joins the sweat on my palms, making them extra slick. The sick one moans again and moves closer. Can it smell my blood, like an animal?

I keep at it, praying the sick one will keep its distance until I get the binding off my hands. Thank the stars Moray used a thin bit of rope. It's strong, but there's less of it to cut through. There's a cold touch on my leg. I kick out, and the creature backs off.

I work furiously, sweat coating my face. I cut myself again, and suck in my breath at the pain. The sick one groans and presses closer. My flailing foot meets flesh this time, but the creature isn't deterred. It hovers over me, its foul breath in my face, its tongue searching. I make myself as small as possible, still working on the rope.

It finally gives. I grab the handle of the knife and scurry around the creature to the other side of the hole.

"I don't know if you understand me, but here's the deal," I say, panting, "I don't want to hurt you, but I will if I have to. So you stay on your side of the hole, and I'll stay on mine, and maybe we can both get out of here alive."

The sick one howls in frustration. The ones above scream and mutter in response. I wasn't expecting it to answer me, but I was hoping it might be closer to human, like the ones I'd heard speak. No such luck. At least my hands are free, and I have a weapon to defend myself with. Not that it will help if the creature really decides to take me. It sounds big, and sick one or not, it's probably the stronger of the two of us.

I crouch against my side of the pit, knife in hand. My ankle aches; I have to shift my weight often. The sick one goes back to pacing. Maybe it could understand me. I wait, wary and watchful.

As the sun follows its agonizingly slow path in the sky, my thirst becomes unbearable. Water is all I can think of. As my tongue slowly swells from dehydration, I start to imagine things again. The sick one speaks to me, only it sounds like people I know—my family and friends, even some from Koolkuna. One groan morphs into Nerang's quiet chuckle. I slap my hands over my ears, almost dropping the knife. It takes all my energy to fight the despair that fills me, drop by drop, like a slow but inevitable trickle of water. As night falls again, I don't know how much more I can endure.

I drift, half-asleep, through memories of happier days: playing tag in the forest with Calli and Bear, sitting around the fire listening to the elders tell their stories, taking walks in the garden with Aloe as she teaches me to identify plants from their feel and smell.

One memory has remarkable clarity: Aloe and I alone by the water hole. She rarely relaxed when I was a child, always busy with her responsibilities, or helping someone else with theirs. But this day was different. No washing to do or water to gather. Just her and me on the shore. I snuggled against her, the scent of rosemary filling my nose as the sun warmed her skin.

Aloe asked if I was happy. That was unusual, too. She usually didn't waste time wondering about things that made no difference. Happy or not, life went on and duties had to be done. I said I was, and she asked what made me happy. I don't remember exactly what I said. I probably chattered about the small things that pleased me at the time—the squirrel Bear captured and caged as a pet for us to share, an evening swim the Three allowed, wildberries we gathered for dessert. Aloe listened, stroking my hair as I spoke.

"Ask me what makes me happy," she said, and I did. "You and Eland. Without you, there would be no happiness or joy for me. Not even a possibility of it."

I don't know why this particular memory comes up, except that there's water in it. But there's some comfort in knowing there was a time, however long ago, when I made Aloe happy.

The night wears on, terrible and interminable, and my world shrinks to two needs: water and sleep. I'd give anything for a few dribbles of water on my tongue, poisoned or not. I can feel it now, pooling in my mouth, coating my tongue, sliding down my dry throat …

I jerk awake as the sick one moans. Is it closer than it was a few seconds ago? Fear pumps through my body, buying me a few more minutes of wakefulness. I clutch the knife.

A thought comes to me. I could kill the creature.

It would be dangerous—I might fail, and end up enraging it. But if I kill it, I could sleep. And anything is better than this waiting game. Waiting to succumb to sleep or thirst. Waiting to die. I'm sick, starving, frightened, wretched. I'm ready to die or to kill.

Slowly, I exhale through parched lips. This is a human in the pit with me. The word echos in my mind. *Human.* And I can't do it. With a trembling hand, I place the knife in my lap, lean my head against the wall, and go back to waiting.

Morning light squints into the hole. As the chill dissipates in deference to the sun, the sick ones above mutter in low voices of relief. At least that's what it sounds like in my delirium. I haven't slept. At least I don't think I have. I can't tell reality from my encroaching nightmares anymore. Nerang speaks to me.

Up, young one. It's time for you to go.

"Can't. Too weak." My tongue's so swollen, I sound like Moray. I turn my face to the wall.

Yes, you can, he insists.

I shake my head, and dirt dribbles down my nose.

Up now. You've found your coat of feathers.

"Feathers?"

They were buried, but you found them. Put them on and fly away.

"Don't know how to fly."

Fennel. Get up. It's Kai's voice now. That's odd.

"Go away," I whisper to the ghosts in my head.

Gladly, if that's what you want. Kai sounds impatient.

"So thirsty," I mumble.

I hear something slide down the side of the pit. It lands next to my head with a sloshing sound. My fingers close over a sack. Water. I fumble with the tie and choke down a few sips. Then I gulp down several long pulls.

You're going to make yourself sick, the Kai-ghost says.

I ignore her, and drain half the sack. A minute later half of it comes back up.

Told you, the ghost says with no hint of compassion in her voice.

I frown. This doesn't sound like a hallucination, this sounds like Kai in the ever-unfriendly flesh.

"Kai?" I whisper. "Is that really you?"

"Who did you think?"

I shake my head, trying to clear it as the water works its magic. "How did you know I was here?"

"I didn't. I saw the sick ones. Thought I'd see what was so interesting." But she sounds like she doesn't find me, or my predicament, interesting at all.

"What are you doing here?" I take a few more cautious sips.

Her voice drops to a mutter. "Peree went crazy after you left. Wouldn't wait until Nerang told him it was okay to go. I caught him sneaking away, and told him I'd bring him back. Now his leg's pretty bad again."

I have to work to hide my relief and excitement that he's back. I don't think it will help Kai's mood, or my chances of getting out of here. A Groundling or Lofty would have run from the Scourge, not have come closer. It was total luck that Kai found me. If she leaves, I'll die here.

"Can you help me get out?" I ask.

The sick one is pacing and almost growling, clearly more agitated since Kai arrived. At least my head is clearing a little, and my thirst could be described as outrageous instead of atrocious now.

I don't hear anything from above. "Kai?"

She couldn't have left.

Could she?

A magpie screeches in the trees. I wait, holding my breath. Finally I hear rustling, followed by a thump in the space next to me. I reach down to find a coil of rope. I exhale gratefully.

"Tie it around you," she orders.

"What about the *runa*?" I ask.

"It won't bother you." She scoffs as if it's a ridiculous idea. Next time I'd like to see *her* stuck in a tiny hole with one.

I don't know how she's going to get me out of here. She doesn't sound very tall or big. She tugs and pulls, and eventually I dangle in the air. The rope bites into my armpits as I rise one excruciating finger-length at a time. The sick one below me moans, and the ones above murmur in response. I hope they don't pick this moment to attack. I keep the knife poised just in case.

When my head finally clears the top of the hole, I grab onto the lip and scramble out. Kai pants somewhere ahead of me. I stand when I'm able to, pocket the knife, and limp over to her. The sick ones shuffle out of my way.

I find her arm to help her up. "Thank yo–"

She shakes me off. "Untie that rope, I need it back."

I try to focus on my appreciation for her help instead of more murderous thoughts as I step out of the loop. "What about the sick one down there?"

"What about it?" She gathers the rope and stuffs it in her pack.

"Should we help it out of the hole?"

"It can take care of itself. They aren't completely helpless—like some people."

I bristle. "Then why didn't it before?"

"Probably waiting to see if you were going to die. It looked hungry."

"Great," I mutter. I drink a bit more water. It tastes unbelievably good. "So, what now?"

She takes off into the woods.

My mouth drops open. "Hey, wait! Where are you going?"

"Home to Koolkuna."

"Where's Peree?" I call, a little frantically.

"In the trees."

"And which direction is that?" I hiss. I hate having to ask her for directions.

I hear her footsteps stop. "I thought you lived here too."

That's it. "Kai," I yell, "I didn't *fall* in that hole, I was *pushed.* So I'm a little disoriented right now. Would you *please* point out the way?"

She stomps over to me, takes one of my hands, and points it. I fight a short but violent battle to keep from pounding her with it when she lets go. "Tell Peree I helped you. He'll be happy."

And with that, she walks away.

I start off in the direction Kai pointed in. Anger keeps my feet moving forward. Not just anger at Kai—now that I'm out of the pit, I have a list of people I want to get my cut-and-bleeding hands on. And they're almost all Groundlings.

When I left home looking for the Waters, I was thinking about my people's needs. Now that I'm back, I'm only thinking about mine. What were Sable's words the morning the Three issued their punishment? I can stand with my people, or I'll stand alone? Alone sounds perfect right about now. If it weren't for Eland and Peree, I'd turn around and follow Kai all the way back to Koolkuna, whether she liked it or not.

As I stumble and thrash my way through trees and underbrush, relying solely on my internal sense of direction, I form a plan. I'll tell Peree and Shrike what happened, then try to get into the caves to check on Eland somehow. The rest of them can rot in there, for all I care, including Aloe.

The forest is unusually quiet this morning. It should be almost midday, but it's much darker, more like twilight. Clouds must be covering the sun. I do the best I can to keep traveling in the right direction, but it's not easy with little to orient me. And although the wild thirst has ebbed, I'm weak with hunger.

After some time, I'm relieved to hear voices ahead. I move toward them, careful not to get too close. If they're Groundlings, I might be caught and thrown in the pit again. If they're Lofties, they may not wait long enough to find out why a Groundling is outside the caves. I didn't come this far just to get shot.

I creep more slowly as the voices grow louder. When I literally run into a large greenheart, I stay behind it to listen, trying to get a fix on where I am. Some of the voices echo, convincing me I found my way to the mouth of the cave. There's movement in the trees nearby. It could be coming from the platform overlooking the caves, where Peree used to meet me in the mornings. I wonder if he's up there now. My limbs tingle with nervous energy.

I hear Fox's voice. His perpetual exuberance is gone, replaced by a weary determination. "You wanted to see your man, and here he is. What are your terms?"

"We can't trust them," I hear Adder say. He doesn't sound well. His voice is repellent as ever, but there's a brittleness to it I haven't heard before.

Someone in the cave says something I don't catch.

"It's not a trick, it's a simple trade." That's Shrike, speaking from his trees. His gruff voice is threatening. "Give him to us, and you can go back to your homes."

"Unacceptable," Adder says. "This Lofty trespassed in the caves, and we know he also killed a Groundling. We demand retribution."

A Lofty went in the caves, killed someone, and got captured? Why? Who? Then I hear a familiar voice from the caves. *Oh, no. It can't be.*

"I killed the Groundling because he was being consumed by the Scourge, not because he set the fire." Peree sounds as if he's already explained this repeatedly.

"You're lying, like all Lofties lie," Adder hisses. There are sounds of a scuffle. "Moray, restrain the prisoner."

I scowl. Moray again.

"You attacked our homes, and murdered one of our women. Our losses are even," Shrike says. "I've told you our terms. Reject the offer, and see how long you can hold out without fresh water or supplies. It's your choice."

"Do you hear that? They admit it," Adder says loudly. "The Lofties mean to starve us out, as I've been telling you. They want to take our land and the water hole for themselves."

The Groundlings in the caves mutter. I hear the thumps of spears on the ground. This isn't good.

"We had no other choice but to contain you after your unprovoked attack," Shrike says, undisguised frustration in his voice. "We don't want the deaths of your women and children on our consciences. Then again, we wouldn't shed tears if you Groundlings left the forest for good." Lofties in the trees whoop their agreement, causing a few Groundlings to hurl curses from the caves.

"Keep your heads," Fox orders. *Where are Aloe and Sable?*

"That's not all this Lofty has to answer for," says Bear. I'm relieved to hear his voice, but it's not like him to sound so somber. He can usually find the humor in any situation, no matter how dire. "He murdered my intended."

His intended? Bear asked someone to partner with him?

"He was her Keeper," Bear continues, "but instead of protecting her, he killed her. Probably when he found out she was leaving the caves."

My mouth drops open. Is he talking about *me*?

"I ... didn't kill her." Peree sounds like he's having trouble catching his breath, making me worry about what Moray did to him during their scuffle. "I came in here ... to find her."

"We haven't seen her in weeks. Stop lying and tell me where she is, or I'll spear you right now," Bear growls.

"Maybe she juth wanted to get away from you, hero," Moray says to Bear.

"Shut up," Bear snaps. A swell of hope fills my chest. If Bear doesn't know I was banished, maybe the people don't really think I'm a traitor.

"Stop this, Bear. Fennel wouldn't want more violence," Aloe says, her voice strangely soft and anemic. Despite my anger, I can't help feeling grateful to hear her voice. Now if I could only tell if Eland is there, too.

"Why would we harm the Water Bearer?" Shrike says. "It makes no sense."

"Nothing you Lofties do makes much sense," someone shouts from the caves. It sounds like Cuda, one of Moray's brothers.

"We're offering you the chance to go home," a Lofty woman shouts back, "and maybe wash away that ferocious stink. But if you don't want to, then feel free to crawl back inside like the vermin you are!"

There's laughter and more taunts from the Lofties. A swell of hostile voices rises from the caves. And I've spent enough time with Peree to recognize the sound of arrows being pulled from quivers and loaded onto bows.

Things are getting out of hand. I have to do something. I step away from the trunk I'm hiding behind, push through some bushes, and emerge into the clearing. There are shouts of surprise as people recognize me. Then my feet leave the ground as Bear crushes me into his broad chest. He does smell fairly ferocious, but also comfortingly familiar.

"You're alive. Thank the stars," he whispers into my hair. "Where have you *been*?" I can't answer; I can't even breathe. He sets me down, but keeps me tucked against his body. He's radiating relief, and it sparks conflicting feelings of gratitude and guilt in me. "I didn't think you were coming back. I thought you were–" He chokes on the word.

I haven't heard him sound like he might cry since his father died when we were children. I squeeze him around the waist, which feels considerably leaner than when I left. "I'm here. I'm okay."

He smoothes my hair away from my face. "You don't look okay. What happened to you?"

"Long story," I whisper. "So, Bear ... did I somehow miss agreeing to partner with you?"

"Oh, that ... I was so happy when you said you would've danced with me at the Solstice, that I kind of let it slip to Cougar, and he told Vole, and Vole told Fox, and Fox told Calli and Acacia—and pretty much everyone knew after that." He sounds sheepish. "I tried to set the story straight, but people assumed if you said you'd dance with me, that it meant we'd partner when you came back."

"Alright, alright, I get it," I grumble, but I smile to let him know I'm not angry.

The startled voices have died down. The air in the clearing seems to throb with tension, like an infected pustule ready to burst. My skin prickles with the physical perception of danger. No one else came out to greet me like Bear.

"Well, well," Adder says, "where did you come from, girl?"

Rage blows full force through me again at the sound of his grating voice. I move a step away from Bear, trying to keep my hands from clenching into fists.

"I think you know." My voice is surprisingly even. "Groundlings and Lofties, listen to me. You may think of me as a child, and dismiss what I have to say. But I've earned the right to speak. I faced the Scourge to collect the water for you, and I found the Hidden Waters. Now I have something to tell you."

"You did it? You found the Waters?" a voice squeaks from the caves. Eland. My heart dances when I hear him, but the feeling is replaced by fresh anxiety that he might be in danger if a fight breaks out. I grin at him, trying to look reassuring.

"Yes, little brother, I found them ... and I found *out* a lot of other things. Things about the Scourge. They aren't what we think they are."

"What do you mean, Fennel?" Fox asks.

"Your minds, all of our minds, play tricks on us. The way you see the creatures isn't real. The creatures aren't monsters, they're ... sick people." As I expected, it sounds ridiculous.

"Sick people?" Adder scoffs. "I've never seen a sick person tear someone's head off their body."

"Listen to her. She's telling the truth," Kadee says from the trees. I'm glad to have her support, but I doubt her vouching for me will change any Groundling minds.

I try again. "When I found the Hidden Waters, I also found a village that was protected from the Scourge. Just like in the legend." There are definite sounds of shock at that.

"How?" someone asks.

"Their water—the Hidden Waters—is pure." Peree says. "Ours is poisoned."

I hear the word *poison* repeated through the caves and the trees.

"And how does a Lofty know that?" Cuda asks, his voice accusing.

I steel myself. "Peree and I found the Waters together."

"You were with *him?*" Bear growls. "Why?"

"You admit you led a Lofty to the Waters? How interesting," Adder says. "I didn't realize you'd become so cozy with our enemy."

I erupt. "Isn't that why you had me banished? And the Lofties aren't my enemies! I'm so tired of your agendas and accusations, Adder. I may be Sightless, but you're blinded by your prejudice against the Lofties." I face the caves. "Groundlings, I came home two days ago, only to be banished—thrown into a pit and left to die." From the sounds of peoples' reactions, I can tell it wasn't widely known. It gives me courage to continue. "Moray told me it was by order of the Three, but I think it was Adder's doing. He's no longer capable of governing us responsibly. His hatred has brought us to the brink of war with the Lofties, and the Three don't seem to have the will to stop him." I direct those words to the spot where I last heard Aloe.

To my surprise, she acknowledges my challenge in a defeated voice. "You're right, my daughter, we don't."

"I learned other things while I was away, too. I wasn't born Sightless. I was made this way as an infant ... so I could collect the water one day." More murmurs at that. "Did you know, Aloe? Did you allow it to happen?"

"Not until after," Aloe says. "I would never have allowed it if I'd known beforehand."

"Be careful, woman!" Adder spits at Aloe. "You're on dangerous ground!" *Dangerous ground*? What does he mean?

"Is this true, Adder?" Fox asks. "We've always thought the Sightless children came from the Lofties."

"Of course it's not true," Adder says. "Can't you see where the girl's loyalties lie? Fennel sides with the Lofties, and challenges the authority of the Three. Either the Scourge has weakened her mind, or she's a traitor."

"I'm not a traitor!" I yell.

"She's a Lofty-lover," Thistle squeals from the caves. "We can't trust her." A few voices agree. *A Lofty what*?

"Fennel's no traitor," Bear says, stepping close to me again. I'm grateful for his solidarity.

"These accusations need to be discussed, but for now we should focus on the negotiations. There are hungry children in the caves, waiting to be fed," Pinion says from the caves. Of all the voices I've heard, hers is the least altered. "Fennel, you've vouched for the Lofties, but how do we know they won't kill us all in our beds if we agree to their terms?"

"Or that you won't burn us out of our homes!" a Lofty yells.

I face the trees. "You Lofties have reason to be angry with us. But since the day you cast out our ancestors and created the Exchange, you've had the upper hand. Instead of fostering goodwill by sharing your most precious resource—the safety of the trees—you kept us low, subjecting us instead to fear and intimidation. If we're going to survive, we have to earn each other's trust, as Peree and I did."

"Show them the necklace," Peree calls.

Confused, but willing to follow his lead, I pull out the carved bird. There are gasps from the greenhearts.

"Peree, you gave yourself to a *Groundling*?" The Lofty woman's voice is a mixture of amazement and revulsion.

Is that what the bird is? A Lofty symbol of partnership, like our bonding bands? Part of me wonders what Peree was thinking, giving me something with that kind of significance without telling me what it meant. Another part is thrilled he offered it to me at all, and long before he told me the full extent of his feelings. But I don't have time to think more about it.

"I'm a Groundling," I say, "but I'm a Lofty, too. Born in the trees, raised on the ground. You can hate me, banish me, kill me—but whatever you do, you do it to one of your own." I pause. "Only a few feet of air separates us. Can't you see that? If Peree and I could find common ground, isn't there a chance we all could?"

"Fennel is right," Adder agrees. People quiet down to listen to him. "She's right that she *is* only a child, with a child's idealistic view of the world. She knows nothing of the deception of the Lofties, and the lengths they'll go to keep us in our place. Children should have no voice in these talks, but I see Fennel has too much of her mother to keep silent. Cuda, guard the Lofty prisoner. Moray, take Fennel into the caves with the other … little ones."

My hand darts to my pocket and Peree's knife. There's no way I'm letting Moray touch me again.

I feel Bear tie something around my upper arm. I might still be muddled from fatigue and hunger, but I know what it is. A bonding band.

"I invoke the privilege of the bond," Bear says. "I'll do what it takes to protect my partner. If you touch her, Moray, you'll have a lot more than a bitten tongue to worry about."

"Think you can thake me, hero?" Moray drawls. He's close to us, in the clearing now.

"Try me," Bear says.

The sounds of a brawl tumble out of the caves behind Moray.

"Cuda!" Moray sounds like he's running back the way he came.

"What is it? What's happening?" I ask Bear.

"Looks like the Lofty thumped Cuda with his own spear. It was a nice move … but they've got him again."

"Peree! Be careful!" I yell.

Shrike speaks, his voice like ice. "If my son is hit one more time, these talks are over. We'll take him back by force."

Someone shouts from the caves. "As if you could!"

Taunts and threats are hurled back and forth. Fox tries to calm the crowd, but his words are lost in the shouting. Bear draws me closer to the bulk of his body.

An arrow zips overhead, heading for the caves. Death in motion. It finds its mark.

"Get down!" Bear says, pushing me into the dirt.

The next few moments stretch out forever as arrows, spears, shouts, and curses are flung over our heads. There are screams of pain, and I can smell the raw tang of blood. Then I hear a new sound. Shrieks, followed by moans. I catch the odor of death, illness, despair—the unmistakable reek of the Scourge. Groundlings that were surging out of the caves a few moments before, hurling spears and expletives, now run back the way they came. The familiar fear engulfs me.

"Bear," I shout, "get in the caves!"

He yanks me up. "You're coming, too!"

He half-drags me toward the mouth of the cave. I'm not sure it's safe for me in there, but I'm positive it's not safe out here in the middle of a hailstorm of arrows and spears. Sweat drenches my hands and face.

A creature near me is hit with a sickening thump. It cries out, sounding horribly human. Several others moan in pain, and one begs to die. I hesitate. They don't deserve to be shot down like helpless animals. Someone grabs my other hand, dragging me away from Bear. It's Peree. I'd never mistake the feel of his hand in mine.

"Come on," he yells, yanking me sharply to the right, toward the trees. "We'll be safer out here."

But more creatures surround us, and it doesn't go unnoticed.

"They're being consumed!" I hear a Lofty woman shout. "Someone shoot them—show them mercy!"

Peree swears, and barks at me to run, pushing me forward. Arrows strike the ground around us.

We almost make it to the line of trees. Almost.

A creature pitches into me. I try to keep my footing, but it knocks me off balance, tearing my hand out of Peree's. As I fall, I feel the cold grip of the sick one, grasping my arms.

My temple cracks against something on the ground—something hard and unforgiving—and pain rips through my head. Blood flows into my ear, and the sounds of the clash garble and begin to fade.

I slip from consciousness quickly. But not before I hear Kadee scream Peree's name, her voice strangled with grief.

CHAPTER TWENTY

I become aware of my surroundings slowly. I'm in the caves, stretched out on some sort of lumpy pallet, and my head's bandaged with cloth—again. A headache cleaves my body like a well-aimed ax. Low voices echo around me, and someone is holding my hand. I squeeze the thin fingers.

"Fenn?"

"Eland," I whisper. I push myself up, but the movement causes the ax to burrow deeper, so I lay down again. Eland puts his arms around me instead. I can feel the outline of every rib in his bowed back, but he's alive and whole-bodied as far as I can tell. And he smells of fresh air and soap.

I smile, my lips cracking. "You've been outside …"

"The Lofties let us go home."

He sounds older somehow, more mature than he did even a few weeks ago. The innocence that was already beginning to fade in his twelve-year-old voice is gone. I feel like a mourner who not only didn't get to say good-bye to the deceased, but also missed the funeral.

A soft sound escapes him, half hiccup, half sob. "I didn't think you were coming back."

"I'll always come back for you, Eland."

There's a screech from nearby. "Fennel! You're awake!" Calli leaps on me, her long, wispy hair pooling in my face as she hugs me. "How do you feel?" Her voice has the same childlike quality as before, but like Eland's, it's changed, too. There's a hard edge.

"I've been worse," I answer, thinking of my most hopeless moments in the pit.

"Where were you?" she asks. "Before you strolled into the middle of the negotiations, I mean. I was in here helping Marjoram, but I heard all about it."

The time is coming when I'll need to tell everyone my story, but for now I sidestep her question. "What happened with the Lofties? I don't remember anything after I hit my head. And where's Aloe?"

Eland's hand stiffens in mine. Neither of them speaks. A spear of apprehension jabs into my gut.

"What is it?" I ask.

"Marj did everything she could … but Aloe had bled too much," Calli says softly.

"We buried her yesterday," Eland mumbles.

My chest tightens and my limbs feel strangely useless, like limp strands of waterweed. Something inside me crawls into a small ball, refusing to acknowledge their words. Aloe's not gone, I tell myself, she's just busy getting things sorted outside. She'll come to me soon. As if I tell myself that enough times, my wish will come true.

"What happened?" I whisper.

They tell me everything. After I left to find the Waters, Adder grew increasingly distracted and paranoid. If anyone questioned a decision of the Three, he accused them of being spies and traitors, calling them Lofty-lovers. He was furious when he found out I'd been in the Lofty trees on the night of my punishment, especially because he didn't hear it from Aloe. She should have told him, as a fellow member of the Council. He became suspicious of her motives.

Adder threatened Aloe. If he found out she was speaking to Shrike or any other Lofty while she collected the water, if she disagreed with his decisions, if she sided with Sable over him—if she went against Adder in any way—Eland would have an unfortunate accident. Accidents happen in the caves.

Eland said Thistle's third son, the one whose name I could never remember, began hanging around him all the time, even sleeping near him. He never did anything overt that would rouse the suspicions of others, but he also never let Eland out of his sight. He just sat nearby, playing with a small knife used for gutting animals. It was enough to terrify Eland and Aloe both, and to buy her cooperation. As Sable's health failed by the minute, Adder cloaked himself with the power of the Three.

He ordered the attack on the trees, believing the Lofties planned to hold them in the caves indefinitely. The people were desperate and afraid. Many were sick from a stomach ailment. They would agree to do anything to get out, even something perilous and ill-considered. And with Aloe and Sable's continued silence, there didn't seem to be another alternative.

After the attack failed, guards were posted at every entrance to the caves. Adder justified it by saying he was protecting them from retaliation, but it kept in people who might have gone out to try to make peace with the Lofties. As far as I can tell, no one knew I had returned. Moray told everyone he bit his tongue while eating jerky.

Then Peree came into the caves, looking for me. Calli said he was limping badly, but he still managed to saunter in like he belonged there. He would have been killed on the spot if Aloe hadn't intervened. She stood in front of him, protecting him from the spears. She convinced Adder he could be used as a bargaining tool with the Lofties. It was the best she could do to spare his life.

On the day of the Reckoning, as people are calling it, right before the negotiations, Aloe finally confided in Fox about Adder's blackmail. She asked him to step in as a de facto member of the Three, to temper Adder's madness. I wondered why she didn't tell someone what was happening sooner. Eland said she probably wasn't sure who she could trust. Adder had allies, and not all of them were as vocal as Thistle and her family.

Adder insisted Eland come to the mouth of the caves during the negotiations while the other children were kept behind, to remind Aloe of what she had to lose if she didn't keep her mouth shut. She died protecting Eland. I wish I could say it was a stray Lofty arrow that killed her, but Marjoram told me it was a spear wound.

My only comfort is knowing that the choices Aloe made were for Eland's sake. She forwent her duty in order to protect him. I would have, too. I try not to think about the times I needed her protection but didn't get it, from being blinded as a baby, right up through the Reckoning. Instead, I remember she was doing the best she could to protect her children under difficult circumstances. Maybe all mothers are.

Sable and Willow succumbed to their illnesses days ago. Thistle, her sons, and a few others are being held under guard, until a decision is made about what to do with them. Adder was killed by Lofty arrows. Scores of them. No doubt he was targeted. With Adder, Aloe, and Sable gone, Fox,

Pinion, and Bream were chosen as temporary Council members. They persuaded the Lofties to let us bury our dead and return home.

That is what I know.

This is what I don't know–

If Peree lives. Eland said Peree managed to wrestle Cuda's spear away from him again when the fighting started. He knocked Cuda out rather than killing him. All anyone could remember about Peree after that was he ran out into the Scourge like he'd suddenly gone mad. Eland thought he was consumed by the flesh-eaters, but Calli said she heard he was shot by a Lofty.

It can't be true. Peree can't be dead. But I'm haunted by Kadee's wail of despair. How could he have survived—a fair-haired, fair-eyed target for generations of Groundling resentment and rage? Or survived the conviction of many of his own people that he was about to be consumed by the Scourge?

I'm strong. The last month convinced me of that. But losing Peree and Aloe in one day is more than my heart can bear.

I sit in the circle of light from the fire, singing softly to Bear as he coughs and shifts on his pallet. The throbbing ache in my head returns with brutal swiftness when I think about Peree, but physically I'm improving. I touch the bandage on Bear's side, under his left ribs, to be sure the wound isn't bleeding again. My guilt grows the longer he remains unconscious.

Calli told me Bear made it to the caves after I literally slipped out of his hands, only to have Moray stab him in the back. Bear's lung was pierced, but somehow he fought him off. I can't say I was glad to hear Moray survived.

Calli started helping in the infirmary when so many people began falling ill from the pestilential conditions in the caves. Marj and she work diligently and without complaint over the long hours. I admire their determination while I sit in a silent stupor of grief.

"Hey, Fenn, guess what?" Calli says as she leans over Bear, probably checking his temperature. He isn't feverish anymore, thank the stars. "Cricket told me last night he was going to ask me to dance at the Solstice. He wanted to know if I would have."

I twitch, remembering Bear asking me the same thing. "What did you tell him?"

"That he'll have to wait and see." Her voice takes on a mock mysterious tone.

I try to smile for her. "I thought he was too short for you."

"Who knows … maybe he'll grow some more before next year."

"Not likely," Bear whispers.

I grab his hand, but Calli pushes me aside, all business now. "How do you feel?"

"Like I was stabbed," he rasps. "Oh wait, that is what happened."

"Nice to see your sense of humor survived," Calli says. "Do you need anything?"

"Water?"

"I'll get it," I say, jumping up.

"No, you stay. Maybe he can tell you where *else* it hurts and you can kiss it and make it better." Calli laughs as she moves away to fetch the water.

I hold Bear's hand in both of mine while she helps him take a few sips. His skin is like tree bark, rough and dry from dehydration, but his grip is strong and steady.

"How are you?" he asks.

I smile. "Better than you."

"That's not saying much. Why are we still in the caves? What happened with the Lofties?"

I fill him in on what he's missed, smoothing his palm with my fingers as I speak. He's quiet as I list the dead.

"I'm sorry about Aloe," he says.

"I'm sorry about a lot of things."

"Like what?"

"That she died. That you're hurt. I feel responsible." I wonder if I look as lifeless as my voice sounds.

"It's not your fault. Aloe made the choices she had to make. And Moray and I had unfinished business. I guess we still do." I can feel him studying my face. "Anyway, that's not why you're sorry."

I swallow hard. "Why am I sorry, then?"

"You're sorry because you're *going* to hurt me."

Unexpected tears leak out of the corners of my eyes. "What do you mean?" I know what he means, but I'm not ready to say it out loud.

"You're going to tell me you don't want to partner with me," he says evenly.

I shake my head. I'm not sure what I'm denying.

"Fenn, when a boy wakes up after a life-threatening injury, and the girl he gave a bonding band to isn't wearing it ... it's not that hard to figure out."

I pull the band out of my pocket. "I have it here."

"Great, maybe I'll see how Marj feels about wearing it," he jokes. "I'd ask Calli, but it sounds like Cricket might still have a chance."

"I'm so sorry," I repeat. I don't know what else to say, so I kiss his knuckles instead.

He exhales. There's suffering in the sound that belies his lighthearted words. "I guess I already knew."

"How?"

"From your Lofty's face when you stepped out of those trees. And from your face when you heard what that bird necklace meant." He pauses. "Although, it doesn't look like you're wearing it either."

I slide it out of my other pocket.

He snorts. "Keeping your options open?"

"I'm not sure where Peree and I stand now ... I don't even know if he survived the Reckoning ..." My face crumbles.

"I'm kidding, Fenn." He squeezes my hand.

"I told the truth when you asked if I'd have danced with you at the Solstice. I probably would have. But I didn't know then that I'd feel this way now." I hang my head. "I hate what you must think of me."

"Fennel, I've known you all my life, you're one of my best friends. I only think the best of you, period."

"See, when you say that, that's when I think I'm making a mistake," I say.

"You *are* making a mistake," he says seriously. "Then again, maybe it's for the best. You really are a terrible cook, and you can't sew worth a damn either. Our kids would be in rags."

My smile wobbles. "You're pretty wonderful, Bear."

"That's what they all tell me."

"All right, Fenn," Calli says as she walks up, "kiss him and be gone so I can check his wound."

"Yes, Fennel," Bear says, "lean way down here and kiss me. Show Calli what it'll be like with Cricket." I laugh my first real laugh since the Reckoning and kiss him on his stubbly cheek.

"Don't stay away," he warns me.

"Stay away? She's been here practically every minute," Calli says. "You two are intended—where else would she be?"

"You really need to try confiding in your friends," Bear says to me.

"About what?" Calli asks.

I hug them each in turn. "Later, I promise."

I wander around the main cavern—it's practically empty now—trying to work up the courage to go outside. I know I should face whatever I'll find in the forest. But every time I think of getting confirmation that Peree's dead, I feel sick.

The stench finally drives me to the mouth of the cave, seeking semi-fresh air. I remember the days, not long ago, when every step toward the Scourge was torture. I keep telling myself it's the poison we need to eradicate, not the sick ones. It's working ... sort of.

Voices approach—Fox and Pinion. They must be coming from the meeting with the Lofties. Maybe they'll know something about Peree. I try to slow my anxious breathing.

"How did it go?" I ask.

"As well as could be expected," Fox says. "They're bitter, we're bitter. It'll take time."

"Who did you talk with?"

Pinion answers. "Two women, Breeze and Blaze, and a few of the men. I thought they carried themselves well, especially considering one of the women lost a son in the Reckoning."

I reach back to steady myself against the ice-cold wall. *He can't be dead. He can't be.* Grief twists my gut. I run out of the caves. The late-afternoon sun hangs heavy on my shoulders as I stumble through the clearing. Groundlings speak to me, but I ignore them.

I end up on the path to the water hole. Birds sing around me as if nothing is wrong. I find the sled, and crumple against it. But the sled reminds me of Peree, and thinking about him feels like being stabbed.

Two voices move down the walkway above, one male, one female. At first I think I'm imagining them. That I want to hear his voice so bad I'm conjuring it. But then I hear it again.

"Peree!" I yell. Silence. Did he not hear me?

"Fennel." He doesn't sound right at all. There's no trace of the warmth and humor I've grown to love. The knots that were loosening inside me suddenly cinch up again.

"Are you okay?" I ask.

"Fine. You?"

"Not really."

"Sorry to hear that." He sounds distant and completely uninterested, as if he's talking to a stranger. Or worse, to a Groundling.

"I thought you were dead." I can't keep the quiver out of my voice.

"Not quite yet."

"Can we talk for a minute? Alone?" He's quiet for so long I'm not sure he's going to answer. "Peree?"

I hear him speak to his companion in a low voice, then one set of footsteps follows the walkway back toward the clearing.

"I'll meet you at the platform by the water hole," he says to me.

What's wrong with him? I chew on my nails as I walk, but I stop quickly. They're filthy. Water breaks on the shore of the water hole, and a few geese honk. It sounds deserted, but it probably won't be for long. Peree steps onto the platform above my head.

"So, what did you want to talk about?" he asks.

"Can you come down here?"

He hesitates. "I don't know if that's a good idea."

"Then I'll come up, if it makes you more comfortable," I offer.

"Always the brave one," he mutters. I frown, hurt by his tone. "I'll come down."

I can't stop fidgeting as I listen to him release the rope ladder and climb down. Why is he acting so strange? What does it mean? Is it because of the Reckoning? Does he no longer feel the same about me?

"Peree, what's wrong?" I ask, the moment I hear his feet touch the ground. He grunts in pain, and I wonder if his leg is any better.

He ignores my question. "Why did you think I was dead?"

I tell him what Pinion said.

"They were talking about my grandmother, Breeze. Shrike's mother. You heard Kadee yelling for me to come to him when she saw he was hit."

It takes me a moment to realize what that means. "Then … Shrike is dead? Oh, Peree, I'm so sorry." I reach out to him, but find only empty space. I drop my hands to my sides. "Aloe, too," I say. Shrike might not have been my father, not really, not in the ways that count. But I can't help feeling like I lost two parents in the Reckoning.

"I heard. I'm sorry." His voice is a little kinder, and it gives me courage.

"I thought–"

What did I think? That we'd run off into the sunset together? That our little fairytale could have a happy ending, like one of Kadee's stories? He's a Lofty. I'm a Groundling. I knew all along we had no future together. The Reckoning just proved it. And now Peree's obviously changed his mind.

"Forget it," I say. "I only wanted to know if you were all right." He doesn't respond, so I turn back toward the path.

"Took you long enough."

I whirl around to him, allowing anger to cover my anguish. "Were you listening? I thought you were dead! And in case the bandage on my head isn't obvious enough for you, I was hurt! You could've come to check on me, too, you know."

"I went in the caves once to find you, and my father was killed as a result."

Is that it? He blames me for Shrike's death? Guilt washes over me again. "I lost people, too."

"How's your …" He doesn't finish.

"My what?"

"Your *intended*. I heard he was injured, and you haven't left his side." Bitterness oozes from his words.

"My intended? You mean Bear?"

"What, is there someone else, too? He put that thing on your arm that meant you were partnered, didn't he?"

I throw up my hands. "And you gave me the bird without telling me what it meant! I feel like a piece of land people keep trying to claim by sticking stuff on me! Why doesn't anyone bother to *ask* me before they decide I'm partnering with them?"

His breath quickens. A cautious note slips into his voice, nudging out the resentment. "What are you saying? You aren't partnering with him?"

I take a deep breath to calm the raging storm of emotion inside me. Peree's alive, and he doesn't hate me. He's only acting like a boar's back end because he's jealous. I can deal with that. I hold my arms out and twirl around slowly.

"What are you doing?" He sounds like he thinks I've lost my mind.

"You told me in Koolkuna that I had ties here, and you were right. But look, not anymore. I'm ... untied. And no, I'm not partnering with Bear."

He almost knocks me over when he grabs me. "I was going crazy the past few days, Fenn. First Shrike ... then I didn't know what happened to you ... then I heard you were alive, but you were staying with Bear–"

I touch my lips to his, quieting him. Then I sketch the curve of his eyebrows and the length of his coarse sideburns. His lips curve under my thumbs. He takes my hands, still cold from the caves, in his, warming them.

"So ... are you still looking for an ending to that story about the boy and the girl?" I ask. "I think I have one you'll like."

"Do you?" Peree murmurs. "What is it?"

"The girl loves the boy, too. She loves him, and she stays with him."

"I don't know ... that wasn't exactly what I was looking for," he says, and I laugh. "Okay, twist my arm. It's good."

"You're the only one I want to be with, wild boy. If you'll still have me."

His kiss answers my question, and a few more I would've been embarrassed to ask out loud. I snake my arms around him and rest my cheek on his chest. His heart is beating at a satisfyingly breakneck speed.

"Peree?"

"*Hmm?*"

"I don't know if Kadee told you, but we're kind of ... related."

"Yeah, I know."

"Does it bother you?" I ask.

"It would if it were true. It would bother me a lot that I feel this ... bothered, about my sister." He nuzzles my neck. "But it's not like we're natural siblings. Does it matter to you?"

I smile. "Somehow I feel like it should, but no, not really."

A group of children run past. Most of them head straight into the water like a flock of gabbling geese, but a few slow down and whisper to each other when they see us.

"I should go back up," Peree says, "before the full-grown ones come along."

I squeeze him tighter against me. "No, I invited you down, and you're staying until you're ready to go." What did the Reckoning accomplish, if we don't take this chance to change some of the rules?

"Always the brave one," he says again, his voice warm this time. "But I have to warn you, I may never be ready to go."

"That works for me."

"Hey, Kadee wants me—us, now—to speak at the next Confluence, to tell everyone more about the Scourge, and present Nerang's offer."

"Confluence?"

"That's what they're calling the meeting today."

"I like it," I say.

"It's a start. So … do you still have my bird? There's something I need to *ask* you."

I retrieve it from my pocket and hand it to him. He offers it back with a very sweet, very formal request for me to partner with him. I accept, and we create our own version of a Confluence, with a not-so-formal meeting of mouths and arms and bodies.

I tug on Peree's hand, pulling him to the water. Soon we're laughing and splashing alongside the children. I help him up from a half-decent float and he gathers me into his arms.

"This is like my dream, the one I had in the caves about us swimming together. Only now I get to show you what else we were doing." He kisses me thoroughly, prompting an outburst of giggles from the children. I wonder if anyone else can see us. I don't care. Let them think what they want.

Happiness pours over me … in sharp contrast to the ache in my heart caused by Aloe's absence. I wish she and Shrike were here to share our joy. I don't know if they would have, but I like to think so. Eland told me Aloe never lost hope that I would come home. He said she never doubted me, or my loyalty. I don't know if that's the truth, or if he's telling me what I desperately want to hear.

I'll miss Aloe's voice, her strength, the comforting warmth of her rosemary-scented skin. She was the only one who really understood the challenges of being Sightless. The only person in the world who knew about my secret scars, the ones I keep hidden away inside. She kept hers hidden, too. I wish I had the chance to ask her all the questions I'd been saving up since I became the Water Bearer. I wish I could have told her what she meant to me.

It occurs to me that collecting the water may not be my responsibility for much longer. What will I be now, if not the Water Bearer? What can I contribute as my people try to shape a new relationship with the Lofties, and maybe with the *anuna?* For the first time I face a future that hasn't been predetermined for me. I get to choose. It's thrilling, and scary.

I hope what we gained the past few weeks will outweigh all we lost. As I hold the one I love—a Lofty, no less—I have to believe it does. But maybe it's not a question that can ever really be answered. Maybe we just have to cling to the faith that because of us, and through us, hope will live on.

AFTERWORD

Thank you so much for reading THE SCOURGE. I'd like to include some information here about the background of the stories included in the novel.

Most are myths or folktales from different cultures. The story about the tiger, for example, was taken from a Chinese myth. The tale of how the first fish came to be and the legend of the flowers are based on Australian Aboriginal Dreamtime stories. The legend of the cassowary woman is a folktale told by the people of Papua New Guinea. I did take a few liberties in my retellings, but I tried to treat these stories with the respect they deserve as treasures of the cultures they were borrowed from.

When Kadee tells Fenn, "*It is not in the stars to hold our destiny, but in ourselves,*" she is misquoting dialogue from the play, *Julius Caesar*, by William Shakespeare. The oft-misquoted text served my purposes, so I went with it. The "first language" of Koolkuna is loosely derived from Australian Aboriginal dialects.

I hope you enjoyed the novel. If you have any questions or comments, I'd love to hear from you.

A. G. Henley

ACKNOWLEDGMENTS

Thank you to my husband and children for their patience and understanding the past few years while I "just finish this one thing" on the laptop. I love you guys.

Thanks also to my parents, Fran and Bill, for always supporting me in whatever I want to do. Thanks especially to Mom, who encouraged a love of literature by helping me check out stacks of books at the library and reading them to me in the front seat of the station wagon while waiting for my sister to finish her kindergarten day.

Speaking of my sister, thanks, Ginger, for always being my biggest cheerleader. And Andy, for being hers.

To Hilary, my BFF and first reader, for encouraging me to keep writing past Chapter Six. To Jenny, for her unconditional enthusiasm and conviction that THE SCOURGE would be a mega best seller. Kim and Shae provided very helpful feedback, and Ande and Nina round out the merry band of moms I turn to for friendship and wisdom.

Lana, Molly, Euell, and Warren were invaluable writing partners and beta readers.

Steve Lamar held my hand as I tiptoed onto the web and into social media. I've met few people as generous with their time and talent.

I owe a big thank you to Sarah Cloots for her excellent editorial work.

And finally, I'm grateful to my agent, Caryn Wiseman, for taking a chance on me.

ABOUT THE AUTHOR

A.G. Henley is the author of the BRILLIANT DARKNESS series. The first book in the series, THE SCOURGE, was a finalist for the Next Generation Indie Book Award.

A.G. is also a clinical psychologist, which means people either tell her their life stories on airplanes, or avoid her at parties when they've had too much to drink. Neither of which she minds. When she's not writing fiction or shrinking heads, she can be found herding her children and their scruffy dog, Guapo, to various activities while trying to remember whatever she's inevitably forgotten to tell her husband. She lives in Denver, Colorado. Learn more at aghenley.com